Peter Henry Emerson

Caóba, the Guerilla Chief

A Real Romance of the Cuban Rebellion

Peter Henry Emerson

Caóba, the Guerilla Chief
A Real Romance of the Cuban Rebellion

ISBN/EAN: 9783337348755

Printed in Europe, USA, Canada, Australia, Japan

Cover: Foto ©Andreas Hilbeck / pixelio.de

More available books at **www.hansebooks.com**

CAÓBA

THE GUERILLA CHIEF

A REAL ROMANCE OF

THE CUBAN REBELLION

BY

P. H. EMERSON

LONDON
DAVID NUTT, 270-71 STRAND
1897

Printed by BALLANTYNE, HANSON & Co.
At the Ballantyne Press

TO

MY FATHER

A BRAVE GENTLEMAN

AUTHOR'S NOTE

THE scenes narrated in this book are founded on fact, and the account of Cuban country life is written from the author's personal experience after some years' residence in the island.

For the story of the execution of the Cuban students, however, the author is indebted to a little book published by one of the exiled students in Madrid in 1873, and entitled *Los Voluntarios de la Habana.*

It is to be hoped that some civilised nation will step in and put an end to the atrocities taking place on the island of Cuba, deeds that disgrace the civilisation of to-day, and the United States of America is the country to interfere and annex the island.

P. H. E.

THE NOOK, OULTON BROAD,
November 1896.

vii

CONTENTS

PART II.—PEACE AND CARE

PART III.—WAR—BLOODY WAR

CONTENTS

CAÓBA:[1]

THE GUERILLA CHIEF

CHAPTER I

THE PLANTER AT THE CASA GRANDE

THE castellated *Casa Grande* of *La Esperanza* estate, in the island of Cuba, crested a limestone hill, and overlooked thousands of acres of waving sugar-canes that covered the rich alluvial plains round about.

The white walls of the great house gleamed in the dazzling tropical sunlight, for the rains were over, and December had come—the dry season had set in with lovely weather.

This mansion of the *Esperanza* was a picturesque pile, solidly built of limestone, blasted from the very hill upon which it stood, and covered with plaster — smooth, hard, and whiter than ivory. It consisted of a large, one-storied *casa*, with a picturesque fringe, beneath which a cool,

---

[1] Pronounced *Kah-ō-bah.*

red-tiled piazza ran, enclosing the front and sides of the structure. The roof of the piazza was supported on pillars of graceful form.

Behind the *casa*, from the left end, projected at right angles a long, low, white wing of rooms, pierced externally with small grated windows, roofed with tiles above, and opening by narrow doors into a covered corridor that looked upon the quadrangular garden within.

From the right end of the house extended another wing of solidly-built offices, store-rooms, servants' quarters, and stables, communicating with the exterior, some by tall doorways, others with the garden by low doors and grated windows.

Behind, a high massive wall, rising some thirty feet from the hill-side, closed the garden from all access save by the front entrance. The wall was railed on the top, and terraced towards the garden, each platform gay with flowers and fresh with ornamental foliage plants. From the left of the terraced wall, at its junction with the corridor, rose a square white tower, its four sides pierced with small gratings, its top tiled and enclosed by embrasures.

In the hollow of the tower hung a heavy alarm-bell.

To the right of the terrace, adjoining the stables, was the hen-house, with tiled roof and cemented floors, its sides enclosed by louvained woodwork. Below it was the sheepfold.

As a further precaution, a solid stone wall, ten feet high, was built round the grounds of the *Casa Grande*—an outwork soon covered with wild creepers that grew with tropical luxuriance —a green screen, gay in patches, with red and yellow flowers.

A winding carriage-drive descended from the front of the *casa* through the grounds to the gates, whence, to the right, an avenue of cocoanut trees led to the king's highway, or *camino real*, as the Spaniards called it, and on the left, for a mile, to the *batey*—the centre of life of the estate.

In this stronghold the planter and his retainers could have well stood a siege by the class of enemy by which they were surrounded ; and, truth to tell, such precautions were necessary, for, besides the *bandoleros*[1] who frequented the primeval forests to the right of the house, a rising of slaves had ever to be guarded against.

One fine December evening, in the year 18—, the wealthy *hacendado*, Don Enrique, the owner of those broad acres, sat in the piazza, gazing at the evening landscape.

Don Enrique was a tall, powerfully-built man, as well set up as a trained soldier. His deeply-

---

[1] Banditti.

bronzed skin showed he had lived long beneath the tropical sun ; but his white hair, closely-cropped moustache, and blue eyes—like the sea—showed he had sprung from some northern race ; and, indeed, such was the case, for Don Enrique was of English stock, a descendant of a Border clan, which had given many sons to the colonies to win distinction in many fields.

Upon this particular evening, the planter was alone but for his three Cuban mastiffs that lay beside him. He was dressed in a black silk coat, negligently thrown open, showing an embroidered linen shirt, confined at the waist by a red silk sash, from which the ivory stock of a long revolver shone. White linen trousers and patent leather shoes completed his costume. His fine plaited Panama hat was pushed back from his forehead, and a long green *vaquero* cigar was fixed in one corner of his stern mouth. A little table stood by his side with a coffee service, maraschino and liqueur glasses, a box of cigars, and a small brazier containing live charcoal.

Don Enrique sat with one arm resting on the rail of the piazza, watching the transparent sky in the horizon, just beyond where the galvanised iron roofs of the neighbouring *La Marguerita* estate gleamed amid the green sea of sugar-canes. In a few minutes the setting sun touched the rustling cane-tassels—for the crop was ripe,—

when suddenly the landscape seemed to brighten and glow—the roosting signal for flocks of green parrots that at once began to fly to the forest that stretched on the right between *La Esperanza* and the Caribbean Sea. Far away on the left a flock of turkey-buzzards circled over some foul carcase —of a mule, perchance—left by the muleteers, whose jingling bells and trappings Don Enrique could hear approaching along the *camino real.* As he puffed his cigar, and watched the peaceful tropic sunset, the drawling voices of the muleteers could be heard singing lazily—

> " *Canta, Filomena, canta,*
> *Canta y yote dare,*
> *Una cinta para tu pie,*
> *Y un collar para tu Garganta,*
> *Y una manta de differentes colores,*
> *Y un grande pucha de flores,*
> *Y si tu no me quieros ami,*
> *Temos a los regores.*"

This barbaric music, stealing across the bright green leaves of the plantains, echoed from the hollows lurking round *El Monte*—the single peak on the right of the house that raised its head from the forest, its foot hidden in dense vegeta- tion—a lonely summit that looked down un- challenged upon the flat land of the estate, a summit from whose bald top the cautious *bando- lero* kept watch, looking over the adjoining estates on the one hand, and the sapphirine sea on the other.

Ere the muleteers' song had faded in the distance, darkness began to gather over the scene; and when the singers' voices were lost in the forest road that led to Maravilla—a secluded little seaport some twenty miles from the estate,—the tropic night had already fallen; and the silence of sunset was suddenly broken by the awakening voices of myriads of living creatures. The forest resounded with strange and mysterious noises, whilst about the grounds of the *Casa Grande* thousands of insects began their nightly concert. The face of the sky, too, had changed from pale blue to violet. Overhead burnt brightly the great belt of Orion, whilst away in the southern sky the firefly-like stars glowed about the Southern Cross, and all around the wondrous violet skies showed sources of pale light, violet abysses, and bright points of fire that filled the beholder with wonder and poetry.

As Don Enrique smoked and gazed upon the magic beauty of the night, a flock of *cucuyos*, those large beetles with eyes and bodies of flame, flew through the grounds at the same moment that a black man-servant, clad in white linen with a red turban on his head, came noiselessly from the house, and removed the coffee-tray.

"How is the señora?" asked Don Enrique.

"Flora says she is well and the child sleeps, my master," replied the slave gravely.

"It is well; light my office candles."

"Yes, my master," replied the man, disappearing into the dark lofty rooms that opened from the piazza, rooms about which turbaned servants moved noiselessly lighting the candelabras.

The planter rose and stretched himself, bored to have to return to the petty details of business, and walked round to his private office, built against the house, but opening on to the piazza.

At the opposite side of the house was a similar room, kept as a guest-chamber for doubtful visitors, for in those wild times, unknown and sometimes suspicious persons came on to the estate and begged for a night's lodging—engineers going to and from distant estates, bagmen, shipwrecked mariners, and others. All these strange persons of unproved character slept in this guest-chamber outside the house, and were entertained indoors according to their position—either with the servants, by themselves, or with the planter.

Don Enrique entered his office, and took his seat at his writing-table that was covered with long day-books and ledgers made of coarse Spanish paper and bound in rough leather, files of letters written on thin blue paper and sealed with wafers, the writing here and there showing traces of the sand-box.

Whilst engaged in correspondence three stalwart negroes entered, each one carrying on his shoulder a long cube of ironwood, some eighteen inches through and six feet in length. Each block was fitted with a short mahogany handle for purposes of portage. These cubes of heavy timber were ranged side by side on the low, tiled window-seat against the iron gratings, and locked in their places by an iron bolt. Thus no one could shoot the planter through the windows, for West Indian landlords were subject to this attention long before the landlords of Ireland. Meanwhile all the windows of the house had been barricaded in a similar way for the night; all the candles had been lighted; and upon the dining-room table was placed a salver upon which stood a carafe of water, some lemons and sugar, some *panellas*, a dish of fruit: oranges, a pine-apple, and some custard apples. Beside this was placed a box of cigars, a flask of maraschino, glasses, and the brazier of *candela*.

The clock had struck midnight when Don Enrique locked his office doors. Standing for a minute, he looked over the sleeping landscape to see that no dread fires were burning in the cane-fields or forest, after which he entered the *sala*.[1]   The lofty white walls, simply decorated with oil-paintings, the marble floor and light cane

---

[1] Salon.

furniture lit up by wax candles, looked simple and inviting enough ; but Don Enrique passed on to the dining-room and drank a *panella* with water. Then returning to the *sala*, he opened a tall cedar door that led to his young wife's room. As he entered, the black waiting-women, with gaily-coloured turbans, white teeth, heavy gold ear-rings, and white muslin dresses, arose and bowed, then stood silently, whilst the master went to his wife's bedside and opened the musquito-nets to bid her good night and kiss his sleeping first-born, after which he returned to the dining-room, and called down the corridor—

"Caoba !"

In response, a bright-eyed, intelligent negro boy appeared in white livery, his short coat decorated with red cord. Bowing gravely, the lad said—

"Yes, my master."

"Call in the dogs ; I am going to bed."

"Yes, my master."

Don Enrique then went to one of the small bedrooms opening into the dining-room, as the lion-like mastiffs walked heavily into the house—*Como-tu*, spotted like a pard ; *Leon*, tawny of skin ; and *Sancho*, white of coat. Reappearing from the bedroom, Don Enrique went round the house examining the bolts and bars, some of the slaves already snoring on the mats before the bedroom doors, whilst away down the corridor some of the men-servants could be heard moving restlessly on their cotton cots.

After Caoba had valeted his master, he said—

"Good night, my master," and withdrew.

"Good night, Caoba," replied the planter, shutting the door.

Having placed his revolver beneath his pillow, he jumped into bed, drew his musquito-nets, and soon that household of eighteen persons was asleep.

CHAPTER II

IN THE FOREST PRIMEVAL

DON ENRIQUE was awakened that night by the loud and furious barking of the dogs. Quickly he lighted the candle by his bedside, and hastened to dress. Whilst he was still putting the finishing touches to his hasty toilet, some one knocked softly at his door.

"Who is it?" asked the *hacendado*.

"Caoba, my master," was the reply.

"Well, what is it, boy?"

"Ramon and Marzial have gone out into the night, and a countryman on horseback wishes to speak with the master."

"What is his business?"

"He will not say, my master."

"Good! Tell him to draw up at Ramon's wicket."

This was a small grated window opening into one of the trusty men-servant's rooms.

Caoba disappeared, and immediately returned, bearing a torch.

The *hacendado* followed the boy down the corridor, past the delicious scents that floated in from the garden on the night breeze, and entered Ramon's room, and cautiously opening the wicket, stood so that he could not be fired at from without, and asked in a commanding voice—

"Who is it?"

"Don Juan Chicadillo, Don Enrique," replied a harsh voice.

"*Hola!* Don Juan.   What do you want at this hour of the night?" asked the planter, looking out of the postigo, for he had recognised the man's voice.

Juan Chicadillo, who was seated upon a small horse carrying a *seron*, or panniers, that hung over each flank of his animal, replied in a low, clear voice—

"The ship!"

"*Hola!*" replied the *hacendado*.   "Wait a moment; you shall be admitted."

Then turning to Caoba, he gave quick orders that Juan should be admitted, and that his own horse, Marikita, should be saddled forthwith.

In a moment all the servants were astir, the dining-room lighted up, fresh cigars, coffee, and *candela* placed upon the table.   Juan Chicadillo was ushered in between the two herculean negroes, Ramon and Marzial, with their machetes in leathern cases at their belts.

The Spaniard was himself a picturesque-looking rascal—a small-featured, black-eyed rogue, with gleaming white teeth, and dressed in the ordinary peasant's costume—a broad-brimmed, coarsely-plaited grass hat, an embroidered white shirt, white trousers ; a long slender machete in silver-mounted leathern scabbard hanging at his side, and large brass Spanish spurs at his heels completed the costume.

When Juan saw Don Enrique, he took off his hat with a bow, saying—

"How are you, gentleman ?"

"Good morning, gentleman," replied the planter, with hidden contempt; "do me the favour of taking a seat, and *tomamos la mañana*," [1] he added, signing to Caoba to pour out a glass of *aguadiente* from a decanter, and to hand it to the Spaniard. The planter himself filled a liqueur glass with maraschino.

"To your health, Don Enrique," said the countryman, raising his glass.

"And to yours, Don Juan," retorted the planter.

When the glasses were drained, the *hacendado* turned to Caoba, and said—

"Boy—leave us."

"Yes, my master."

"And so the *Cruz de Mayo* is in at last, Don Juan ?"

"Yes, Don Enrique, with two hundred *bozales*, —young and handsome."

[1] Let us drink the morning.

"Does El Conde of La Caridad know ?"

"No, no, Don Enrique. I have heart—when a gentleman pays as you do. *Caramba*—El Conde may go rot."

"When do they land ?"

"At seven in the morning; it will be high water then, and she can slip over the bar if we are disturbed."

The planter thought for a few minutes, and replied—

"Good! we must start in two hours, Don Juan."

"As the gentleman pleases," retorted the Spaniard, now more at his ease.

"We'll have breakfast first. Eh, Don Juan ? The house is at your disposal.

"Many thanks, Don Enrique," said the Spaniard, bowing and helping himself to a *trabuco*, lighting it with a flint and tinder which he drew from his pocket.

Caoba was recalled, and promptly answered the summons.

"Order breakfast for two as soon as possible."

"Yes, my master," the lad replied, and ran off to the kitchen.

Whilst breakfast was being prepared by the Chinese *chef* and his black assistants over the charcoal fires, Don Enrique went to his safe, built into the wall of his bedroom, and filled a leathern belt with golden *onzas*, securing them about his waist; the Spaniard, meanwhile, smoking and drinking coffee.

Having visited his wife, and explained to her the journey he was about to take, he found, on returning to the dining-room, that the covers were laid, the silver and glass sparkling on the white napery beneath the candles. A vase filled with lilies and tuberoses—still dripping with the heavy tropical dew—shed a rich perfume through the cool dining-room.

After some delay, a gong sounded from the kitchen, and a file of comely young negresses, all gaily turbaned, led by matronly old Flora— a trusted slave—walked into the dining-room, each one bowing and muttering—

"Blessing, my master,"[1] as she placed her dish upon the table. Then they withdrew as they had come, down the corridor, to the kitchen, looking in the gloom like phantoms; but their merry laughter, as they reached the kitchen, dispelled the illusion.

Meanwhile, two men-servants and Caoba entered and stood silently behind their master.

"Come, sit yourself down, Don Juan," said the planter.

Don Juan deposited his dirty hat, in the crown of which was rolled a bandana handkerchief, upon the floor, boor that he was, and sat down

[1] Bendicion, mi amo.

opposite to Don Enrique; but never a smile passed over the *hacendado's* face, for apart from good breeding, he knew the Spanish peasantry and small farmers only too well: their pride was boundless, and he knew them to be touchy as tinder.

The alert and well-trained servants took off the covers, disclosing a sumptuous breakfast. There were omelette garnished with fried sweet peppers, fried ripe plantains and rice, fried green plantains, guinea-hen stew, fried fish from the river, soft-shelled crabs, fried oysters from Maravilla, avocado pears, cheese, Boston water-crackers, preserves, caraffes of water, and St. Vincent wine.

They ate their meal hurriedly, finishing up with a glass of maraschino and a cup of coffee, after which they lighted their cigars and walked on to the piazza, where the grooms stood with flaring torches, holding the horses, Ramon and Marzial standing at attention by the steps.

"You come this time, Ramon; and you, Marzial, re-lock the doors and keep watch," ordered the *hacendado* after he had mounted Marikita.

The grooms bowed, and Juan on his hack, and Don Enrique on his beautiful little chestnut, for all the horses of the island are small, being of Spanish descent, walked down the winding drive, Ramon following. At the gates there was a pause, whilst Ramon unlocked and re-locked them.

The party then took the road to the right, leading to the King's highway, and set off at a walk, for the roads were bad. The lovely tropical night was cool, and ere they reached the highway, Ramon was wet to the skin by the heavy dews that dripped from the long slim plantain leaves, rustling in the grove, and the tall wild plants that grew beside the road. Puffs of sweet perfume, swept by the gentle breezes, met them at every turn, while at intervals a cry came from the woods as some bird or beast fell a prey to the snakes or wild dogs. The sweet-potato fields looked black as they rode through them. After passing them, they rode through a tall strong gateway, and the little party found themselves off the *Esperanza* and on the highway. Beside them was the black mysterious forest, and every one instinctively loosened his weapon; and Don Enrique, digging his spurs into Marikita, cried to his companion—

"*Vamos, Don Juan.*"

Ramon seized his master's crupper, and both horses broke into that quick run so familiar to Cuban riders; and they passed along the highway, startling a *hutia* here, a *campanero* there, who cried his bell note. On reaching the foot of the mountain, they stopped beneath the violet sky and formed single file, Juan leading, for they were about to make short cut by a bridle-path, through the forest. Lighting fresh cigars, they passed beneath the tall, mast-like trees whose crowns far aloft hid the sky. The darkness deepened, and the night was filled with the music of myriads of musquitos that at once attacked the riders, so that they were compelled to break branches from the undergrowth to beat them off. They moved through an arcade walled on either side by thick vegetation, black depths filled with strange voices, matted growths impenetrable to daylight. After half-an-hour's ride, they passed the mouth of a cave in the mountain, when suddenly a negro ran across the path, and disappeared on his hands and knees into the thick vegetation.

"See, see! Don Enrique—a runaway negro."[1]

"I saw him," said the planter; "one of the Conde's people, I believe."

"Ah, he told me Alfonso, one of his carters, had run away on Monday."

"Why?"

"He had ordered him twenty-four for going with his *mulatta*, Rosa."

"*Hola*," said the planter, staring in the direction the fugitive had taken, "*sinverguenza*."

"I'll take him, my master," volunteered Ramon.

[1] Cimarron.

"No, man, it is not worth it."

"Ah! my master has heart," said Ramon sententiously, for it was well known that Don Enrique would never go out of his way to catch a strange fugitive.

"And Ramon, too," remarked the planter.

"Blessing, my master," said the negro.

Just before sunrise the little cavalcade emerged from the dark woods with blood-stained faces, for the mosquitos had played havoc with them. Riding side by side, they traversed a cart road with deep ruts on either hand.

It was now a little before five o'clock, and a deep silence had fallen upon the woods, broken only by the cries of some wild birds, among which the clear whistles of the meadow-larks, the calls of the *torrero*, as it pecked a rotten *quebrahacha* branch, and the call of the *campanero* could be distinguished.

"The morning has come," ventured Juan.

"Yes, there comes the light," replied Don Enrique.

"Yes, my master, and the parrots call, the morning is here," remarked the negro.

"The first glimmer of light brightened, the formless vegetation began to shape itself, when suddenly the red rim of the sun appeared.

"The sun, my master," said the stalwart negro, pointing to the glowing disc.

"Yes, like a fire," acquiesced the *hacendado*.

In less than half-an-hour the full day was upon them, the foliage glittered with heavy dew gems, and beams of golden light shimmered through openings in the scrub; flocks of parrots screamed as they fed on the wild oranges, great bees buzzed by, and gorgeous butterflies flew across the road, and alighted on shrubs to sun their metal-like wings. The temperature was delightful, and the riders soon recovered from the slight chill of the night, and began to chat cheerily, Ramon joining in.

"This way, this way, Don Enrique," shouted Juan, turning his horse into the forest again.

It was like going into a cave after the bright sunshine, for the light scarce penetrated the dense vegetation and twining creepers that crowned the tall, twisted tree-trunks. Strange and fantastic were some of these forest giants, twisted like mighty lianas wound together, whilst others were round and smooth, and others again had buttress roots—the ironwood, the caoba, the *quebra-hacha*, the cedar, the *sabicu*. All grew there, bound together by thick ropes of creepers. Some of the living ropes were covered with gorgeous yellow flowers, whilst others were lost in the thick glossy leaves of the tree-tops. Here and there the sun streamed down into the forest, through an opening left in the dense overgrowth, whence some hoary monarch had fallen, having crashed through the undergrowth, and was now lying on the ground—a corpse covered with lovely arums and gaily decorated with orchids.

Ramon ran up to the trunk and wrenched off a parasite, resembling the top of a pine-apple, and, raising it to his lips, he drank the pure water preserved in the cup.

"How beautiful it is!" cried Don Enrique, pointing to a tree, the trunk of which was covered with gorgeous red flowers.

"Lovely," said the Spaniard; "a bunch of flowers for the señora."

After riding another ten minutes, they emerged from the forest, and before them lay the sea—a sapphirine flood of indescribable hues, a background to the straggling but stately royal palms that grew along the coral reefs.

"The sea, the sea!" exclaimed the Spaniard, "we are nearly there."

Riding along the shore, they startled the crabs, that scattered over the coral, and dived into the water. Following the shore they turned a bend in the coast, and at once came in sight of the little bay of Maravilla. Outside the bar, a beautiful brigantine, with white, yacht-like canvas, tacked to and fro, awaiting a preconcerted signal.

"There it is—the ship!" said Juan excitedly.

Ramon stopped suddenly, and gazed at the vessel, then turning to Don Enrique, he said quietly—

"People, my master."

"Yes, Ramon."

The negro did not reply.

"Go, Ramon, and tell Don Eustaquio to hoist the flag."

Don Eustaquio was a Spanish clerk, who had charge of Don Enrique's warehouses on the far side of the bay—warehouses where the hogsheads of sugar were stored, ready for shipment to the United States. About these buildings stood a wharf knee-deep in the tropical sea. Near by was a cheap Spanish inn and some adobe cottages, in which lived poor whites, who trafficked with sailors in the ships—the men selling the seamen fruit and vegetables, fish and fowl, the women kisses and shells; but the population of the hamlet was small, not numbering seventy people, all told.

Ramon ran along the shore like a buck until he reached the clerk's house. Don Eustaquio stood before his door smoking a cigarette, and trimming his long-pointed finger nails.

"Señor, the master asks you to hoist the flag," said Ramon.

"Good, Ramon: and how is his Excellency?"

"Ah, señor, he is, as always, a good master. God preserve him."

"Well said, Ramon."

Immediately the Spanish flag was run up on the warehouse, and the yellow and red bars of Ferdinand and Isabella floated on the sea breeze that still blew landwards.

Immediately the signal was answered on the brigantine, and she altered her course, and steered for the wharves.

When Juan and the *hacendado* reached the Almaçen, a small party of swarthy Spanish villagers, dressed in half-sailor, half-countryman attire, took off their hats and cried—

"Good morning, your Excellency! Good morning!"

"Good morning, gentlemen," replied the planter, raising his hat; "*vaya*. Here is an ounce to drink the morning."

A grizzled old man ran up and seized the large gold coin, kissed the planter's hand, and muttered—

"A blessing upon you and yours, Don Enrique"—all the party repeating the patriarch's words.

Dismounting at the Almaçen, Ramon took the horses to the stables in the rear, and went in search of a feed of *maloja*.[1] Having fed the

---

[1] Maize fodder.

horses, and secured a roast *bônato*[1] and some pieces of *tasajo*,[2] broiled over the embers of a wood fire, Ramon took a small sack, and went down to the mangrove trees, to gather oysters that grew on their fantastic roots.

Whilst engaged in this work, he saw the brigantine cross the bar, lower her canvas, and run towards the wharf, propelled by a jib and a pair of long sweeps; and Ramon propped himself on a mangrove root to watch her actions, for his oyster-sack was full.

[1] Sweet potato.   [2] Jerked beef.

CHAPTER III

As Don Enrique and Juan Chicadillo and Don Eustaquio walked down to the black wharves, the graceful *Cruz de Mayo* with her sharp lines took in her jib and dropped anchor by the wharf. On her deck, flushed fore and aft, stood several swarthy men in blue guernseys and loose trousers, all wearing red caps. They were heavily armed with cutlasses and pistols.

The rakish-looking craft's large hold, fine lines, and mountains of canvas, proclaimed her to be a slaver, built in some Maryland dockyard, and laden with *bozales*.

A gang-plank was run on to the wharf, and a long line of negroes, chained together in pairs by the wrists, began to leave the ship, and huddle together on the wharf. They were emaciated, for the captain of the *Cruz de Mayo* was short with his rations ; but still they laughed and talked in their unknown tongue, casting their rolling eyes round the little harbour and pointing to the stately ceibas that towered into the sky.

Ten fierce-looking desperadoes — all Portuguese—followed them ashore, and the chief, a tall, black-whiskered Spaniard, went up to Don Enrique and said—

"Good morning, Caballero ; you keep good hours—time is money. Let us to business."

"Good morning, captain," said Don Enrique ; "will you do me the favour of walking this way?"

And he led the way to the wretched *posada* where the Spanish mob were drinking *San Vicenti* and playing dominoes. Two horses with panniers were tethered to the low, projecting roof of the *posada*, and eating fodder out of rough mangers, about which pigs, fowls, dogs, and naked children disported.

As Don Enrique entered, followed by the captain and Juan and Eustaquio, the skipper greeted the wine-bibbers with the " Good morning, gentlemen ; " while Lola, a handsome wench with lustrous black eyes and cream-coloured face, curtsied as the party removed their hats.

"Wine, cheese, and bread, Don Natan," ordered the *hacendado*.

"Yes, señor," said the proprietor, coming forward.

The villagers resumed their dominoes, but Lola's dark eyes wandered from the *hacendado* to the swarthy captain and back, as the simple refreshments were spread before the little party seated in the shop. Eustaquio meanwhile had ordered rations of bread, plantains, and oranges to be sent the *bozales*.

The slaver was full of talk, telling how he had sold the rest of his cargo to Don Miguel, how a French corvette was in search of him, and what a fearful storm they had weathered off Lagos.

"Well, captain, how much for the people?" demanded the *hacendado*, interrupting.

"Five hundred dollars apiece, and cheap at the price."

"Come, captain, five hundred dollars apiece! —that's a big price—very big, say four hundred dollars apiece, and it's a bargain. Why, there are twelve women and eight children."

"Four hundred, ah, very good. Do you think, Excellency, I pick people up on the sand-banks? No, thank you."

"Ready money is always good, and no questions asked," replied the *hacendado*.

"Four hundred for lucumis: you know the tribal marks, Excellency. Go and look; they are lucumis—all."

"Well, well; will the captain say four hundred dollars?"

"No, Excellency, but let us not play; the time runs away," said the captain, with smothered temper.

"Good, four hundred, and it's a bargain."

"And a dress for Lolita, Excellency," interrupted Lola.

"Just so, señorita—the dress," said Don Enrique.

The captain thought for a moment, and said in a more conciliatory voice—

"Come, come, Don Enrique, you are a *caballero;* let it be four hundred and fifty; the time runs away."

"*Bueno*, say four hundred, and it's done."

"Ah, Excellency, you are hard."

"No, señor," said Don Enrique, with decision. "Times are bad; the rats and the cane-fly have played the devil with the fields this year."

"Well, well, let it be four hundred dollars apiece, and twenty ounces for the captain."

"*Bueno, ya esta, *"said Don Enrique; and turning to Eustaquio, he gave him a sign, at which the clerk wrote out a receipt, which the captain signed, and then Eustaquio began to count out the gold from the canvas bags to which the planter's belt money had been added.

"*Vaya-te,* an *onza* for Lola," said Don Enrique, spinning the great Spanish coin on the counter before the girl.

"*Ah, muchas gracias,* Excellency, how brave you look!" said the girl, eyeing him with genuine admiration.

"If I were as brave as the señorita is beautiful, I should die happy," said Don Enrique gallantly.

Ramon, who had returned with his sack of oysters, was waiting outside with his master's horse and that of the Spaniard, Juan Chicadillo.

When the money was counted out, the party left the *posada*, and the planter and Juan mounted, Don Enrique slipping five ounces into the clerk's slender hand as he mounted.

"*Bueno gente*," said Ramon, as they rode towards the chattering *bozales*, round whom the fierce crew stood smoking *vaqueros* and drinking wine supplied by Eustaquio. As the *hacendado* approached, the sailors lifted their caps, and said, "Good day, *caballero*."

"Good day, and have something to drink the morning with," said Don Enrique, giving the nearest sailor—an evil-looking man, with a white seam across his cheek—a handful of small coins.

The *bozales* looked better already after their food, and were laughing and joking, whilst Juan formed them into line for the march home.

As soon as Don Enrique had taken charge of them, the sailors saluted and went off to the *posada*, to lay in fresh vegetables, fish, cigars, and *aguadiente*, and the *bozales* started for *La Esperanza*, Chicadillo riding in front, Ramon and Don Enrique bringing up the rear.

The crew of the brigantine soon got their

needs supplied and hastened aboard, and before
the *bozales* had turned the promontory that hid
the bay from sight, all hands were getting the
ship under canvas, much to Lola's disgust, for
she had hoped for a merry night with the black-
bearded Spanish captain of the *Cruz de Mayo*,
but she consoled herself that the Yankee skipper
after the *Esperanza* sugar would soon arrive.

As the *hacendado* and his *bozales* walked along
the shore, they saw the brigantine—which had,
in addition to the usual square fore-and-aft sails
of a brigantine, a mizzen-mast stepped well aft
close to her taffrail, upon which was spread a
spinnaker and gaff topsail—cross the bar safely;
and when Don Enrique and his party entered the
primeval forest, the *Cruz de Mayo* was already a
speck on the sapphirine sea, a dot, over which a
frigate-bird hovered in the æther.

The chain-gang walked through the silent
tropical forest in the mid-day heat, only stopping
once on the way to the *Esperanza* to watch a
large hubo snake chase a *jutia* to the end of the
long branch of a tall ebony tree, catch the prey,
and begin to swallow it, after having crushed the
creature's bones with its strong coils, for these
snakes are often fourteen feet in length, and,
though non-venomous, are deadly to fowls and
small animals.

When Don Enrique, who was now riding at

the head of the shackled gang, debouched from the forest, the plantain grove of the estate came in sight, and the *Casa Grande* gleamed in the bright sunshine, the faithful Marzial standing at attention at the distant gates.

As they rode along the cocoa-nut avenue, the *bozales* began to chatter and gesticulate, for they recognised the sweet potatoes, plantains, and cocoa-nuts. When they arrived at the gates of the house, they stopped, and Marzial took off his hat, and said—

"Good day, my master."

"Good day, Marzial; and the mistress?"

"Is well, my master, and the child too: but the señora has had much fright."

"In the name of God, why?" asked Don Enrique eagerly.

"The wild cat, my master."

"Tell me quickly, man."

"My master, the señora and child, whom may God bless, were sleeping, when suddenly the señora screamed out 'Maria.' That, my master, woke the house, and they saw a big wild cat, my master, jumping up at the señora's big looking-glass. The house began to shriek—like women, and to call 'Caoba, Caoba;' and, my master, the young Caoba seized the big iron bar from the front door, and ran in and killed the wild cat, and called the women cowards."

"Good God! how did it get into the room?" asked Don Enrique eagerly.

"My master, it must have entered the house when your Excellency departed this morning, and it must have got into the señora's room when the women took in the herb tea at five o'clock."

"Good! And Caoba—where is he?"

"We cannot find him, my master."

"Why?"

"My master, he broke the long glass in killing the cat, and has fear. You see, my master, the wild cat kept jumping at the glass."

"Bobo, tell him I shall reward him. I must go on now to the *batey;* but tell the señora we are well, and I shall return in two hours."

"Yes, my master," said Marzial, looking down the newly-purchased *bozales*, for he, too, was a lucumi : but he recognised no one.

And the gang started at a slow walk over the cracked earth, leading by a stone wall to the *batey*. As they passed along, the road to the right was walled in by the tall cane-crop, the ditch bordering the cane-fields being filled with dead cane leaves.

On the left, however, was the *corral*, a slope of ground reaching to the walls of the *Casa Grande*, an enclosure overgrown with weeds, and studded with rounded and crenellated outcrops of lime-

stone boulders. In this *corral* the young steers
recently branded and freshly caught in the great
run, or in the far lands of the estate, were confined, ready to go under the yoke for the coming
grinding season, in harness with others broken in
years before.

Passing beneath a tall gateway, the procession
entered the *batcy*, as the works and negro quarters
are called. Before them stretched the long white
boiling and purging houses with galvanised
roofs, and tall chimneys with smoke-blackened
mouths. On the right was a bagazo-house, resembling a large and picturesque Norwegian barn.
As they approached the archway perforating the
long buildings afore mentioned, they saw a
white cooper with some negroes busily making
hogsheads, whilst the cold empty feeding-pits
to the boilers yawned on the right, for as yet
the dead season had sway.

The gang marched beneath the archway over
which the sugar trains ran on rails ; and when
they had passed through they came upon a cart-
way leading to the right, where the *bagazo* fell
from the rollers into light horse-carts. At right
angles to this road stretched the roofed engines
and boilers and feeding stairs—several horses
munching the corn in open stalls by the engine-
house.

Don Enrique waved his hand to the Spanish

engineer, who with his black assistants was getting the machinery ready for the grinding season.

On the left stretched the quarters of the white mechanics, the head-carpenter, master-mason, engineer, and major-domo. Beyond their common kitchen stretched the Chinese quarters palisaded with whitewashed boards, and on their left the roar and hum of the saw-mills and knocking from the carpenters' and blacksmiths' shops could be heard.

The gang marched across the *batey* and turned to the right, leaving the large granary raised on poles on the left, and the administrator's square white house in the orange grove by the river behind them. Ahead they could see a quadrangular barrack of low buildings pierced with small grated windows, and entered through a pair of massive iron gates hung under a staircase leading up to some wooden rooms placed on the second story.

In front of this staircase they were drawn up, and stood facing the open gates.

They gazed up at the overseer's quarters; rooms flanked by the hospital wards, for contagious diseases were removed to palm-leaf huts at a distance.

It was past two o'clock when the gang drew up before the *barracon*, and the heat was intense, the thermometer standing at 94° in the shade. Every bird was silent; even the petals were dropping from the flower stems into the river that ran behind the *barracon*. The plants drooped in the intense heat, and the sun was almost insupportable to Don Enrique, hardened though he was to the climate. The negroes, however, showed no signs of discomfort, but chatted in their unknown tongue, their eyes staring curiously at each new sight.

Don Enrique dismounted, and bade Ramon ring the call-bell to summon all hands from the fields. No sooner did the loud-voiced bell begin to clang forth in the hot stuffy air, from the belfry above the overseer's quarters, than negroes in the sick wards began to peep curiously through the slanting slats before them, whilst children and old people past work came toddling from their quarters and staring at the *bozales*. At the same time the administrator walked over from his house.

He was a short, one-eyed Yorkshireman, and though a good administrator, was never liked by Don Enrique, for he was reticent, avoided good cheer, was ever nursing his health and calculating how to advance himself—nor was he a gentleman.

"Ah, good morning, Don Enrique," said the softly-spoken man as he came up.

"Good morning to you, Don Martin. Taking a *siesta*, eh ?" queried Don Enrique with a contemptuous gleam in his eye.

"Yes, yes ; the sun is fearfully hot ; but what have you here ?"

"A hundred and three lucumis—landed this morning."

" Fine upstanding men and women too. Cheap ?"

"So, so," replied Don Enrique.

The agile figure of the overseer, Don Leonaldo, then appeared galloping on to the *batey*, which he entered at a furious pace, drawing his horse up as he came to Don Enrique, his machete and heavy stirrups gleaming in the sun, as he took off his hat with a sweep, and said cheerily—

"Good day, Don Enrique, *ay, Dios mio!* I thought it was fire, but I see—more people ;" and he ran his eye intently over the gang, remarking, "Good strong lucumis."

As the masters talked together, the field hands came filing in Indian fashion, the men dressed in straw hats and cotton shirts and trousers, and the women and girls in handkerchiefs and cotton skirts—all carrying machetes, for they had been weeding. At the head of the men walked a tall negro—the contra-majoral—with a whip, whilst at the head of the women walked a magnificent negress with a cow-hide.

The gang marched up and formed a hollow square before the overseer's quarters, as was the custom for night and morning roll-call.

In the square stood Don Enrique, the administrator, the overseer, and the *bozales*.

"Send for the major-domo," ordered Don Enrique.

The contra-majoral repeated the order to a lad, who ran over to the white men's quarters, and returned with a black-eyed little Spaniard with a big moustache.

Meanwhile the blacksmith had arrived, and was standing ready to strike the manacles from the *bozales*, who looked on timidly at this new scene.

"Who speaks lucumi?" asked Don Enrique of the people.

"I do, my master," volunteered a stalwart carter.

"Well, tell these people I have bought them, and that they are going to have their fetters knocked off. Tell them that they must work for me, and I will treat them well; but tell them that if they disobey, they will get the lash; and if they run away, they may be killed."

"Yes, my master," said Pablo; and drawing himself up to his full height, he made the speech ordered in lucumi, the *bozales* listening eagerly to every word.

The blacksmith then knocked off the shackles, but even then the savages crowded timidly together.

Pablo then marshalled them into line, the major-domo distributing to each shirts, trousers, hand-kerchiefs, and to the women and children dresses and handkerchiefs. When this was done, Don Enrique said—

"Now, my people, take your black brothers and sisters to your *boheas*, and show them how to cook *funchi* and *tasajo*, and treat them well. Arrange it amongst yourselves."

Then bidding his people good day, Don Enrique mounted his horse and set off with Ramon for the *Casa Grande*.

Meanwhile the majoral called the roll, and with Pablo billeted the new-comers on the old hands, preparatory to their occupying the new huts standing ready for them.

This was done to promote friendship between the old and new hands, and to educate the savages before entrusting them to housekeep for themselves.

After this ceremony the people were dismissed to their quarters, and the new arrivals went through the gates, surrounded by a mob of eager-spoken and gesticulating old hands.

And Juan Chicadillo took a *libranza* to the major-domo to be cashed, and left the estate, after a glass of gin with Don Leonaldo, with a smiling face, a big cigar, and his panniers filled with flour, *tasajo*, and rice, which he had bought from the estate stores, for it was customary to supply, as a favour, certain people with these commodities, together with sugar and *aguadiente*.

CHAPTER IV

WILD CATS

WHEN Don Enrique arrived at the *Casa Grande* the first gong had sounded for dinner, for it was after four o'clock, yet this man of iron, after dismissing Ramon with a peseta to buy tobacco, ran into the house to his wife, who had recovered from her fright. Kissing her, and hugging the baby boy, he said,—

"What shall we do to Caoba?"

"You must reward him, dear," said his wife, an English lady.

"Yes—reward, yes ; but I must go and bathe, and dress for dinner, for I'm all perspiration and dirt. My very mouth is caked with dust."

Going out to the bath-house he met Caoba.

"How brave !" said the planter, patting the negro youth.

"If I ever grow to be as brave as my master, it will delight me," said the youth sincerely.

"You will. I'll talk with you after dinner, boy. Pour a bottle of Florida water into the bath—quickly."

.   .   .   .   .   .

In another half-hour the planter was sitting at his lonely dinner-table, as fresh-looking as the tuberose in his button-hole.

He had dismissed the two other waiters, and turning to Caoba, who looked so smart in his Zouave-like, white linen jacket, trimmed with red braid, he said, as he broke an avocado pear into his soup—

"Would you like to be free, boy?"

"No, my master, I should not. I like the master and the señora; no, no."

After the fideo soup, delicious pargo, fried to a turn in oil, was placed upon the table.

"Well, lad, what would you? for I want to reward you."

"Oh, nothing, my master."

After the fish the negresses brought up a number of dishes from the kitchen, minced "jerked beef" dressed with wild tomatoes and peppers, ajiaco, fricasseed guinea-fowl, roast turkey, beans, yams, yucca, boiled sweet potatoes.

The planter ate hurriedly, for he was excited, and more or less worried, for the planter of a great estate leads a patriarchal life mixed with barbaric splendour, and is judge, doctor, lawyer, farmer, manufacturer, consulting engineer—all in one.

After the roasts followed the cheese and guava jelly, which the planter ate together, as is the habit of the country, finishing with a delicate apple banana gathered from the garden behind him, and an orange.

When the dessert was cleared away and the coffee, liqueurs, and fire were brought in, the master said—

"Caoba, come here!"

The smart and intelligent negro came, and stood by his side, saying—

"My master."

"Caoba, I like bravery above all things. You won't take your freedom—you may if you like. But if you don't wish to be free, you can choose what girl you like from the *bohea*, and you can choose your own work."

"A thousand blessings on my master," said Caoba, visibly overcome.

"It is true; go now, and tell me after the grinding is over what you would like."

"Master is too good to a poor slave."

"*Vaya-te, vaya-te!*" said the planter, rising and going out on to the piazza to smoke and enjoy the cool of the evening.

CHAPTER V

THE following afternoon Don Enrique left his office, and lingered in the verandah to gaze over the burning landscape—the forest on the right, with the plantain grove cowering at its feet; the seas of sugar-cane glancing yellow in the sunlight, right away and beyond the *Marguerita's* iron-roofed buildings, that seemed to irradiate heat in the fierce tropical light—his own works and *barracon* on the left, the noise of riveters, at work on a new boiler, sounding through the still, hot afternoon, right up to the house and down to the river-course winding away to the left, marked by giant royal palms, whose white, smooth round trunks, with tufts of huge green leaves, dozed against the fierce blue sky.

All was silent. Even the little hawk with her young that lived over the office, dozed, and the meadow-larks no longer whistled *whee-wheet*; the very cacti in the ground looked hot, and all ironwork burnt the hand. Suddenly the planter's sight was focussed to a corner of the estate edged by the woods, belonging to a Spanish squatter.

A Peninsularian, Sancho Gomez, and his two sons lived there in the heart of the woods, too lazy to fell the timber and clear the land, content merely with raising a few cattle, which they allowed to run wild through their scrub.

Don Enrique looked long at that corner of the estate, when he suddenly called out, "Caoba !"

"Yes, my master," answered the boy, appearing from the *sala*.

"Go and tell Joaquin to saddle El Moro, and tell Marzial and Ramon to come here at once."

The boy ran off to give the message.

In a few minutes one of the grooms led a horse to the piazza, followed by Marzial and Ramon with lassoes twisted round their torsos, and their long knives hanging on their hips.

"Call the dogs, Marzial. Gomez's cattle are in the cane. This is the third time. I have warned him many times ; now let him look to his own."

Marzial ran round the house and collected the four great Cuban mastiffs.

"*Vamos*," said the planter, mounting his horse in the burning heat, and starting off at a swift run, the negroes jogging alongside, each holding by one of the stirrups, and the great dogs following like lions. They passed the *corral*, crossed the *batey* by the corn-house, and forded the river by the gourd-tree, now loaded with green shiny globes.

A shag flew up from the river-bed, and a water-hen called as they waded across and struck off into a lonely road between two cane-fields, disturbing coveys of quails that ran into the crops, and startling flocks of little yellow birds and swarms of butterflies. After riding a mile, they came to Gomez's woods, separated from the estate by a ring fence, bristling with a young prickly pear hedge. The fence was freshly broken down in one place, and they could hear the stray cattle breaking through the sugar-canes and munching the leaves.

"*Carajo!*" said the planter, drawing up his horse. "*Anda* Watche, *anda* Leon, *anda perros*," urged he to the dogs, at the same time loosening his revolver. "You, Marzial and Ramon, go and round them off."

The negroes dived into the cane with the dogs. The planter sat his horse by the forest, and listened as the dogs, cattle, and men broke through the cane. Suddenly the dogs began to bark furiously as they came up with the stragglers, and the negroes began to shout; and the huge beasts could be heard crashing through the cane, coming towards the planter. Suddenly a half-wild bull burst from the cane-field, worried by the great dogs, who were jumping at his throat. The enraged animal, with gleaming eyeballs, tried hard to toss one dog and then the other, but they were too alert.

"*Anda perros*," urged the planter, as the bull tore past him, when suddenly the tiger-like Watche made a spring and seized the bull by the throat. The huge beast charged at the broken fence, but fell in the ditch, when the mighty Leon then sprang upon him and tore out his throat, the blood gushing over the dogs, the bull's mighty sides heaving ; but after a short struggle the beast was dead, and the dogs were greedily lapping its blood, when Don Enrique rode up and beat them off with a riding-whip. There was another crashing in the cane, and three cows burst into the open, followed by the negroes, who held their lassoes ready in their hands. Immediately the animals were clear of the cane, each man threw his lariat and secured his prey. The dogs made a rush at the nearest beast, but the planter again beat them off. The lassoed cattle were restless and tried to struggle, but the negroes quickly bound their heads to their hind-legs, when they gave in and stood quietly. The third beast had meanwhile escaped through the opening into the woods. The planter dismounted, and going to the fence, examined it critically. He found that the old bast thongs had been *cut*.

"Ah ! I thought so," he said. " Let in on purpose ; curse the Spaniards!" then turning to the negroes, he asked, " Any brand on the cattle ? "

" No, master."

" Gomez again. It is good ; he shall pay dearly for this."

Then, taking charge of the ropes securing the cows, he ordered the negroes to gather some bast and re-make the fence — a job they soon finished.

" Now, drive the cows home," said the planter.

The negroes looked wistfully at the dead bull.

The planter noticed their looks, and said, " It is good. You shall have fresh meat to-night in *barracon*, but leave the bull alone."

The party then set off for the estate, the captured cows being driven in front. Before they reached the ford, the sky above the dead bull was black with circling turkey-buzzards.

And that night Gomez's cows were served out as fresh rations to the hands.

CHAPTER VI

THE BANDIT'S THREAT

THE following Monday was the negroes' holiday, and also the day of the grinding dinner, a yearly feast looked forward to by all the white employees on the estate, for they were always entertained handsomely upon this occasion.

That morning the negroes had scattered, as was their custom on holidays, to amuse themselves. Some had gone to work in their gardens, where they grew tobacco, which they sold; where they kept bees, whose wax supplied them with candles; where they grew their favourite pea-nuts, bananas, plantains, yucca, and yams. Some even grew flowers, every man on the estate that wished it being allowed an allotment, most of them abutting on the river.

Others spent their day in killing their pigs, for nearly all of them possessed their split palm-log pig-styes on the river's edge behind the *barracon*. Truly they smelt somewhat in the hottest weather, and the timid, one-eyed Yorkshireman wished to do away with them; but the planter would not listen, knowing that the negroes valued this privilege greatly, for they made a considerable sum of money over the sale of their pork.

Some, who were to be trusted, had permits to go to the nearest village, some three miles off, to make purchases, and sell their pork and tobacco to the little shopkeeper.

A few fished in the river. Others set figure-of-four traps for wild pigeons, or others went to the high woods, hunting *hutias* or crested pigeons, when in season, and parrots. Every one did as he pleased, but all were due at roll-call, at half-past five o'clock.

Each estate held the holiday upon a different day, so that the negroes should not meet and conspire to rise, a danger ever present to the planter's mind.

At five o'clock the big bell was rung, and the holiday-makers trooped in with hoes and rakes, with birds and fish, with purchases and sweets from the village, and by half-past five had formed into a hollow square in front of the overseer's house to answer to their names. After the roll-call they were locked into the *barracon* for the night.

On holidays they generally cooked a great feast in the common kitchen, their rations of mush, broiled jerked beef, and sweet potatoes or plantains, which each family supplemented with kalalu soup, joints of savoury roast pork, fried fish, or roast pigeons, and often guava jelly, luxuries provided by themselves.

After the feast the great tom-toms were heated before wood fires, the players standing astraddle, beating on the stretched skins with their palms; whilst the men and women gathered round the different tom-toms and began their African dances, shrieks of laughter from dark corners or uninhabited *boheas* breaking in upon the dancers, the jokes of amorous couples who had straggled from the dance. Everything was permitted to these happy negroes except spirit drinking. To smuggle that in to the *barracon* was a grave offence, punished with the lash.

When the negroes were locked in after roll-call that night, the white employees, dressed in their best, walked up to the *Casa Grande*, to the grinding dinner.

The first to arrive was the Spanish engineer, a dark, short, good-natured man, dressed in a black frock coat and white linen trousers. His jovial nature made him everybody's friend. No sooner had he sat down in one of the rocking-chairs than the Cyclopean Yorkshireman, the administrator, entered, having ridden up on his bay. He was dressed like Don Enrique, in silk and linen, but his manners were provincial and cold, and, after the usual salutations, he sidled off to look over the papers that lay on a side table.

The next arrival was the master-mason, a grave, middle-aged Spaniard, who came in with the major-domo, a Spanish dandy dressed like Don Enrique. They were followed by the master-carpenter, who with the master-mason was dressed in a blue linen suit. The carpenter was a jovial but sly Canary Islander. Last to come in was Don Leonaldo and the *boyero*, or cattle manager, a light-haired Biscayino, together with a sharp, rough-featured *Gallego*, the head-carter. These three men were dressed in the usual countryman's attire.

After shaking hands all round, the party began talking cheerily of the coming grinding season, when Don Enrique interrupted :—

"There is only the distiller to come now : where is he. Where is Don Ramon ?"

"I saw him by the river this afternoon, under the plum-trees, with that wench Louisa," said Don Basileo, the carpenter, slyly.

"Hola! likes the women, eh ?" replied Don Enrique.

"Yes, we have got two mulattos too many now ; we shall have more if he stays," said Don Leonaldo.

"Yes, I don't like mulattos," said Don Enrique ; "they are devils, and as lazy as trashy whites."

"It's true," said the overseer ; adding, "a

mulatto works like a trashy white, and thinks like a bad nigger."

"The females alone are bearable," said the dandy major-domo; "they are handsome."

At this juncture, the distiller, a tall and sedate Spaniard, entered, clad in white, and making a sweeping bow to the company, he begged a thousand pardons for his tardiness.

"It is granted, *caballero*," said the planter; and turning, he called—

"Muchacho!" when a man-servant entered with trays of Cuban cocktails, one of the most delightful mixtures ever compounded by any artist in drinks.

After the cocktails had been drunk, the planter led the way to the dining-room.

It was a warm night, and the jalousies opening into the garden had been thrown asunder, and the sweet smells of oleanders, mignonette-trees, lilies and tuberoses, were wafted into the dining-room. Behind the rustling banana leaves, the great planets burnt brightly in the violet sky, and far away in the *corral* could be heard the sounds from the cattle, whilst every now and then an owl or other night-bird flew over the garden.

The planter took the head of the table, the administrator the foot, and the men ranged themselves according to their position, at the right and left.

And the repast began. The drip of the water from the porous stone filter into the huge earthenware jar below, could be heard through the slats of the *tinajera* : this and the rustling of the banana leaves were the only sounds audible during the lulls of conversation, so peaceful was the night.

As the dinner progressed, the comely negresses going to and from the kitchen with the dishes would occasionally be startled by a large, hairy-legged tarantula that crept in from the garden through the open door.

The cigars, coffee, and liqueurs, a case of varied bottles, had been brought in, and with them the fire in the braziers, when Caoba brought a letter which he handed to Don Enrique.

The master took it, and breaking the wafer, began to read, and as he read, a frown settled on his face.

" *Sinverguenza,*" he muttered between his teeth, laying the letter down.

"What is the matter ?" asked Martinez the engineer.

" Listen, *caballeros,*" said Don Enrique, " to the threat of that *sinverguenza,* Lorenzo the bandit.

"'LA LOMA.

"' MY DEAR SIR,—You in person killed a bull belonging to Don Sancho Gomez, so injuring a poor Spaniard. I hereby warn you, by the

Blessed Virgin, that unless you leave fifty ounces at the *posada* of Don Juan Tinente, addressed to me, before Monday next, I will burn your estate, and give you a *machetaso.*—I remain, my dear sir,   LORENZO ALMENDAREZ.'"

The keen eye of the planter ran round the faces of his guests, for he knew few of the lower-class Spaniards were to be trusted ; but he felt pretty sure of his men, with the exception of the *boyero*, and old Basilio the Guacho carpenter. Don Leonaldo was noisily indignant, exclaiming, " Dog to write to a gentleman !"

"A dangerous man, a dangerous man," whined the administrator ; "he must be bribed."

" By God, never !" said Don Enrique, slamming his fist on the table ; "I will kill him with my own hand first."

"Shoo ! shoo !" said Don Martinez, turning instinctively towards the carpenter, who was looking attentively at the end of his cigar.

" *Vaya*, gentlemen," said the planter suddenly, throwing the brigand's letter into one of the braziers. " Let us play cards—come, a game of *espada.*"

They played for several hours, smoking and drinking and changing money, until, tired of gaming, the noisy revellers, heated with good old Catalan wine, strolled into the garden, disturbing the two parrots, one of which spoke Spanish, and slept in the cotton tree, and the other, which spoke English, slept in the South Sea rose. But the birds immediately began to scold each other, much to the amusement of the guests.

It was nearly three o'clock when the party broke up, the distiller and the dandy quickly separating from the rest, and disappearing in the thick herbage round the house, whither two of the comely black waitresses could have been seen gliding a few minutes before.

The planter sat brooding over the bandit's threat for long, thus giving the love-lorn maidens time to return to the house before it was locked for the night.

OLD FLORA'S DEATH

ALL the following week the *batey* was a busy scene.

Machetes were being ground at the carpenter's shop, wheelwrights were busy fitting tires to the new wheels, heating the great iron hoops in wood fires, and bracing them to the great, solid cart wheels. The negro carters had been appointed to that most distinguished of positions amongst the field hands. These men were busy greasing their axle-trees, fitting the poles to the bodies of the tumbrils, and lashing them together with ropes, so that they could safely carry the huge loads of cane. They were also fitting the yokes to the shafts, and repairing the gear generally.

The negro youths who drove the light bagasse horse waggons, were fitting up their harness and oiling the joints of their tilt-carts.

In the dark, cool boiling-house the boilers were cleaning the pans, greasing the windlasses, and fitting up their skimmers and other tools. In the purging-house the new hogsheads—pierced at the bottom—were being arranged over the drainage baulks.

Everywhere the work pressed, and no one was idle, for the great harvest and manufacture of the year was at hand, the net result of which might yield from £10,000 to £16,000 profit to the great planter.

For Don Enrique himself it was a restless, wearing time ; the machinery might break down, the cane-fields might take fire, for the crop was like tinder, and the sugary stalks would burn like spirits.

In the midst of this worry of the beginning of the grinding season, the faithful old negress Flora fell ill of an apoplexy and died. This was a great grief to the family, and especially to the señora, who had just left her bed, and it was with heavy heart that Don Enrique welcomed the Spanish priest who came to bury her.

The funeral procession was formed at the big house—the priest walking ahead, bareheaded, the men-servants following with the brass-nail studded coffin, the other servants and old Flora's relatives from the *barracon* following them, wringing their hands and wailing in unknown tongues, the planter bringing up the rear, as they descended the drive, and turned towards the burying-ground, which lay beyond the river, distinguished by a single royal palm. This primitive Campo Santo was surrounded by a prickly-pear hedge, and in the centre stood a rustic cross, overgrown with tropic creepers.   In this lovely spot were laid the remains of the faithful old servant.

CHAPTER VIII

THE BANDITS

AT the end of the week the American Consul—a well-known commission merchant, who bought most of Don Enrique's sugars, came to stay for the week, escorted by Caoba, who had been sent off with horses to the railway terminus, some three miles away, to meet him.

On arriving at the house, the Consul bathed, and after dressing for dinner, went into the saloon, which was empty. To beguile the time, he took up the last copy of *Harper's Weekly*, when Caoba suddenly ran into the room and hastily bolted the doors.

"What is it, lad?" asked the Consul, turning from his paper.

"Bandits, sir; where is my master?"

"Dressing."

Caoba ran to his master's room, and said quite coolly—

"The bandits, master! Rosa saw them coming."

"*Carajo!* the brutes," said Don Enrique, seizing his revolver, and running into the *sala*, where stood the tall, fair, honest-looking Consul, quite composed, and the señora, white and anxious.

"They will murder us all; there are thirteen of them—look," said the señora.

And sure enough thirteen armed men, dressed like peasants, were riding slowly up the drive— amongst them two negroes. The chief, Lorenzo, rode ahead—a tall, fine-looking, black-bearded Spaniard, armed to the teeth. The party rode up to the verandah, when the chief knocked carelessly with the butt of his pistol on the rail.

"What do you want? Who are you?" asked Don Enrique from the window.

"Ah, good day, Don Enrique. How are you, gentlemen? May we alight?" asked the Spaniard, with a sneer.

"Who are you, and what do you want, gentlemen?" asked the Consul coldly.

"Don Lorenzo Almendarez and his *gentlemen* come to visit Don Enrique and his señora."

"Ah, dogs!" said Don Enrique.

"Take care, the balls fly quickly," said Lorenzo, with ill-concealed anger, and several of the band began to finger their machetes.

Going to a corner of the saloon in which always stood three loaded carbines with fixed bayonets, Don Enrique took one and handed one to the Consul, saying, "By God, we'll kill that lot."

Turning to Caoba, who stood coolly looking on, he said, "Run and fetch Ramon and Marzial."

The negro giants soon came in and saluted.

"The bandits, men; have you got your machetes?"

"Yes, my master," and they drew their short, broad blades.

"Now you, Caoba, take the señora to the back room."

"God help us!" said the poor lady, going to the bedroom and hugging her baby to her.

Meanwhile the bandits had dismounted and were tying their horses to the verandah.

Don Enrique's rage knew no bounds.

"Dogs!" he cried; "the first man who walks up those steps I'll shoot like a cur."

"How brave!" said Lorenzo with a sneer, as he cocked his pistol.

"See you, I am the American Consul," said the visitor, "and this gentleman is my friend. If you harm either of us you will answer for it with your lives."

"Americano, eh?" said the chief, a little staggered. "It's worse than the English; but we want money."

"Let me shoot the brute," said Don Enrique in an undertone to the Consul, at the same time raising his carbine.

"For God's sake don't; are you a madman?" asked the Consul in a low, quick voice. "They will murder us all if you do, and burn the estate."

Don Enrique dropped the barrel of his weapon.

Then, turning to the bandit chief, the Consul said coolly, "How much do you want?"

"Fifty ounces."

"For what, *caballero?*"

"Don Enrique killed a poor Spaniard's bull on his land, and then drew it across the fence on to the estate, to make believe the bull had broken through."

"It's a lie, coward," hissed Don Enrique, now mad with rage, and threatening death in every line of his severe countenance.

"How a lie?" asked Lorenzo, smiling cynically.

"The cattle were let into my cane from Gomez's land to fill their starving bellies, for their master is like you—a lazy scoundrel who won't work; he is no man."

A flush of anger passed over the leader's face, and some of the bandits began to murmur and talk together, whilst others seemed to be examining the house and looking for weak points for an attack.

Suddenly the Consul threw a purse out of the window, saying, "*Tenga*, Don Lorenzo Almendarez, my friend is a gentleman of honour, and what he says is true : the cattle were let into the cane piece ; *vaya*, there are your fifty ounces ; begone, and don't trouble gentlemen any more."

"Why did you throw the dogs the gold ? it is rank cowardice," said Don Enrique, sullen as a thunder-cloud.

"For God's sake, think of your wife and child, my friend. If they were not here I would fight to the death with you."

"By God, perhaps you're right, *amigo;* but, by the Lord, I would like to drill a hole through that Lorenzo."

The bandit had picked up the purse, and was holding a consultation with his men. The consultation was short, when the chief turned and said—

"Gentlemen, a thousand pardons for having disturbed such honourable gentlemen as yourselves. We offer you our apologies for having frightened the señora, and wish you a very good evening," and, taking off his hat, the rascal bowed like a courtier.

The party soon mounted and set off at a run down the hill, turning off to the right towards the highway and the forest. The ironwood blocks were immediately put up, Marzial and Ramon were sent as watchmen to the tower, and the family sat down to dinner, whilst Caoba ran off through the brush at the back with a note to the administrator, warning him of what had occurred, and putting him on the *qui vive;* but the villains did not return that night, as was half anticipated.

CHAPTER IX

EL PADRE

As Don Enrique and the Consul sat the following day, after breakfast, in the piazza, the portly figure of the little priest could be seen riding towards the house, for he had been summoned to christen the new-born heir to the estate, several newly-born negro children, and the savages that had been bought from the slaver.

Don Martin was a jovial man of the world, who liked the planter, and was liked by him, for, though not of the Roman Catholic faith by choice, it was, in such times and in such a country, necessary to profess that faith. Indeed the priest took this view of religion himself, and confessed to the planter that he looked upon religion as a civilising agent, and a necessary deterrent to the lower classes : so they were good friends. Moreover, the good cheer of the *Casa Grande* was very acceptable to the good-natured little *gourmet*, living, as he did, in a dull Spanish town. These visits were, then, looked forward to by both parties, and always remembered as red-letter days. Moreover, the fees netted by the little priest upon these occasions were considerable.

After his arrival at the house he donned his canonicals, and the tapers were lit in the saloon, and the little son and heir given the holy wafers, the long row of savages—already improved in appearance—and slaves with their children looking on reverently. The negroes were then given the salt, and after the ceremony was duly finished the planter's child received a handful of coins of different values, strung upon gay ribbons, and each negro child was given a silver *real* on a piece of red ribbon.

There was not much time after the ceremony before dinner was served, and, of course, the chief topic of conversation was the recent visit of the bandits.

"Ah, my friend," said the priest, "time is money, and money buys all things, even bandits."

"I'll never buy them," said Don Enrique sternly.

"Ah, but, my son, we must be wise in this wicked world. A few ounces a year, and your estate is safe ; is it not worth it ?"

"No ; it is a coward's way."

"Ah, you are a fire-eater, my son. Listen. What can you, a man of peace, do against the sons of darkness ? You work and they lie in wait, and murder you, and your señora too, and child. Is it not worth a few ounces?"

"Be sensible, Don Enrique," said the Consul; "this is not war. It is not cowardly to pay for security under the circumstances."

"No, no," said the little priest soothingly. "My son will let me pay them a hundred ounces a year, and they shall not trouble him, I'll promise."

"Oh, Don Enrique, what is a hundred ounces after all?" urged the Consul.

"They are such cut-throats that they will probably take the hundred ounces, and stab you in the back the first chance."

"Tut, tut," said the priest; "they look to the future. Look, my son, there is security of my holy office: I swear it. Lorenzo is my godson."

Don Enrique repressed an expression of disgust, and said resignedly—

"Father, as it is so, pay the dogs."

"Ah, that is wise, my son; now let us have some music from the señora," said the little padre, and the party adjourned to the saloon.

CHAPTER X

ON the following Tuesday—the first Tuesday in January—the great plantation bell rang at five o'clock, an hour earlier than hitherto, and while it was yet night.

But the torches in the corridors of the great house had been gliding to and fro, like comets, an hour before, and the planter was already breakfasting when the big bell rang, for it was the first day of the grinding season.

That morning the fires were lighted beneath the boilers of the engine, and below the great copper boilers, and they would be kept burning night and day till May—till the rains began.

That morning the field hands would separate into night and day gangs, each shift getting six hours' sleep, for the work would never cease. All through those months the gangs would cut cane by day under the burning sun, and by night under the fiery-red planets and brilliant starlight, the sentinel giant ceibas and lofty royal palms looking on. Sometimes the night gangs would have their nostrils filled by the scent of the night-blooming cereus, hanging from some dead ceiba trunk, looking like ghostly flowers. The carters, too, would creep by night and day, with their slow ox-teams, along the roadless ways, now jolting over stones and stumps as they went to and fro between the cane-fields and *batey* with their freight of sugar-canes—calling loudly to the bullocks as they goaded them through the deep ruts, or singing Spanish songs to the stars in the intervals of peeling and sucking stalks of sugar-cane.

Soon after five the planter mounted his horse, and rode towards the *batey*. In the *corral* the cattle-boys were lassoing the few extra bullocks required for some of the carts, shouting to the cattle as they rode about on their ponies seeking Lorenzo or Joaquin, for they knew all the beasts by name.

The planter stopped for a moment, and watched them flitting about in the dark amongst the frightened beasts, the perfumes from the bursting morning glories scenting the air. On his right rustled the leaves of the canes, and a little farther on he could hear the swish of the machetes and the shouts of the contra-majoral as the gang began to cut into the golden harvest.

On reaching the *batey*, he rode across to the right, passing the bagasse boys loading their carts with dry bagasse stored in the bagasse-house during the previous year, a valuable supply of fuel to go on with until fresh fuel could be prepared. On coming up with the cane-cutting gang, he beheld a line of men and women advancing in open order against the crops. Each hand seized a cane, cut it with one stroke from its root, sliced off the leaves and tassel with another cut, and with a third dividing it, if it were over long, then throwing it beside them, whilst a few stragglers ran about piling the cane into heaps ready for the carters, or collecting the cane-tops for fodder.

The cane carts, with four spans of oxen yoked Spanish fashion by their horns, with the drivers standing on the shafts, were coming towards the field. Above the shouts of the carters, jets of steam could be heard panting from the engine that had already begun to work. Leaving the field hands, the planter went to the stables by the engine-house, a negro running up and taking his horse as he alighted. Going into the mill, rattling with the stamp of the engines and the whirr of belts, he heard the weird song of the feeders, a gang of negro boys and girls, clad in cotton shirts and frocks, who threw the canes on to an endless platform of slats that travelled upwards and onwards, carrying the canes to the massive triple rollers which squeezed them dry, the juice running into a tank to be pumped to the boiling-house, and the bagasse being carried on another moving platform of slat into the ever-waiting carts. Finding the engineer, Martinez, near the governors, the planter said—

"Hola, *caballero*, it is a good sound, a good sound."

"Oh yes, señor," said the engineer, thrusting his hands into his white apron, "everything goes well; the engine runs as smoothly as a duck on the water; and look at the bagasse—not a drop left in it."

They went to one of the carts of bagasse, and carefully examined the crushed greenish stem with its pith-like interior, and seemed well satisfied, leaving the boys to carry it out to be cured like hay in the hot sun, for no other fuel was used. The glimmering day was coming up quickly, and the sun had already begun to gild the iron roof of the engine-house standing open to the air, when the planter passed down the cane stairs to talk to the comely Louisa, the splendid negress with golden earrings and red handkerchief, who was superintending the feeders with a short cow-hide in her hand. Close by a train of carts were dumping their loads of cane round the feeding stairs, the cattle all leisurely chewing the sweet cane-tops, whilst their drivers raked the cane into heaps.

Don Enrique then went back and looked at

the tank where the juice collected and was being pumped into defecators heated by exhaust steam passed through pipes, the condensed steam feeding the boiler, which a bright negro, José, the sub-engineer, was stoking with bagasse and wood.

Bidding the engineer good morning, the planter walked into the large, gloomy boiling - house, where four trains of huge triple coppers were already steaming with the sweet fragrant smell of the boiling cane syrup, into which the raw juice had passed, skimmed of its froth.

The scene was most picturesque—the mysterious gloom of the long tall house, the boilers with the negroes stripped to their waists standing before them, skimming the froth from the caldrons, and twisting the windlasses with the boxes of boiled syrups to be delivered into the cooling trains on the metals overhead. Every now and then some figure would flit about the misty gloom, or cry in musical voice to the fireman below—

"*E-e-cha, e-e-cha, candela!*"

Then the tender of another train would begin some wild native chant or some Spanish cry, whilst some one far down the house would shout—"*A-a-bla, a-a-bla, e-e-cha, e-e-cha, candela!*" and these would be answered in the same tones by the men feeding the furnaces below, their voices sounding far away like voices at sea.

The planter took the saccharometer from a rail, and tested the boiling juice in the nearest train. As the syrup was ladled from one caldron to another, the sweet, healthy fumes filled that part of the house. The planter was satisfied with his test, and walked to the cooling trains above, where the first cooler was already full of syrup that had begun to crystallise here and there.

Leaving the boiling, Don Enrique walked over to the administrator's house, and sat down to wait. At seven o'clock that individual appeared.

"Good morning, Don Enrique; all goes well."

"Yes, Don Natan, all goes well, and the barometer promises fair, so we shall be able to make some good bagasse to go on with."

"Yes, that's so. Will you have breakfast with me? I have ordered it now, as I wish to go and examine that cane lying by Gomez's land; it is ripe, I think."

The planter accepted, and breakfast was served in the dining-room, looking out on the orange trees, golden with fruit and white with blossom.

After breakfast they walked to the sick quarters, the planter prescribing for some simple ailments, and looking at two lying-in women who occupied two rooms; then giving the majoral a few directions, they went back, and, mounting their horses, they rode towards Gomez's land.

As they passed the spot where the bleached

bones of the dead bull lay, already well-nigh covered with weeds, a voice cried from across the fence, "*Buenas dias.*"

The riders stopped.

"*Buenas dias*, señor," exclaimed the planter, and peering into the trees he saw the evil face of the montero Gomez, with his palm-leaf hat, a red handkerchief round his shoulders, partly hiding a dirty cotton shirt, reaching to his white trousers that led to two huge brass spurs that hung below the flaps of his highly-decorated Spanish saddle.

"I have been waiting to see you," said the montero coldly. "Why do you kill a poor man's cattle ? "

"*Sinverguenza*," retorted the planter hotly. "Why do you and your two sons cut down my fences, and fatten your wild beasts on my cane ? "

"It is not the truth ; they were let into the señor's cane by some of his negroes."

"*Mentiroso*," mentally ejaculated the planter. "Why were they not branded ? "

At this awkward question the montero dropped his threatening attitude, and said, with assumed dignity—"*Ya esta.* I don't like many words. The *ingeñio* shall pay me. *Buenas dias*," and digging his spurs into his horse, he disappeared into the depths of the wood.

"Scamp," said the planter.

" He'll give trouble, he'll give trouble," crooned the administrator.

" Yes, yes, these low Spaniards are blackguards enough to do anything ; but let him look to himself."

"Silver his palm," said the administrator, with a knowing wink of his one eye.

"Drill him with a bullet sooner," said Don Enrique.

On reaching the estate the riders parted, and Don Enrique returned to the *Casa Grande*, to find his wife looking on at the gaily-dressed negresses drying plantains in the bright sun.

CHAPTER XI

TETANUS

THE weather continued fine, and the work pressed day and night, the gangs taking half-an-hour for breakfast and half-an-hour for dinner.

The same routine went on from day to day, with the addition that the white carters had now got to work, and were busy carrying off the great hogsheads of *muscovado* to the seaport of Maravilla, where the *Cousin Jonathan* lay loading, whilst her skipper was whiling away his time with Lola — black-eyed, cascarilla-powdered, naughty Lola — or else drinking *aguadiente* with Lola's father.

The purging-house was now also a busy scene, in which gangs of negroes played their parts, shovelling the sugar through holes in the cars into the hogsheads below, which stood upon cross-beams over the huge, copper-lined tank into which the molasses dripped and drained, to be taken thence and distilled into rum, or to be placed in hogsheads, and sent to market if the price was high—a little being reserved, however, to make white sugar and liqueurs for the house.

Don Enrique was busy from morning till night, often taking his meals with the administrator, and generally riding home of an evening to take his wife for a ride through the cleared cane-fields, by fields of maize, through plantain groves, or more rarely to the great wild *potrero*, where a trusty negro, Leon, lived in a cottage of palm leaves, and looked after the wild cattle.

The *batey* was a lively scene at this season, for, in addition to the never-ending work, pedlars came with cheap jewellery, sweets, combs, glasses, and beads, to sell to the negroes at the dinner hour ; countrymen laden with panniers of dried cod, jerked beef, bananas, big oil-jars, or demi-johns of wine were constantly riding in and out and delivering their goods, generally carrying off bags of sugar and bundles of cane-top fodder that almost hid their horses.

It was an anxious time for the planter—bad weather, fire, or a break-down of the machinery being a constant dread ; so that one night in March, when Caoba knocked loudly at his door and reported that the administrator had ridden up and been admitted, Don Enrique said to himself, " At last ! " and asked the lad excitedly—

"What's the matter ? Has the alarm - bell rung ? "

" No, my master ; but the administrator wishes to see you immediately."

Putting on his clothes, and slipping his revolver into his sash, Don Enrique hurried to the office, which was already lit up, and after greetings had been passed, asked what was amiss.

" Poor Martinez (the engineer) caught his hand in the machinery early last night, and now has lock-jaw. We cannot open his mouth."

" Good God ! how was it done ? "

" Oiling the bearings."

Calling Caoba, who was standing without, Don Enrique said—

" Saddle the grey."

" Yes, my master."

When the horse appeared with the torch-bearers, the two mounted and rode through the cool tropical night to the works, whence the cries of the fire men—"*E-echa, e-echa, candela !*" sounded musically.

On nearing the works, the feeders could be heard crying, " *Aya mañana nami, aya mañana nami,*" as their figures moved mysteriously under the bright, starlit night.

Dismounting at the stables, Don Enrique left the horses to eat cane-tops in the roar of the machinery, as he hurried to the engineer's room, whilst the administrator, an engineer by profession, took charge of the machinery, much to José's disgust.

As Don Enrique entered the engineer's white-walled room with its simple furniture, lit up by a candle, he saw Martinez lying on a low cot, an old negress trying to soothe him. Immediately the injured man was seized with a fit or spasm, and lay stiff on his back, his dark face pale and full of pain, his brow knit, his eyes half closed, and the corners of his mouth drawn up into the *risus sardonicus*, froth dribbling from his lips.

As soon as the planter reached the bedside, the patient was again seized with a spasm, his legs and arms became rigid as poles, his back arched, and the poor fellow, struggling for breath, grew livid with starting eyeballs.

"*El pobre*," said the planter in a low voice to the old negress, who was standing and muttering, "*Bendicion, mi amo.*"

Feeling his pulse and skin, Don Enrique said to the negress—

"Go and call three Chinamen from the night-gang. I hear them coming in."

The three Mongolians soon appeared, and stood impassively in the porch, waiting for their master to address them.

"The engineer has lock-jaw; get everything out of the room quickly," ordered Don Enrique.

These men, dressed in their blue cotton shirts and trousers, moved noiselessly round the room at their work.

When everything had been removed except the cot, Don Enrique ordered baskets of dry *paja* to be brought. Each man soon returned with a large flat basket on his head, filled with the dry corn-leaf.

Making a sign to the strongest Chinaman, Don Enrique and the man lifted the engineer on to the floor, whilst the other two removed the cot ; then spreading the *paja* in a ring round the invalid, who was now lying on the stone floor, Don Enrique took a candle, and going round the circle, lit it in several places, ordering the Chinaman to pile on plenty of leaf whilst the others kept him supplied. Don Enrique and his patient were soon in a ring of flame.

" Pile on the fire !" he cried, the perspiration streaming down his face.

The spasms soon began to abate, and the invalid looked round and whispered—

" Ah ; Don Enrique !"

The planter took his hand.

"Go it, men ; pile on the *paja* !" ordered the master.

The room was already like an oven, the smoke blinding, and the men all streaming with perspiration. As the heat increased, the planter called for water, which he drank eagerly, and his face brightened as the invalid's spasms gradually relaxed and he spoke with greater ease.

"Blankets!" cried Don Enrique from the furnace; "and ask the major-domo to be good enough to spare us his bed."

Wrapping the invalid in blankets, an opening was kicked in the burning ring, and a cold bath was placed in the fiery circle, which was now allowed to die down. Eager hands carried the engineer into the major-domo's room, whilst Don Enrique stripped and plunged into the cold water, and dressed hastily in a suit of clothes supplied by the carpenter; then going to his patient, he called for coffee and cigars whilst he kept watch. . . .

When he left for the big house, the next day at noon, the engineer was out of all danger, as Dr. Rios, who had been summoned, confirmed.

CHAPTER XII

THE INSOLENT COBRADOR

THE grinding season progressed favourably, the fine weather having been broken only occasionally by thunderstorms ; but before these tempests all the field hands were rung in to cock the greenish white bagasse, as hay is heaped, that which was already sere being carried off by the women in large flat baskets, on their heads, to the bagasse-house, where the precious fuel was stored.

One morning, towards the end of the grinding season, a cold *norte* was blowing, confining Don Enrique to his office, where he was busy and not in the best of tempers, for your *norte* acts on the liver as does an English east wind.

Don Enrique was disturbed by Caoba announcing that a *cobrador* was without, and wished to speak with him.

Before the house, upon a small Spanish horse, sat this officious-looking man, dressed in the costume of a townsman of the lower class. Upon his breast he wore a brass star, the badge of office of the tax-collector, for such he was.

When Don Enrique appeared, the man said with an insolent air, and tendering him a paper—

"*Papel, para Usted.*"

"*Sinverguenza,* dismount, and hand me the paper properly," said Don Enrique.

"I am no slave," sneered the boorish Spaniard.

"No, nor man either," retorted the planter.

The Spaniard felt for his machete handle.

"*Que, sinverguenza,* do you wish to fight?" asked Don Enrique, looking the pigmy between his black shifty eyes.

"It will wait—*toma el papel,*" said the boor, tossing the demand note into the piazza; and wheeling his horse, he went off at a run down the drive.

Don Enrique bit his lip, and with mighty effort suppressed his passion, for he knew full well that to attack a Spanish official would bring the whole nest of corrupt officials on to his back, for the foreigner and the native are ill protected by the laws of Spain.

Caoba picked up the paper, and hissed, as he looked at the vanishing figure of the horseman, "Coward!" and then turning to his master, the bright, regular-featured negro, born on the plantation, said—

"Let me follow him, my master, and fight him with machete."

"No, no, my boy—a brave boy like you; no,

they would swear your life away, and give you *four shots in the back.*"

" It is true, my master, the big men are bullies, and the little men cowards."

" Yes, 'tis true, Caoba; but here's a peso for you. Go down to the boiling-house and take a bunch of manzana bananas, and get them boiled in the syrup for the señora, for we shan't have the chance much longer."

" *Bendicion,* my master," said the negro, taking the little gold coin and kneeling.

Don Enrique placed his hand upon the boy's head, and said—

" *Dios, te haga Caoba.*"

CHAPTER XIII

MURDER AND SUICIDE

A FORTNIGHT after, Caoba came to his master as he returned from the works, and said—

"Has my master seen the turkey-buzzards in the great *corral* by the ceiba tree?"

"Yes, Caoba, what can it be? Look at them moving like a corkscrew in the sky. No ox can be dead there. Call Ramon and Marzial."

When the squidgy-nosed, big-lipped retainers came stepping along like Greek gods, their machetes swinging by their sides, Don Enrique said—

"Come, let us go and see what the birds are about."

Digging his silver spurs into the bay, he rode down the back road from the *Casa Grande*, passing the limekiln that was still burning. Riding over stony ground, under cover of large trees that resembled oaks, they came upon open ground, where they frightened a flock of parrot-beaked *jutias*, that kept flying before them, and calling, warning the wild pigeons and guinea-fowls that had, years before, escaped from the house.

"Ah," said the planter, "we must come some moonlit night and shoot these guinea-fowl : they are too wild to stalk by day."

As they approached the buzzards, the planter's horse crushed the yellow thumburgias that grew in luxuriance over the ground, and startled chameleons and limber snakes whose heads could be seen projecting from holes in the rocks. Riding along, Marzial said—

"I am making a leathern glove to catch some chameleons for the American Consul, my master."

"It is good, Marzial ; but take care they don't get hold of you."

Passing beneath some creepers of cupy, they left the last large trees and entered the chapparal, where grotesque cacti, tender myrtles, castor-oil plants, red-berried Cayenne pepper plants, and morning glories, now drooping in the sun, all grew in luxuriance.

They drew up to a thick clump of chapparal, from which a cloud of nauseous, fleshy-headed turkey-buzzards rose with flapping wings.

"*Ay, Dios mio,* how it smells !" said the planter.

The great dogs had run forward, and now stood baying, a few sluggish turkey-buzzards hovering over them.

"What is it, what is it ?" asked the planter of Marzial, who had run forward.

" *Caramba miamo,* a dead man !"

"May Heaven protect us ! it is Kakuta," said Ramon.

By this time Don Enrique had reached the spot where lay the corpse of a negro, his eyes and face already eaten away, and near by sat two buzzards, gorged and unable to fly.

"How do you know it is Kakuta ?" asked the planter.

"See, master, his right toe is gone, and Kakuta lost his toe—the *nigua* got into it."

"I remember," said Don Enrique ; "and it is about his build."

The nauseous turkey-buzzards kept hopping and flopping away, followed by the dogs, who dared not touch them, however.

"He ran away last week," continued Don Enrique ; "but how did he come to die ?"

Marzial had turned the carrion over, notwithstanding the fearful stench, and after examining the back, he said—

"See, my master, a stab in the back."

" *Caramba,*" said Don Enrique, dismounting, and examining the corpse with his nose buried in his handkerchief.

"And look," said the quick-eyed Ramon, "here is Chinos or white man's hair in his left hand : there has been a fight."

"Very strange," muttered the planter, "very

strange; this will bring trouble." Then re-mounting, he said, "Ramon, go at once to the carpenter's shop and get a coffin knocked up, and bring a *seron* here on a horse, and take the body to the Campo Santo; and you, Marzial, ride over to Santiago and ask the padre to come and bury it to-day if he can; and at the same time ask the captain of the Partido to come over at once, but don't tell him anything."

The planter rode home, stopping to pluck a bunch of wax-like poinsettias on his way; but nevertheless he was much troubled in his mind, and he had reason, for that very evening, as he sat at dinner, a jingle of arms and the tramp of horses was heard on the drive.

"Go and see who it is, Caoba."

The lad returned with a long face, and reported Captain Baro and ten guarda-civiles.

"What's wrong?" asked his wife.

"That dead negro, Kakuta," said Don Enrique, going to the piazza.

The little troop, dressed in brown linen trimmed with red facings, all wearing Panama hats with red cockades, and all armed with carbines with fixed bayonets, were drawn up before the piazza.

"Good day," said the planter, bowing.

"God day," replied the captain, taking off his hat.

"Won't you dismount?" asked Don Enrique.

"Yes, señor, I have some business."

Caoba led the captain's horse to the stable, and Captain Baro entered the piazza.

"Will you have any refreshment?" asked Don Enrique.

"Yes, thank you. I should like a glass of *horchata*, but let us to business first.

"Then kindly walk this way," said Don Enrique, leading the way to the office.

When they were seated, and Captain Baro had lit a cigar, he began :—

"You know, Don Enrique, a murdered negro has been found on your property, and I need not tell you it is a very serious matter, especially as you have enemies. A *sitero*, Gomez, lodged a complaint that he heard you threaten to kill a negro only last week, and the *cobrador* of this district reported that you threatened to shoot him whilst doing his duty ; morever, it is reported that you are in league with Lorenzo and his brigands."

"Captain Baro," said Don Enrique calmly, "I need not tell you that these are all falsehoods, the fabrications of jealous and low-minded men. You are a Spanish gentleman of heart, and know it would be as impossible for me to think of killing a slave or an insolent official as it would for yourself."

Captain Baro bowed gravely.

"That is well, señor," said the captain, "but you know my duty: I must proceed in regular form."

"I am entirely at your disposal, captain, as is this estate."

Again the captain bowed.

"Then, if it is not taking too great a liberty, will you send for your major-domo, and order him to bring writing materials ?"

"With pleasure, captain;" and Caoba, who was standing outside, was sent to the works for Don Pablo. Meanwhile Captain Baro entered the dining-room, and having saluted the señora in Spanish fashion, sat down to dessert; sending out a message to his troop to disband, which they did, and were provided with refreshments in the servants' quarters.

In due time the major-domo arrived, provided with long sheets of rough Spanish paper, an ink-horn, quill pens, and a sand-box.

"To horse, to horse !" said Captain Baro ; we will go at once to the scene of the murder.

Having reached the spot, Captain Baro dictated a long description of the surroundings, which the major-domo took down.

"He may be buried now," said the captain. "I examined his body on the way up."

After they returned to the house, the troop of civil guards marched with Don Enrique and the captain to the estate, halting at the negro quarters, where the troop drew up on guard.

The majoral was sent for, and cross-examined by the captain, every word being taken down. After that they proceeded to search the negro quarters, going first to the common kitchen, where an old woman was cooking mush in a great caldron over a wood fire. Passing the well, they began at the first hut, that of the contra-majoral.

These huts were built of stone with earth floors hardened by the feet of the inmates. There were a hundred of these, each like the other. A little square room, lighted by a grated window, and furnished with low wooden cots and blankets; whilst gourds, home-made candles, dried plants, palm-leaf hats, pea-coats for wet weather, cotton shirts and trousers, dresses, cheap prints of the Virgin, bundles of dried tobacco leaves, corn-cob pipes, iron kettles, boxes, bamboo cages with cucuyos, and garden tools were arranged according to the taste of the occupants. Here and there they found old men and women past work, who were allowed to do nothing, but sleep or play with the naked little boys and girls, who ran about amongst the black, long-eared, thin-flanked wild dogs, that some of the negroes had tamed.

The search was a farce.

After dictating several more notes to the major-domo, the party left the negro quarters, and went over to the Chinese, beginning at the kitchen, where an old Chinaman was acting as cook.

Here the furniture differed, for many of the Chinamen had bamboo pillows to their cots, and most kept pets, chiefly wild pigeons. Beyond finding two illicit opium pipes made of the necks of wine bottles, which the planter confiscated, they found nothing incriminating. Indeed, knives were scarce among the Chinese, for they used chopsticks. After more sheets of paper were filled and sanded, the captain ordered the people to be formed up in front of their quarters.

The roll was then called, and a full description of every missing negro taken down by the major-domo. After this ceremony, the captain went round, and himself examined the knife carried by each; but none were confiscated, the captain being contented with the names of those who carried knives, short, stout-bladed implements with wooden handles, such as used by sailors, and worn in leather cases.

The captain then walked through the works, and continued his examination, even entering the sick-house; the same examination was gone through with the Chinamen, a ceremony which they bore with supreme indifference. And finally Captain Baro said to Tangu, their head-man—

"Tell them in your language that Kakuta, a slave of this estate, has been foully murdered, and that evidence goes to show that the murder was committed by a Chinaman ; now ask each one if he did it."

Each man on being asked, replied, " Yes."

Captain Baro turned with a look of triumph to Don Enrique, and whispered—

" One of these Chinamen did it ; I congratulate you, señor."

Don Enrique knew this from their replies.

After again dictating to the major-domo, Captain Baro turned to Tangu, and said severely—

" I shall take your gang in charge, and march you to prison to Santiago to-morrow morning, where you will in due course be all garrotted ; but if you give up the murderer before to-morrow morning, nothing more will be said."

After Tangu had translated the message, not a muscle moved in those pale yellow faces ; and to make the matter more difficult, it was noticed that every man's hair was cropped short, though many had worn pigtails but a few days before, for many were fresh from China.

The Chinamen were then locked into their quarters, and the troop settled down to bivouac before them for the night.

At this juncture the administrator rode in

from the *potrero*, where he had been all day ;
and when he heard how matters stood, he
volunteered—

"If a Chinaman committed the crime, as is
evident, it was Amu, that weak little cowman's
helper, for he was caught with Rosa, Kakuta's
girl, in Louisa's garden, at the dinner hour.
Louisa and Rosa went to bathe in the river,
and whilst Louisa was digging some yucca, after
bathing, Rosa disappeared, but Louisa found her
hidden in a corner of the garden under some
plantain leaves with this little Chinaman. That
night Louisa told Kakuta, and he beat Amu with
a stick in the *corral* last week. Thomas, the
cowboy, told me, and that is why he ran away,
for fear of punishment."

"Call Louisa, Rosa, and Thomas," said the
captain, "and let me take their depositions."

The captain held his court in the major-domo's
room. Louisa was the first called, and the handsome negress, with jovial face and regular features,
entered, and, after curtseying, she told her story,
having previously crossed her fingers and sworn
Spanish fashion.

Thomas, a strong, bad-tempered, mulatto boy
was next called, and he gave an account, after
having been sworn in the same manner, of
Kakuta's beating Amu.

"Did Amu threaten him ?" asked the captain.

"No, captain, he said nothing ; but, *shoo!* he is a coward ; he is afraid of a wild bull."

As the boy left the room, the captain said, "A fierce, bad-looking slave, Don Enrique ; these mulattos are bad people."

"He is stubborn, but clever ; he can lasso better than any man on the estate," replied the planter.

Rosa was called next. She was born on the estate, and, like all creole negroes, was handsomer and more intelligent than the *bozales* or imported negroes—a fine upstanding wench, whose figure would have run the Venus of Milo's hard, was Rosa, as she stood boldly facing the captain with smiling face and glittering eyes.

"Do you know Kakuta is dead ?" asked the captain.

"Yes, captain, I have just heard so."

"He lived with you ?"

"Yes, captain, since two months."

"The girl does not seem to care whether he is dead or no," whispered the captain to Don Enrique.

"Of course not. They care for nothing but cheap jewellery," replied the planter.

"What happened when you went to bathe in Louisa's garden last Thursday ?" asked the captain.

Rosa smiled a wicked smile, and in the coolest

and most unabashed way said, " I had taken off my clothes and was bathing in the pool, when I heard some one go p—s—s—t, and I looked and saw Amu's yellow face in the plantains.   He beckoned to me, and held up a necklace of beads ; so I ran to the plantains, and he offered me the beads if I would lie with him ; and, Señor Capitan, what was a poor negress to do ?   The Chinos are very free of hand."

" It is good ; that is enough ; you may go," said Captain Baro, the men smiling at one another.

The depositions were duly read aloud by the major-domo, and signed and sealed by the captain before witnesses.

" Now to the house," said the planter : " the señora will be getting anxious."

" At your service, señor," said the captain, rising.

Outside the horses were ready, and the gentlemen rode to the *Casa Grande*, where Marzial reported that Kakuta had been buried, and that the priest was within.

.   .   .   .   .   .

About three o'clock in the morning the household was aroused by a loud knocking, and the administrator was admitted.

" Amu has hanged himself," reported the Yorkshireman slowly.

"Ah, hanged by his mates," said Don Enrique ; "by-the-bye, Rosa is one of your servants, is she not, Don Natan ?" asked the planter coldly.

"Yes," said the one-eyed man, looking down.

"Well, see that in future she does not meddle with the Chinese, or I will sell her. This matter will cost a pretty pile as it is, and it might have been very serious indeed. As it is, a good negro, worth eight hundred dollars, is gone, and a Chinaman that cost four hundred dollars, as well as his keep and twenty dollars a month for the last two years ; and all these depositions to be paid for, and the captain to be paid, all over that girl Rosa. What a wicked face the girl has."

"I won't detain you longer. Shall the China-man be buried?" asked the administrator, changing the subject.

"Yes, before daylight, on the north side, and outside of the Campo Santo. Captain Baro, who is now dressing, and I will be down in half-an-hour. Let no one touch him before the captain sees him, and awake Don Pablo."

It was not yet sunrise when the captain finished his new taking of depositions, and the party were returning to breakfast at the *Casa Grande*, as Amu, the assassin and suicide, was put into his unconsecrated grave on the north side of the prickly-pear hedge.

After breakfast, Don Enrique took the captain

to his office, and, over cigars, said : " You have conducted this affair like a gentleman.   What do I owe you, captain ? "

" The depositions : twenty ounces say, señor."

" Allow me to make it fifty, and to thank you for your courtesy, captain."

" Oh, no, no ; impossible," said Captain Baro, with an aggrieved air.

" A thousand pardons !   Well, here are the twenty ounces, captain," said Don Enrique, placing a bag with fifty ounces upon the table.

The captain said, " Thank you," in an offhand manner, and placed the bag in his pocket ; but his manner soon showed by its amiability that he knew that fifty were there.

Before the heat of the day, the troops started off for Santiago, the padre going with them, some sixty-eight golden dollars jingling in his pockets also.

CHAPTER XIV

Amongst the negresses at the great house was one Francisca—city bred, who had been bought for the señora at a high price, as she was an accomplished sempstress and milliner.

Francisca was a middle-aged woman, thin, proud, and bad-tempered, who looked down on her fellow-servants as rustics, disliked the ways of the country, and made them discontented with exaggerated tales of the pleasures of the city. On her weekly holiday she was very fond of resorting to the village of Santiago, and flirting, if no worse, with the trashy white bar-loafers that frequented the only *tienda* and *posada* in the place.

There she often met the widower Gomez, whose love of cock-fighting took him to the village, and not drink; for your true-bred Spaniard is, as a rule, abstemious, and does not frequent the tavern for drink, as would his English equal.

But Francisca's acuteness soon led Gomez to make love to her, and she wheedled many presents out of him. Upon one of these holidays, he had the luck to win several ounces at the cockpit, and in his exuberance he asked Francisca whether he should buy her.

"No, *caro*," she said familiarly, "for the master won't sell me."

"Hola, girl! Does Don Enrique then love the black Señorita Francisca?"

"No, *sinverguenza*. I would that he did; he never has any dealings with the women."

"*Vaya-te*, señorita, you joke," said old Gomez, leering at her.

"It is the truth; even the beautiful Louisa smiles upon him in vain, and, as for Lola at Maravilla, she is really in love with him, and, though she is not a lady of colour, he'll none of her."

"Ah, the English and Americans are cold."

"Yes, *they are* cold," said Francisca; "and for that reason I am getting tired of *La Esperanza*. Don Enrique is very particular, and won't let the gentleman visitors call the girls to their rooms, as they used to in Havana, and so we cannot earn much."

"Then, child, I cannot buy you; for, as you say he uses you well, the law will not help you."

"Yes, he is a good master, but doesn't understand the ways of the country. *I* like the Spaniards."

"Make him use you badly," suggested old Gomez.

He then took her aside, and held a long conversation in a low voice, at the same time showing her a little bag of gold. And Francisca returned to the estate wrapped in thought.

CHAPTER XV

FEAST AND DANCE

THE last week in May had come, and with it the last day of the grinding season.

All the people and the cattle and horses looked fat and happy, for the sugar-cane fattens man and beast as well as filling the pockets of the planter.

At four o'clock of the afternoon of that auspicious day, the last canes were tossed into the endless stairs, the feeders singing their weird, Africo-Spanish songs more lustily than ever, as they filed off to their quarters immediately after the steam was shut off.

Before roll-call the fires had been raked out for the year, the cattle unyoked and driven to the *corrals*, and the cane-carts drawn up in a line before the grinding-house.

That evening, in the negro quarters, the people were dancing to the beat of their tom-toms, and the last night-gangs of boilers were at work shouting louder than ever—

"*E-echa, e-echa Pablo, e-echa, candela,*" the busy stokers below crying back through the night—

"*E-echa, e-echa, la candela !*"

The next few days were spent in storing the carts under the corn - house, in driving the bullocks to the *potrero* to feed at large, in cleaning the great boilers and trams, in carting the last hogsheads of sugar to Maravilla, and cleaning up the purging-house and still, so that by the first Sunday in June the former busy haunts of work and song were as silent and deserted as a ruined city.   Upon that Sunday the white employés donned their best attire for the great dinner at the *Casa Grande*, a feast always given at the end of the season, as well as at the beginning.

On the Monday the people went to their holiday tasks with light hearts, for easier work was before them for the next seven or eight months.   Moreover, they were looking forward to the festivities of the following night, for it was customary at the end of the grinding season to give the people a great feast to celebrate the harvesting of the crop.

On the Tuesday morning the major - domo selected the best pigs that belonged to the negroes, and paid them their price, varying from fourteen dollars to twenty-three dollars apiece, the blackbirds with their yellow bills flitting to and fro excitedly as the pigs were removed from their palm-wood pens, and killed by the side of the river, whose course was marked by pools and rocks green with rank herbage, through which the stream trickled to other pools, for the river was very low at the end of the dry season. Sometimes, indeed, it was completely dried up, and its bed was marked by a stinking mass of decaying fish.

On the *batey* oxen were being killed and dressed, and carried off to the quarters to be roasted in great joints. Extra rations of plantains, ground maize, sweet potatoes, and jerked beef were served out, and, best of all, a cart heavily laden with bales of hats, shirts, trousers, pea-coats, dresses, handkerchiefs, and new machetes came in from the station, for new clothes were served out upon this day, each negro receiving in addition a present of cotton stuff and handkerchiefs.

Towards four o'clock the feast was ready, but before anything was touched, the two contra-majorals, bearing dishes of stewed beef and rice and kalalu, a negro soup, together with rolls of cigars of their own manufacture, walked solemnly to the great house, clad in their new clothes and hats, with gay handkerchiefs used as belts for their long machetes.

Picturesque they looked as they walked through the grounds, scaring the lizards that scuttled away among the star cacti and red-flamed ipecac bushes, and announcing their arrival by knocking on the stone steps.

Caoba answered the knock.

"Will you ask the master to accept these offerings, and to give us his blessing?" said the head contra-majoral.

Caoba carried the dishes, and placed them on his master's dinner table in a position of honour. Don Enrique appeared, and after thanking them, said—

"My people, may God bless you all."

After this ceremony, Caoba gave each man a glass of *aguadiente*, and they walked back to their quarters, where all hands, with their wives and pickaninnies, fell on the abundant feast.

At the planter's table every one ate from the dishes brought up by the contra-majorals; and after dinner the planter smoked one of the cigars, for such was the custom; and had he omitted to do so, the house servants would have told the people, and it would have been looked upon by them as a slight, and never forgotten, for this custom they had doubtless brought with them from Africa.

After dinner, Don Enrique gave all the house servants permission to go to the *batey* to the dance, and himself rode down with his wife and the nurse and child, seating themselves in the administrator's piazza, where refreshments and cigars, with braziers of fire, were prepared.

Before long, the negroes, dressed in their best,

the men walking ahead, Gangas and Carabalis, short Congos, Macuas, Molembos, and Araras, intelligent lucumis, and the more refined-looking creole negroes—a wildly picturesque procession in palm-leaf hats and handkerchiefs, the women in gaily-coloured cotton dresses, with massive gold earrings and red handkerchiefs, boys and girls running in and out, some naked, some in cotton shirts and dresses. Many of the men carried long, hollow trunks of trees, their ends covered with leather. The procession filed past the administrator's house, each slave kneeling quickly, and muttering, "*Bendicion*, señor," or "señora," as they passed the master and mistress, who replied continually, "God keep you, my people."

The reticent Yorkshireman said nothing, but sucked a fat trabuco cigar, and looked listlessly at the scene.

The people then formed a crescent round the piazza, and in the hollow space little fires of corn-cob and *paja* were quickly made, the long tom-toms being laid with their heads to the fire, to warm and tighten the leather.

Whilst these preparations were being made, the white employés strolled over in little groups from their quarters, and shook hands with the planter, bowing to the señora, and took up their positions on the verandah rails or the piazza steps.

After them the dismal, melancholy-looking Chinese filed out of their quarters, and crossing the *batey*, they walked past the piazza, each man silently taking off his hat as he went, and muttering some unintelligible greeting or curse, the planter replying cheerily, "God keep you. God keep you."

The two contra-majorals, who were the chief drummers, then took their tom-toms from the fire, and feeling the leathers, tapped them, muttering, " It's good."

Then all the tom-tom players, some fifteen in number, followed suit, each man astraddle his long, hollow drum as a boy rides a stick, these instruments being supported by straps worn round the waist. Suddenly, at a signal from the contra-majoral, they began to play wild African music with the palms of their hands on the heated cow-hides.

No sooner had the tapping begun than the orderly crescent of solemn Chinese broke into groups, and collected round the corn-cob fires, many of the negroes and negresses beginning to beat time with their feet and hands. The drummers grew more excited as they played, and began chanting wild songs in their own tongues, writhing, wriggling, and throwing themselves about with wild gestures, and suddenly a comely wench stepped forth and began a wild dance, soon to be joined by a big black fellow, who bounded into position opposite her. The example having been set, nearly all the grown-up people who were not too old joined in parties, and soon the people in the piazza were looking on at a wild carnival of savage song and dance—the dancers throwing themselves about and writhing, clapping their hands and singing wild songs, or mimicking battle scenes, or expressing sentiments of love, jealousy, and hatred.

It was a savage and impressive sight as the fires burnt more brightly in the quickly-gathering night, and silhouetted the sensuous features of the dancers, or lit up the solemn yellow faces of the Chinamen, who looked on stolidly at the savage carnival. The drummers were getting drunk with excitement, some frothing at the mouth, whilst the dancers were striving hard to weary their *vis-a-vis*. Occasionally a drummer would stop and unstrap his tom-tom, and lay it before the fire, which the negro children kept replenished. The great planets burnt steadily and brightly over this scene, but the peaceful sounds of the wild fowl and the rustling of the soft breezes in the trees were all drowned by the savage uproar.

The alert eyes of the majoral would note a Chinaman slipping off with some strapping negress to the deserted engine-house, or some precocious negro boy might be seen sauntering off with a bright-eyed negress, the air was so narcotic and love-compelling ; but no notice was taken of such little irregularities.

It was truly a golden day of a golden age that is gone for ever, with its poetry and antique spirit.

In the midst of this scene, a phosphorescent cloud floated over the orange grove at the back of the administrator's house, and voices called—

" Ah, see the *cucuyos*," as this shower of living light flew over the vegetation towards the river. Their appearance was hailed with delight by the lookers-on, for it boded rain, but to the dancers they might have been the stars leaving their appointed places, for they were intoxicated with emotion.   Several of the elder negro boys ran off to the river, caught numbers of the cucuyos, and brought them back to the negresses, who secured them with pins to their dresses, bright jewels indeed, for a few of these insects give as much light as a candle, and the reader may imagine the effect of a comely negress, in a light cotton dress, all besprinkled with living points of light.

It looked a fairy scene indeed when another cloud of insects, attracted by those worn by the dancers, flew softly through the night.

At length, when the bright Southern Cross stood erect in the heavens, proclaiming midnight, Don Enrique arose and waved his hand. At the signal there fell a solemn silence upon the scene.

" My people, midnight is past ; see the Cruz de Mayo begins to bend. Good night, and many thanks. May God keep you all." And from those dark throats rose a wild cry of—

" Long live our master and mistress !" and the fires were kicked out with naked feet, and the people went chatting and laughing to their quarters; the Chinese, sedately and silently, with bent heads, as if full of thought, following suit.

"What great children !" sneered the administrator.

"No matter, they have hearts," said Don Enrique shortly.

The house servants then filed across the *batey* on their way to the *Casa Grande*, and the white employés, after bidding Don Enrique and the señora good night, strolled off to Don Leonaldo's to drink "square face" or *aguadiente*, and gamble at draughts or dominoes.

The planter and his family mounted their horses, and, followed by Ramon and Marzial, made their way through the heavy dews to the *Casa Grande*.

CHAPTER XVI

A WEEK afterwards the estate had settled down to the wet season's work. Gangs of men and women arose at six, and went to land cleared the year before, and now covered with wild cherry-tomato plants, which they proceeded to hoe, afterwards planting sugar-cane, burying the greenish cuttings diagonally in the earth. A gang of picked men, provided with long machetes and axes, went to clear new land, for fire was never used for the purpose in that country. These worked in the primeval forest amid the blue-birds and wild parrots quarrelling over the bitter oranges. These men often captured the young parrots, and took them home to stew, leaving the pedoreras, campaneros, golden-winged woodpeckers, paroquets, and wild crested pigeons, as they felled the precious woods—such as ebony, majawa, sabicu, ironwood, cedar, and caoba—cutting their way through great jaguey creepers, crushing many-coloured orchids and arums, and ruthlessly cutting down blossoming frangipani and trailers of wild passion-flower, avoiding only the poisonous manchineel.

These woodmen only returned to the estate at night, sometimes bringing with them dead *jutias*, at others carrying large snakes, which were let loose in the corn-house to kill the rats, or taken to the *barracon* to extract from them snake-oil—a specific for their pains. Sometimes they brought home strings of pigeons, snared in wooden cages; sometimes humming-birds' nests as big as a thimble for their pickaninnies; at others a big spray of wild flowers or a banana leaf filled with wild honey, for their women. When they worked near the river, they brought home fish, an ibis or two, or a yellow bittern, or else a dead heron, caught with their African traps.

The field hands came home at eight to breakfast, and were allowed an hour for the meal, going afield again and working till twelve, when they rested a couple of hours for dinner. At this time many of them bathed in the deepest pools of the river, men and women together in savage fashion; and after their siesta they filed off again to work until sundown. The cane-feeders were employed under the magnificent Louisa in chopping weeds round the works and on the roadsides.

The engineer was busy working the saw-mill,

cutting ironwood sleepers for the new light railway that was to be built for rolling the sugar-cane from the fields to the *batey*, to save the weary and slow bullock work.

It was an easy time this wet season for the negroes, but they preferred the grinding season for many reasons, and after the first downpour of rain had come and gone, and swollen the slender river, so that it rushed a turbid stream by the pig-styes, the people began to lose the cheery appearance which they bore a month before.

At the end of the first month of the wet season, Don Enrique was engaged one morning in his office over his books, when the damp heat made him call for a bottle of wine and a carafe of water.

Caobo brought the refreshments, and placed them on a side table.

Don Enrique poured out a large tumbler full of wine, and drank it off without stopping, then resumed his writing. Some half-hour after he turned pale as death, and his life seemed to slip away. Staggering to his feet, he made for the door, but was terribly sick before he reached it.

Caobo, who always stood outside, ran in and cried—

"*Ay, Dios mio!* what is the matter, my master?"

"Call the señora quickly," he said, and staggered to a chair.

His wife appeared pale and agitated, and asked anxiously what was wrong.

"Poison, dear. Quick! some sulphate of zinc from my medicine-chest."

Caoba turned pale beneath his black skin.

"Gallop for your life to Santiago for Dr. Rios," ordered the señora, turning some sulphate of zinc into a glass.

Caoba was soon galloping as hard as his horse would go through the bare cane-fields on his errand. Meanwhile the patient was suffering agonies from sickness, lying on his cot, whither he had staggered, supported by his wife.

"Shut the door ; tell nobody," said Don Enrique in his agony.

"It is yellow fever : the vomit is black," said the señora.

"No, no," muttered the planter ; "give me milk, plenty of milk."

When Dr. Rios arrived, streaming with perspiration from his hard gallop, he found Don Enrique in a state of collapse, with a feeble pulse and a drawn face, looking like a cholera patient.

"*Ay, Dios mio!* what is it?" asked the good-hearted little doctor anxiously.

"Arsenic," moaned Don Enrique.

"Cowards!" said the little Spaniard contemptuously, hastily fitting up his stomach pump and calling for warm water. Passing the tube down the pharynx into the stomach, he filled the viscus with water, and pumped it forth, giving orders that the liquid should be kept.

For a whole week the planter lay between life and death, and his wife was worn to a shadow with anxiety; but at the end of that time the doctor, who had remained by his side night and day, said to her—

" He will pull through, but only one man in a thousand would have done it—he is made of iron."

" Thank God," murmured the señora.

.   .   .   .   .   .

A month afterwards, Don Enrique, worn to a shadow, sat on one of the rocking-chairs in the *sala*. Dr. Rios, with an analysis of the liquid pumped from the stomach, sat opposite him, whilst opposite them sat Captain Baro and a secretary.

" It was arsenic you swear, doctor?" asked the captain.

" Arsenic, I swear," said the doctor, crossing his fingers and repeating the words. " And Don Enrique here was saved through the dose being too large—that together with his superb constitution."

"Do they know in the house what your illness is supposed to be, Don Enrique?" asked the captain.

"No, it has been kept from them."

"Good! Who brought you the wine?"

"My boy, Caoba; but he had nothing to do with it, I'll swear."

"May we call him in, señor?"

"Everything is at your disposal, captain."

The captain called Caoba, and the boy entered with a grave, composed face.

"It is not," muttered the captain.

"No, no, he is no coward," replied the planter in a loud voice.

"The day that your master was taken ill, whence did you take the wine?" asked the captain.

"From the *tinajera*, captain."

"Is it always kept there?"

"Yes, captain—to cool."

The clerk took down every word.

"Where is the wine stored?"

"In the almaçen, captain."

"Who keeps the key, boy?"

"The master."

"It is good. How many days had that bottle been in the *tinajera?*"

"One week. A dozen are placed there at a time, but the master has not had much company lately."

"Does all the household know that the wine is kept there ?"

"Yes, captain."

"Retire from the room a moment, but wait outside, boy."

When Caoba had withdrawn, the captain said : "That lad is innocent as a baby, but he knows something. I saw by his eagerness that he wished to tell us all he knew : he is a faithful slave."

"Yes, captain, I know the boy is as brave as he is faithful ; I already owe him much," said Don Enrique.

"Well, I'll call him back, señor. Come here. Caoba," cried the captain when he returned. "You know your master has been poisoned ?"

"Ah, señor, I think I know who did it."

"How—you ?"

"Yes, captain."

"Have no fear ; tell us."

"Francisca Habanera."

"*Hola!* And what makes you think that ; be careful, but have no fear."

"Juan de Dios told me, captain."

"Aha! And what did he say ?"

"He said he saw Francisca go to the *tinajera*

and take a bottle of wine and take it to her sewing-room ; but he said nothing, for he thought she had stolen it to drink ; but when he heard the master was ill, and came to get a bottle for the dinner-table that night, he found that no bottle was missing, so he suspected."

"It is good. You are a faithful slave ; go and send Francisca here."

"Thank you, captain, and a blessing, my master."

"God keep you, Caoba, and I will reward you," said Don Enrique.

Francisca came in bridling, for she was a nasty-tempered, sour-faced wench.

The captain looked her steadily in the face and said : "Francisca Habanera, I accuse you of poisoning your master by putting arsenic into his wine."

"*Ay, Dios mio!* what shall I do ? " said she, clasping her hands ; and falling, she cringed at his feet.

"Confess your crime and you may be pardoned," said the captain sternly.

"Oh, captain, captain," she cried convulsively, "it was all Gomez's fault."

"Señor Gomez! a Peninsulare. Be careful, slave," said Captain Baro haughtily.

"Ah, mercy."

"Woman, confess, or I'll have you flogged to death," hissed the enraged officer.

A flood of convulsive tears was her reply.

"Señor! Do me the favour of sending for the majoral. Ah, my God," she cried hysterically, "don't kill me."

"Confess, or it will be too late," said Baro sternly.

Raising her body into a kneeling position, she said with hysterical sobs—

"Ah, my master, and Captain Baro, Señor Gomez offered to buy me and take me to his *casa* as his mistress. I thought" (sobs) "my master would not sell me" (sobs), "and I had heard in Havana that, unless your master treated you badly, you could not ask to be sold" (sobs), "so I determined to poison him, thinking the señora might sell me after his death.

"Coward; infamous woman!" hissed the officer; then, calling Caoba, he said, "Send Ramon and Marzial with a rope."

Not a word was spoken until the giants appeared, when the captain said sternly, "Bind this woman and carry her to the *batey*, and place her in the stocks."

They obeyed with alacrity, for Francisca had got herself disliked for her airs by all her fellow-servants.

When she was gone, Captain Baro said gravely: "Don Enrique, I condole with you; you must lose your slave—fifteen hundred dollars, I have no doubt, at the lowest. I shall have her publicly whipped on the estate, and then she will go with me to Santiago."

"As you will, captain; she has nearly cost me my life; let her suffer the just punishment."

After some further talk, Captain Baro mounted his horse and rode down to the *batey* at the head of his troop, halting before the majoral's quarters. He commanded the alarm-bell to be rung, and in due time all the hands filed in and formed up in a hollow square.

"Where is the administrator?" asked Captain Baro.

"Gone to San José, captain."

"It is good; it is good."

"Go to the stocks and bring forth the woman Francisca Habanera."

Don Leonaldo gave orders to the contra-majorals, and the shrinking criminal was led forth.

"Strip her," said the captain; then turning to the people—

"People, this woman has confessed that she tried to kill the master. She is to be flogged first, and afterwards leaves you for ever."

A murmur of surprise went round the hollow square.

"Begin!" said the captain shortly.

The great Ashanti contra-majoral raised his whip, and as its loud report cracked through the silent air, the prisoner fell on her face and began to shriek—

"Mercy!"

As the man proceeded, weals rose on her back, and the blood began to flow, but she only moaned, lying prostrate on the ground.

"Twenty-five," counted the second contra-majoral.

"It is enough," said Baro; "dismiss the people. Slave, arise."

But the woman only moaned.

"Arise, I tell you," shouted Baro angrily, and she tottered to her feet.

"Now dress yourself."

With trembling fingers she put on her cotton dress.

"Now, follow me," said the captain, and giving the order for the troop to form on either side of her, the word for the march was given.

"For life," said Don Leonaldo, looking after the troop as they filed off the estate.

"Too good for her," said the major-domo.

Francisca staggered along, holding on to the captain's stirrup.

When Santiago was reached, Francisca was put into the imprisoning stocks for a few days, after which she became a perpetual slave and prisoner, having to wait upon the prison officials for life, and thus justice and economy were practised by the Spanish officials.

CHAPTER XVII

THE first freshening showers of the rains had grown into a prolonged downpour, the water falling in sheets that masked the surrounding scenery, and turned every depression into a tiny torrent. The hard-baked earth, full of cracks, was now soft and sticky, and the roads were quagmires.

Don Enrique had been advised to go down to the sea to recruit, so one morning in June the large travelling-cart, painted in gay colours and covered with palm-leaf thatching, crept up to the house drawn by four bullocks.

Into this springless cart were placed several chairs, in which Don Enrique and his wife, the nurse and child, took their seats, Caoba jumping in after them, and sitting on the tail of the cart. The baggage was packed in front, and the head-carter took his stand on the long shaft, and at a word from the administrator, who rode beside them, the heavy conveyance started off as the cattle were urged on by name. Ramon and Marzial, with their long machetes, walked behind, followed by the big dogs. When they reached the miry roads, the cart sank to the axle in the mud, the oxen struggling with the sticky bog, drawing forth their limbs with sucking sounds. Occasionally they would jolt over a large boulder buried in the mud, when the occupants were shaken like people on a rough sea. On reaching the *camino real* travelling was better, for in places palm-tree trunks had been thrown into the soft mud to prevent the wheels sinking. Travelling along the primeval forest, and skirting the fields of the *Marguerita* estate, they came to a ford which they had to wade, and a mile more of rough travelling brought them up to the little station of Santiago, where the lightly-built American cars were standing, the big, bell-chimneyed, wood-burning locomotive throwing off smoke, for the planter was a few minutes late, and the train had been kept waiting for him. When the cart drew up, the Cuban stationmaster ran down with a tall-backed chair, covered with leather and studded with brass nails, and taking his hat off with a sweep, begged Don Enrique to descend. The servants were getting the luggage into the train as Don Enrique and his family took their places in the light, cane-bottomed seats.

The administrator shook hands, Ramon and Marzial knelt and asked for *Bendicion*, when the negro porter rang the bell, and with many jolts, and much rattling and banging of springless buffers, the train started, passing with much clanking through a sparsely-cultivated country, grey with cleared cane-fields, dotted with royal palms, and lit up by the white buildings of the estates, with here and there the adobe houses of small farmers. Here and there the line ran through the forest, past a montero's hut made of yaque, or of palm-leaf sheaths laced to a framework of sticks with bast, and roofed with dry palm leaves. Around these primitive houses were pigs, fowls, and naked children, some of them mulattos, for though the Spanish law does not allow a white to marry a " person of colour," the mulatto girls and negresses are often kept as concubines by these little farmers.

After an hour's ride the train drew up at La Boca, a small Spanish town situated at the mouth of the Santiago River, and overlooking the emerald sea.

The American Consul was at the station with his long volante, and, after salutations, the señora, with her baby and nurse, were seated in the carriage. The gaily-attired postillion cracked his whip and drove off to the Consul's house; Caoba, who had come to valet his master, supervising the luggage being loaded in a bullock waggon, whilst the Consul and Don Enrique walked slowly to the official's beautiful one-storied villa, surrounded by a lovely garden, gay with blue clitorias, fuchsias, South Sea roses, Maréchal Niels, Amaryllis, verbenas, and dwarf palmetto trees. After cocktails, dinner was announced, and after that they strolled to the beach, gathering some of the lovely shells scattered on the coral, and watching the hermit crabs, or the yellow soft land crabs stalking up towards the town, where they became a nuisance, being crushed by the horses and carts as the countrymen brought in maloja and vegetables to the markets held in the plaza.

It was a quiet, restful life, for company was scarce, a few planters and merchants occasionally dropping in to dine with the Consul.

Every morning the men went to a bathing-house built between some dark black wharves, and fenced about with iron bars to keep out the sharks—an uncanny sort of place to bathe in, for when one entered the water, all around was the gloom beneath the black wharves, and to the imaginative mind sharks were gazing through the bars, watching the helpless wight.

The family used to watch the Cuban youths amusing themselves by playing hand-ball in the arcades and streets, or gaze at the picturesque groups of countrymen who frequented the *tiendas* and *posadas*, smoking their cigars or cigarettes, made of corn-leaf, taking their medios to pay for their *café* or *vino* or *aguadiente* from purses made from cured pigs' bladders, gaily decorated with ribbons, or lighting their cigars with flints and yellow tinder. But they were a temperate set of men, as far as drink was concerned, yet intemperate gamblers, although gambling was forbidden by law, except the Royal Lottery, and even in this remote town the lottery-ticket sellers passed regularly, crying, *La Lotteria, numero dos ciento y vente-quatro,* or some such number, every now and then stopping to sell a whole ticket, or a portion, to one of the country-men. The shouts of these men, the cries of the orange-sellers with their "China oranges, sweet and good; two for a medio," and the voices of the vendors of confectionery and preserved sweets, made the old-fashioned town the more picturesque. Much amused, too, were they by the milkmen driving their cows from house to house, and milking them before their customers. Baskets of sea-fish of brilliant hues packed in ice, and the gay handkerchiefs of the negresses, added bright spots of colour to the scene, which was lit up by the light muslin dresses of the ladies as they walked bareheaded, with their parasols, followed by negresses, or other chaperones, from shop to shop.

A few days after the family's arrival a *dia de festa* fell, and they went forth after Mass to see the sports held in the plaza, now crowded with soldiers, civil guards, shopkeepers and their families, and country-people.

The graceful, black-eyed señoritas, dressed in delicate white muslin, with bright shawls and large tortoise-shell combs, were divided into two parties, wearing, the one yellow ribbons, the other red, each galaxy of beauty having a queen, a lively creature that flirted her fan, smoked her cigarette, and used her eyes and body with much persuasive eloquence. As a foil to these were parties of laughing, white-eyed negresses, with gay handkerchiefs, and smoking long cigars.

Already the goose fight had begun in one corner of the plaza, where two poles had been set up, and between stretched a strong rope from which hung a live goose by the feet. The competitors, always countrymen, for they had to be good riders, gathered on their little horses, and ran at the goose in turn, trying to wrench its greased neck from its body at full gallop, the successful competitor carrying off the goose.

Leaving these scenes, the Consul and Don Enrique went to the cockpit, a circular, two-storied building. After paying a dollar *fuerte* (pillared with the Pillars of Hercules), they were admitted into the galleries, which encircled the sawdust-covered arena edged with wooden seats. The galleries were filled with a promiscuous crowd of countrymen, negroes, clerks, and a few gentlemen, an old priest looking calmly on the babbling crowd. Around the edge of the pit sat several countrymen with their cocks by their sides. Two of the competitors were standing before the weigher, who was engaged weighing a cock placed in a sling, balanced by a long arm with a weight, a primitive and picturesque pair of scales held with even justice by the umpire. When two birds were found of equal weight, their respective owners began to trim up their spurs with their daggers ; and, at a word from the umpire, the owners uncovered the heads of their birds, and the rivals were dropped into the middle of the arena, the feathers having been previously plucked from their necks, and their combs trimmed and hardened with rum. The umpire then took his seat, and the crowd in the galleries grew wild with excitement as the birds eyed each other, the people yelling and betting, holding up their fingers to indicate the amount of the bet, crying ten to six on the black, or evens on the white, or an ounce to half an ounce on the black. The two birds continued to eye each other, or made feints pretending to pick up grain, when suddenly they dashed at each other, and the black cock nipped the white one by the comb, the white one freeing himself by ducking.

"Two ounces to one on the black," shrieked a

negro ; but the white bird, as if hearing the bet, flew at the black and knocked him over, giving him a good spur-thrust that drew blood. The betting and gesticulations grew more furious, and the birds began to fight in deadly earnest, until they were covered with blood and dust, when their owners, having filled their own mouths with rum, seized their birds, and spurted the rum over their heads, then wiped the blood off with their handkerchiefs, replacing them in the pit. After this refresher the fowls fought more furiously, dodging and nipping and spurring, when at last the white cock thrust his spur through the eye and into the brain of the black cock, which fell dead amid hisses, shrieks, curses, and cheers.

Then there was heard the jingle of money, as the bets were settled amid much jabber, and the weigher was again busy, and so the sport continued.

After dinner, Don Enrique and the Consul sauntered out to see *guachiros* dance, in a large room with a sanded stone floor, where was assembled a motley crowd of countrymen and their señoritas, the men and women keeping in separate parties at either end of the room.

Some countrywomen began dancing *zapatero* to the music of the guitar and a chorus of song by the men, who sat with their hats on their heads and their cigars in their mouths. The object in this dance seems to be for each one to tire her *vis-à-vis*, the girl every now and then giving a sign to her partner to retire, until with loud *bravas* and plaudits another takes her place. In another large room hard by was a mixed dance for professional men, tradesmen, and officers. The girls were all *decolletées* and armed with fans, dressed in muslin, the hair dressed Spanish fashion, with a tall comb. Some were fat and languorous, some bilious-looking, with sharp features and glassy eyes, but others were perfect in build, with full figures, beautifully modelled, with small hands and tapering fingers, and dainty little feet, shod in French slippers. And they can dance, those Cuban girls; they are as light as sylphs, and, clad in their muslin and lace dresses, glide through the voluptuous figures of the *Lanza* or *Dansa Criolla* like fairies. Every motion is full of grace, every movement full of a voluptuous languour; they are as elastic and supple as a panther, and to see these beauties, with their melting or sparkling black eyes, raven hair, and cream-coloured complexions, and to hear their low sweet voices, is for a man to be lost. And added to this is the witchery of their gesture, their flirtations with their dainty, sandal-wood fans, so that the most experienced dancers have more than once avowed that there are no dancers to be found like the Cuban girls.

The planter looked on at this festive scene for some minutes, when he espied the lovely daughter of the storekeeper who supplied the estate with negro clothes and provisions, one Laura Nargas. Going up and paying his respects to her with Spanish courtliness, he and Laura joined in the dance, and soon they were the cynosure of all eyes, for Laura danced wildly, and so voluptuously withal, that some of the young men whispered to each other passionate words, and went forth to a by-street, where some beautiful Spanish girls, dressed in short frocks, sat in rocking-chairs before a long grated window.

These girls were kind, and invited the young Spaniards in to see them, after which they returned to the dance wiser if sadder men.

CHAPTER XVIII

FIGHT WITH THE BANDITS

A MONTH later the planter returned in health and
spirits to the estate, with mind invigorated by his
sojourn on the strip of golden sand, dotted with
stately palms, greener than the emerald waters
that flashed like an opal in the sunlight, and
faded away to a double blue distance where the
sea and sky met.

One evening towards the end of July, the gang
of young girls were making a fire of the weeds
recently cut round the house, and dried by two
or three lucky days of sunshine, when suddenly,
as if in response, a fire burst forth at the foot of
the hill to the right of the highway.

" What is it, Caoba? " asked Don Enrique.

" A runaway's fire, my master ; it has caught
the rotten ceiba trunk."

Always suspicious, the planter looked intently
at the faces of the negro girls lit up by the fire in
front of the house, whose flames shot up higher
than the piazza roof, as fresh loads of dried weeds
were thrown on to it ; but he could not detect in
their young faces that they knew aught of the

fire at the foot of the hill, for, of course, to the planter's mind it might have meant a signal for a rising of the slaves, an ever-menacing danger.

" It's no signal," muttered the planter to himself. But he would have been still worried had he known that round the fire sat Lorenzo and his bandits roasting eggs and plantains in the hot ashes of the dead giant ceiba, and thus accidentally setting it afire. But he would have been happier still had he known it would be their last good night on this earth, for such indeed it was.

The alert and energetic Captain Baro had, by aid of negro spies (for the poor Spanish countrymen and villagers were in league with the bandits), received information of their whereabouts : indeed, he was at that moment on the march—a negro tracker riding ahead with two bloodhounds in leash, and a troop of twenty-four *guarda - civiles* coming after in their grey uniforms with scarlet collars and cuffs, armed with carbine and sword bayonet.

The next morning at breakfast-time Captain Baro and his party arrived at the burning tree trunk, and halted, examining the ground, Don Enrique watching them from his piazza, their gun barrels shining in the morning sun.

Loosely closing his hands, with the palms out-

wards, the planter signalled to Caoba, Spanish
fashion, to come to him.

"See the *guarda-civiles* at the old ceiba. There
were people there last night."

"Yes, my master, and not runaways, or the
guarda-civiles would not be out."

"What, bandits, do you think ? "

"Ah, who knows, my master ? "

"By God, if it were, I should like to reckon
with that insolent Lorenzo." Then turning to
Caoba, he said, "Run and get the grey saddled,
and bring him here quickly."

Don Enrique had called his three dogs, and
when the horse was brought he jumped into the
saddle, and galloped recklessly over the boulders,
knocking a pathway through a forest of trembling
sensitive plants, crushing a snake, scattering a
flock of *jutias*, and pushing his way through a
newly-made gap in the prickly-pear hedge that
separated his plantation from the highway. All
round the gap were the footmarks of shod men,
and stray plantains showed that the bandits had
helped themselves from his plantain grove the
night before.

"May the lightning blast them !" said the
planter, grinding his teeth as he waded through
the heavy mud in the highroad ere he reached
the foot of the hill where he picked up the *guarda-
civiles.*

" Good morning, Don Enrique," hailed Captain Baro. " What is this ? "

" Good morning, captain. Lorenzo, I think. I saw the fire last night, and thought it that of a runaway, but white men have been robbing my plantain grove, and a large party too."

" Yes, about fifteen, señor," said the tracker, whipping off Don Enrique's dogs, who wished to exchange greetings with the bloodhounds.

" Yes, they are the *bandoleros*; this will be a dark day for them," said Captain Baro. " I think we have got them at last."

" They must have gone to the cave on the hill," said Don Enrique quickly ; " their tracks all lead in that direction. Curse them ! May I accompany you ? "

" By all means: brave men are always welcome," said Captain Baro, taking off his hat.

" And to follow a brave man is always a pleasure," said the planter, returning the salute and compliment.

The party moved on towards the hill-top, the captain falling behind and listening intently to Don Enrique's description of the ground round the cave.

After riding slowly for some time over scrub and rock, they came to the band of forest fringing the cave.

" We must all dismount here," said Don

Enrique, " and tie our horses to the guava bushes, and I will show you the way," he said, drawing his revolver.

Captain Baro drew his sword, and the tracker bared his machete, the troop fixing bayonets and falling in Indian file, the dogs following at the heels of the tracker, who led the bloodhounds.

The forest around the cave was not thick, being at a somewhat high elevation, so that after about twenty minutes' walking, Don Enrique signalled, " Hist," and pointing in the direction of the cave, he said, "It lies there, some two hundred yards to the right." The well-trained dogs merely snuffed the ground as they slouched along. The party moved forward cautiously, and suddenly debouched before the cave.

"The entrance is on the left hand," whispered the planter.

Captain Baro gave a signal to halt, and whispered a signal to the sergeant for the troop to defile to the left and advance in open order, himself and Don Enrique leading.

Suddenly, in the quiet, one of the bloodhounds bayed.

" *Car-r-ajo !*" cursed the captain under his breath. Then aloud he shouted, " At the double. Forward."

A pistol squibbed amongst the rocks before them, and a bullet whistled over their heads.

Running on, they surprised the bandits, their horses hobbled behind the cave, and themselves hastily concealed in the crevices of the rock round the entrance, for they had been surprised asleep, and were only aroused by the shot fired by their lookout.

" Halt, ready, present, fire ! " shouted Baro in one breath, and a volley echoed from the silent hill-top.

" Charge ! " shouted Baro, leading the way.

The little band of civil guards dashed at the bandits, who had risen from their hiding-places, some of them trying to jump to their horses. There was a sound of clashing steel as the bayonets met the machetes, for the brigands fought desperately, as they knew there was no quarter.

Don Enrique was standing by Captain Baro, using his revolver freely—for he had no other weapon—and every time he fired he rested his revolver on a rock, taking deadly aim, and watching Baro's hand-to-hand conflict with one of the bandits in the interval, ready to kill the opponent if the captain was too hard pressed. One brigand dashed past on a horse, cutting at Don Enrique with a curse as he rode by, but the planter was too quick for him ; the revolver cracked, and the man toppled over with a crash into a cactus bush.

The fight had been short but fierce, and but three living men were to be seen when Captain Baro cried—

"Surrender, and your lives shall be spared."

The three men, who stood on a tall rock, and behind a boulder, cried—

"Never ! come and take us."

Among these they recognised Lorenzo.

The captain gave the order to take them, and a zealous civil guard dashed up with his bayonet, but Lorenzo's bright blade flashed in the light, and cleft his skull in twain.

"So will I serve you all, cowards," shouted the bandit chief with rage.

"Aha, Lorenzo Almendares, once thirteen of you attacked me in my house. I would have shot you then but for the American Consul," said Don Enrique ; "but to-day I swear by the God in heaven you are mine ;" and aiming his deadly revolver, the planter fired, the brigand falling forward shot through the head. The other two then threw down their arms.

"Too late ; no quarter now. Bayonet them," ordered the captain. There was flash of steel, spurts of blood and curses, and the last of the bandits was dead.

Captain Baro then ordered a large fire to be made in the cave, whereupon a string of bats flew forth, and a couple of thin-flanked wild dogs.

By the bright firelight they examined the cave, but no hiding-places could they find, though they prodded their bayonets all over the stone walls. There were merely a few blankets, and bunches of bananas and blackened stones, where the bandits made their fires : no plunder of any kind rewarded them.

Whilst this examination was going on, Don Enrique was busy dressing the shoulder of one of the civil guards, who had it cut open by a machete. This casualty, and that of the man killed by Lorenzo, completed the losses of the civil guard.

When the troop came forth from the cave, Captain Baro said, "Carry your dead mate to the horses, and do him up in a *seron*. As for these sons of—well, leave them for the turkey-buzzards and wild dogs—all except the head of Lorenzo." This he ordered the sergeant to cut off and take charge of.

The troop then rode back from the hill, and accepted Don Enrique's advice to dine on the estate.

Captain Baro, after the meal, ceremoniously presented Don Enrique with a handsome little silver-mounted and richly engraved dirk, as a memento of their little adventure, and the whole troop rode away after dinner in high spirits with the head of Lorenzo, to send to the Captain-

General with the report of the complete destruction of the band.

And their annihilation was fortunate for Don Enrique in more senses than one, as well as the part he played in it, for his enemies could no longer say that he was in league with Lorenzo the brigand.

CHAPTER XIX

LOLA OF MARAVILLA

TOWARDS the end of the wet season, disease broke out amongst the negroes, intermittent fever and dysentery being the commonest complaints. The little Spanish doctor shook his head gravely, too, at the number of diarrhœa cases, and ordered three of the worst to be taken to Maravilla by the sea, both for their own sakes and for the planter's—for the possibility of cholera always hung over the wet season like a baleful *ignis fatuus*.

Don Enrique decided to escort the invalids himself, for now that Lorenzo's band had been destroyed the roads were safe. The family cart was drawn up to the hospital, and the convalescent negroes laid in blankets at the bottom, Don Enrique, Ramon and Marzial, Caoba and Sabicu, and the great dogs escorting it along the muddy roads. After a long and dirty journey, they drew up at the little *tienda* and *posada*, in the verandah of which Lola was sitting fanning herself, for she had seen them turn the point of the bay. By the time the invalids reached the

Almaçen, Don Eustaquio, who had been fore-warned by Ramon, was ready to receive them, for a room was kept on purpose for such cases.

The three invalids were helped out of the cart, and given in charge of the clerk.

Already night was falling, and the bay was bright with phosphorescent light where the returning fishermen's oars struck the water. Turning to Ramon, Don Enrique said—

"I shall sleep at the *tienda*. Take the cattle out and give them a feed, and start back for the estate at daybreak. You can take the dogs with you."

Don Enrique walked to the *posada*, where the old negress nurse was buying wine and food for the convalescents.

When the planter entered the dimly-lighted *tienda*, with its flickering oil lamps, two half-wild dogs ran forth, evidently belonging to three sinister-looking Spaniards in montero dress, who were sitting playing dominoes.

"As Cervantes says," thought the planter, "poor Cuba is a sanctuary for the homicides of the Peninsula. What cut-throats these villains look!"

But they were forgotten as the bright Anda-lusian girl, Lola, who had followed him into the *tienda*, touched his arm. Turning, he saw her cunningly standing under an oil lamp, that lit up her olive complexion, jet-black eyes, fringed with long dark lashes, and the luxuriant coils of her bluish-black hair that sat high upon her head, bound there by a large, square, tortoise-shell comb.

She was standing with her head on one side, fanning her youthful but exquisitely-moulded figure, with an expression of the deepest interest on her face.

"Good evening, señorita," said the planter.

"Good evening, Excellency; how goes it?" she replied, with a melting look in her large eyes, giving her fan a witching flirt.

"Well, thank you, señorita, and how is Lola?" asked he, patting her hand.

"Well, then, señor, and have you no present for Lola?"

"Not to-day, Lolita."

Lola made a *moue*, and kept opening and shutting her fan in vexation.

"I came with invalids," explained Don Enrique.

Lola's eyes flashed, and giving her fan a graceful wave, she said—

"Ah, señor has heart for the poor things; señor is very good."

"Thank you, child," said Don Enrique, as she fanned herself quickly, looking every now and then wickedly at the planter from over her fan.

The three villainous-looking Spaniards were whispering together and gazing on the scene, for they did not know who the planter was, but saw he was wealthy.

"Come, Lola, child. Show me to the *comedor*. I want dinner. Where is your father ?"

" He has gone fishing ; we expect him every moment. Señor, will you walk this way ?" and opening a hinged part of the counter, she led the way to the dining-room at the back, and said gaily, "Seat yourself, señor ; and what shall Lola get you for dinner ?"

" What have you, little one ?"

" Dolphin and crayfish, oysters, sweet potatoes, eggs, jerked beef. . . . Shall I make the señor a tortilla and fry some dolphin? Or say, a crayfish salad, and a dish of picked tasajo and rice, with a little cheese and guava, and a bottle of English ale or catalan ?"

" Excellent!" said Don Enrique ; "and give my servants tasajo and sweet potatoes, bread and wine."

"Now, if the señor will allow me, I will go and get the mother to cook," said the girl, with an arch look, leaving the room.

" *Hasta luego*," said the planter.

" *Hasta luego*," she replied, putting her smiling face round the door.

After giving the orders to her mother, she

went to wait on the Spaniards, who had called, when they asked her, saying—

"Who is the *caballero*, señorita?"

"Don Enrique of the *Ingeñio La Esperanza.*"

The men looked at each other, and one asked—

"Does he return home to-night?"

"I do not know, gentlemen."

They thanked the girl, and resumed their gambling.

As the women were preparing the dinner, the girl's mother said—

"Your father is late to-night. Go and take the Spaniards' money for the wine, and shut up the doors. We shall have no more custom to-night ; they owe a peseta.

Lola went into the *tienda*, and said—

"Gentlemen, do me the favour to pay me, for we must now shut up."

One of the grey-headed, sun-dried Spaniards drew out his bladder purse and paid the reckoning, after which he and his companions shuffled out into the mud streets, and stood talking together in low voices, whilst the active Lola locked and barred the windows and doors. After she had extinguished the lamps, she returned to her mother, and said—

"They are bad people those men."

"Warn Don Enrique then," said the mother ; "I think they are freshly-arrived Peninsulares."

Lola then laid the cloth and set on the dinner, after which she took a seat in the rocking-chair, and began flirting with her eyes and her face as Don Enrique ate his meal.

"Is Don Enrique, the brave, afraid of nothing?" asked the girl.

"Only of Lola's eyes," said the planter, with Spanish courtesy.

"Ah, mother mine, if Don Enrique only loved me ever so little!"

"So he does," said the planter, draining his glass of catalan.

"Ah, but Don Enrique loves as an American. Don Enrique is cold."

"What would you, Lola?   I am married."

"Ah, in Spain that is nothing—when the heart loves——"

"Well, Lola?"

"They love; and to show Don Enrique that I love him I will tell him there are bad people lying in wait for the wealthy *hacendado*."

"Aha, Lola!   How?   Where?"

Lola came up with blazing eyes and burning cheeks, and leaning over his shoulder, whispered—

"On the Maravilla road—three armed men—I heard them talking;" then giving the planter a passionate kiss, she swept from the room.

A feeling of indescribable tenderness seized the

strong heart of the man, and the loyalty and love of the poor, illiterate, but beautiful Andalusian, aroused in him a sudden passion, and going to the door he called softly—

" Lola ! "

But instead of the girl's voice, he was answered by the rough cheery voice of the father, who had just returned from fishing, and who came up in his jovial manner to tell the latest news over a glass of catalan.

.   .   .   .   .   .

Next morning, after an early breakfast, Don Enrique mounted his horse, after Lola had pinned a spray of tuberose to his coat; but before he started Lola beckoned him to stoop down, and she whispered in his ear—

" Señor, remember a *Spanish* girl loves you."

" Good-bye, little one," retorted Don Enrique, squeezing her hand affectionately, "and may God preserve you ; " and digging spurs into his horse, he started for home.

As he entered the silent forest he pondered on this strange girl's affection for him, for he knew Lola would be his slave unto death—for he knew that a Spanish woman who loves, loves unto death. As he was thinking of her, the three men she spoke off were brought to his mind, and taking out his revolver he examined it carefully, and replacing it rode on, overtaking Ramon and Caoba, who had purposely hung back.

" How is this?" said Don Enrique.

" My master, there were bad people at the inn last night. I tried to find out where they were going, and they said they were going eastward by the sea ; but I did not like their looks, and I hope the master will forgive us for hanging back."

"A blessing on you both, but it's all the better for them if they have gone eastward by the sea," said Don Enrique.

.   .   .   .   .   .

It was high noon when the planter and his servants reached the estate, and never a " bad person " had they met or heard ; so perhaps they had gone eastward by the sea, guessing doubtless that the planter would be well armed.

CHAPTER XX

THE DUEL

THE rainy season had nearly passed, with the depression and dulness incident to plantation life during this period, for society was scarce; the neighbouring planters were many of them absentee landlords, for such was the custom amongst the Spanish grandees who owned estates; indeed, Don Enrique himself usually went to New York for the greater part of the wet season, so that besides the little doctor, the padre, the American Consul, and the captain of the partido, visitors were scarce; and what with the bad weather time hung heavily. The roads were almost unfit for riding, except upon occasional short spells of fine weather, so that reading and music were the chief recreations.

One incident, however, occurred at the end of the season, which was the talk of the estate for some time.

One day as Don Enrique, followed by his faithful Caoba, went down to inspect some new cane carts recently made by the wheelwright, they came upon the majoral and boyero fighting with poignards in the deserted boiling-house. The two combatants were madly excited, shouting loudly, and fencing round each other with their drawn dirks like crazy people.

Before Don Enrique could dismount, Caoba ran forward and seized a stick lying upon the ground, and, darting into the house, ran between the combatants, Don Enrique jumping from his horse and following. When he came up to the two men, still glaring at each other, he said—

" What, what, Don Leonaldo and Don Joaquin —fighting on the estate ! "

" Pardon, señor ; pardon, señor," they both said, taking off their hats ; " it was in a moment of passion," added the majoral.

" I pardon on one condition," said Don Enrique—" that you shake hands and be friends. Nothing but honour is worth fighting for like that."

" Ah, Don Enrique is a gentleman," said Don Leonaldo, sheathing his dirk, and holding his hand out to the cowman, who still held his dirk in his hand, and, after some hesitation, sheathed it, and shook the overseer's hand rather sullenly.

" Now that's settled : let it be forgotten," said Don Enrique.

As the two white men went to their quarters, Don Enrique said—

"Caoba, you ran great danger in what you did—to lay a hand on a Spaniard, too. Had he stabbed you he would have got nothing."

"No, my master, he is a Cuban, which is better than a Spaniard."

"Ah, that's different. A negro is better than a Cuban in the eyes of the foolish Peninsulares; . . . but you are a brave lad. Have you thought over what I said to you some months ago?"

"Yes, my master. If the master will give me Maria Lucumi, the mistress's maid, for wife, and let us live on at the *Casa Grande*, Caoba will be a happy slave."

"It shall be done, Caoba; she is a neat, bright, upstanding girl. I will see to it."

"A blessing, my master."

And Don Enrique walked over to the wheelwright's, whilst Caoba got some heads of maize and threw them into the manger for his master's horse to chump in the silence of the sleeping machinery.

PART II

PEACE AND CARE

CHAPTER I

FIRE

THE slaughter of the bandits had effectually stopped all lawlessness in the interior, and for several years the planters and farmers round *La Esperanza* enjoyed their lives peacefully. Don Enrique himself had given up going out with his bodyguard, Ramon and Marzial. Through those tranquil years he had worked hard during the grinding seasons, and in the wet seasons taken his pleasure in the United States with his family—a son and a daughter. These children were the idols of the servants at the *Casa Grande*, but the brother and sister preferred to wander alone through the chapparal, for they were as simple and innocent as Paul and Virginia. Pedro, the boy, was a great lover of birds and beasts, and his joy knew no bounds when at six he was put on an old white horse and allowed to take his first ride ; but by practice he soon learned to ride barebacked, and at thirteen could be seen in the *corral*, throwing a lasso over the half-wild calves, a sport which he varied by making figure-of-four traps for the wild

pigeons, baiting them with maize; or killing
snakes with sticks when they thrust their heads
from their holes; or collecting eggs or throwing
great pieces of yellow pumpkin to his pet pig;
or chasing some of the lambs to a corner of the
sheepfold, not to kill them—as did Areo, the new
dog, one night, for which Areo was muzzled and
tied to a post and flogged—but to tie ribbons
round their necks, for the children then called
them their lambs.   He knew where the little
hawks nested in the roof of the *Casa Grande*,
where the eggs of the *peteri* were to be found
in the orange trees; the egg-shells he strung on
pieces of bast for his little sister Juanita; then
the evening walks with Juan de Dios, one of the
servants, to the old platanal, where the children
built a grotto, in the centre of which the faithful
African had built a miniature palm-leaf hut, in
which he placed a little clay figure, telling the
children that no evil spirits would come near
them so long as the figure remained.   Juan de
Dios too would gather melons that grew in the
platanal, and the subacid fruit of the rat pine.
But Pedro and Juanita were not allowed to go
alone to the *batey*, for divers reasons, so that
a visit to the works during the grinding season
was a great treat, as was the sip of guarapo
punch which the major-domo always made upon
these occasions.   Nevertheless the children were

always happy and occupied, for when not with their governess they were always busy; one of their chief delights being to tie dry corn-cobs to a long stick, and go forth amongst the cacti-decorated rocks in the grounds, and search for the papery nests of the angry yellow wasps, which they burned by applying their primitive torches. One day Pedro and Caoba, who were great chums, had decided to burn the dozens of nests that hung from the wooden rafters of the piazza, round the house; and having prepared their long torches, they went round, setting the nests alight, being often compelled to run from the piazza, chased by the angry broods of wasps; and they did their work so well that never a nest was left, when Pedro, tired with the exercise and excitement, went and sat in a rocking-chair in the saloon by his father, who was dozing. Presently there were loud crackling reports like that of a whip-crack, and Don Enrique started up, asking—

"Who is cracking a whip, Pedro? Go to the window and see."

The boy did as he was told, and looking out at the postigo, he said with hesitation—

"Why, sir, the house is on fire! the ceiling is falling."

"What?" yelled Don Enrique; "go and ring the alarm-bell;" and seizing a carafe of water, he ran out into the sunny piazza, where, sure enough, the rafters were blazing and smoking. In his excitement he hurled the carafe at the fire, at which the boy smiled. Servants were now flocking from all parts, and Don Enrique crying for water, and the alarm-bell in the tower was ringing, and answered by the alarm-bell on the estate; and people could be seen running by different roads to the house. Buckets of water were passed along from hand to hand from the rain tanks, built under the dwelling-rooms, and in a comparatively short time the flames were extinguished.

"No more wasp-burning about the house," said Don Enrique. "It is an expensive and dangerous amusement."

And the extemporary firemen were given each a dram of *aguadiente*, and returned to their work.

CHAPTER II

DEATH AND WARNINGS

AGAIN the grinding season had returned, and work pressed all over the estate, the songs of the firemen and negroes resounding by night and day, under the torrid sun or bright tropical stars.

January had nearly passed when one night Don Enrique was awakened by Caoba, who said—

"The administrator is outside. One of the people burnt, my master, stealing sugar."

Don Enrique sent for his horse and rode with the administrator down to the infirmary, where a tall Ganga African, with his tribal marks, lay on a cot moaning, for he was terribly burnt from head to foot, having filled a large tub with the boiling syrup, and tripped as he ran in the dark with his stolen sweets.

Don Enrique approached the man, but feeling his pulse and seeing his state of collapse, he shook his head gravely ; nevertheless, mixing a cordial, he forced some down the patient's throat. The man gradually recovered his senses, and Don Enrique began to dress his scalds, when the poor negro, in a faint, jerky voice, said—

"Thank you, my master; but, before I die, listen to a poor negro—you will all be eaten up."

"How eaten up?" asked Don Enrique.

But the negro's head fell back on the cot, and he was dead.

"Ah, poor man," said the planter, moving out of the room; "send for the padre in the morning to bury him."

CHAPTER III

THE HIGHWAYMEN

THE following wet season Don Enrique and his family did not go to the United States, as he wished to superintend the laying out of the iron-wood sleepers for the light railway to Maravilla, Don Enrique's great project, which was to save all carting of sugar, railway, and dues to other ports. Besides this, he amused himself by shooting partridges that ran through the young cane, and crested pigeons that frequented the woods in great numbers at this season ; for, as I have said, the country had now grown quite quiet, and even Gomez did not annoy, owing to the offices of the captain and the padre. The early months of the wet season passed with the usual thunderstorms, torrents of rain, and spells of fine days.

It was upon the evening of one of these fine days, that Don Enrique sat in his piazza watching the sheet-lightning after dusk flashing on the distant horizon, recalling the opening and shutting of the huge eyes of some sombre giant, when the gingle-te-tingle of horses could be heard passing the cocoa-nuts and coming towards the house.

Horsemen at such an hour were always received with a certain amount of uneasiness and suspicion, and Don Enrique was more disquieted when three low-class Spaniards entered the drive, and, riding up to the house, saluted him with the usual "Good evening, gentleman."

"Good evening," retorted Don Enrique, rising; "what is there to do?"

"Will the master mind sending the *niño grande* indoors: we would speak privately to him."

Don Enrique turned to the fair-haired boy and told him to go in and order Caoba to place lighted candles in the office; then turning to the Spaniards, he said—

"Won't you dismount, gentlemen, and take some refreshment?"

"No, señor, thank you; we wish to tell the master that a cargo of *bozales* is to be landed off the coast near Remedios."

"Whew! Remedios! it is a long way off."

"Oh no, señor—only sixty-three miles, and they are a handsome lot—Ashantis."

"And you—where do you come from, gentlemen?"

"From Remedios—from Don Chicadillo, who has sent this letter."

The planter took the letter, written on coarse paper, and broke the wafer. It was in truth from Don Chicadillo.

"Gentlemen, I will go, if you will await me."

" Till the gentleman pleases."

Then, calling Caoba, he ordered Marikita to be saddled.

The planter ran indoors to tell his wife of his journey, then dressing for a long ride, he came out and mounted his horse, and rode off with the three Spaniards.

" Is the señor armed ? " asked one of the men as they entered the highway.

"Yes, enough for six men," said the planter coldly.

" *Vamos !* then," retorted the man, digging his spurs into his horse, and started off at a run, followed by the others.

They rode along the highway till nearly daylight, when they emerged upon an open savannah where the grass grew tall and luxuriant ; and owing to the boggy nature of the ground, the riding was heavy for the horses ; but the Spaniards whiled away the time singing muleteer songs under the bright starlight, songs accompanied with the jingling of their trappings. Just before dawn, as they entered a clear place at the edge of a forest, the Spaniards suddenly wheeled their horses, and the eldest said—

" Señor Chicadillo is unknown to us ; the letter was a forgery. We want twenty ounces, or you are a dead man."

The planter's hand went to his belt, but his heart sank within him for his revolver was gone, and he was unarmed. He saw the three men handling their machetes, and he knew, had he only his revolver, he would be more than a match for them, for at that time the low Spaniard was mightily afraid of the bullet, though not of a dirk or a machete.

"Come, gentleman, the money and that clock," pointing to his watch, ordered the eldest man.

"Go to the devil!" said Don Enrique, holding up his left hand, as though it were a revolver, and catching his thumb with the index finger of his right, a simple ruse that deceived the ignorant Spaniards, unaccustomed to firearms—a ruse rendered all the easier by the dim light. "The first man who moves, I'll shoot dead as a stone," continued he.

"Take care," said the Spaniard.

"Go, ride off, *sinverguenzas*, or I fire," said the intrepid planter.

The rascals consulted together.

"Are you going ? One——"

"Ah, good morning, *caballero !*" said the old man, digging his great brass spurs into his horse, and wheeling they rode off into the forest.

"Cowards !" yelled Don Enrique, turning his horse back into the savannah. But he was trembling, man of iron nerve that he was, for this miraculous escape had shaken him.

As he rode across the savannah the morning broke, and mists began to rise from the sodden earth.

"I must have a drink," said he, parched from the excitement ; and alighting, he drank from a runnel with greedy thirst. The draught of muddy water was a great relief, and remounting his horse, he turned off his old trail to the left, striking a road that skirted the forest edge, but soon lost his bearings. Presently the jingle of a mule caught his ear in the morning air, and an old Spaniard, with his panniers full of melons, rode past.

"Say, compadre, is this the way to Remedios?"

"Nor am I your compadre, nor is this the way to Remedios," retorted the old countryman curtly.

"Where am I, then, gentleman ?" asked Don Enrique.

"Ah, that is another matter. You are on a highway that, if you left it at the proper time, would take you to Remedios, and there is a posada two miles farther on."

Famished, the planter made the best speed towards the little *tienda* kept by an old bachelor. Riding up, he called, but no one replied ; so, dismounting, he led his horse into the bar, where a little *Gallego* was eating a dish of piccadillo and *frijoles*.

"Good morning, gentleman," greeted the planter.

"Good morning, gentleman," replied the unkempt host, raising his eyes.

"Can I have anything to eat ?"

"No."

"How no ? I am starving."

A shrug of the shoulders was the *Gallego's* reply.

"Come, man, catch me a chicken—I saw some outside—some eggs and rice—anything."

"No ; my fire's gone out."

"*Caramba !* let me have raw eggs, then ; I am starving. I'll pay you well."

The Spaniard's eyes glittered, and he asked coldly—

"How much for a dozen ?"

"A dollar, if you'll get them at once."

"Ah, that is another thing," said the *Gallego*, rising ; and shutting his dish of beef and beans in a drawer, he went out to look for the eggs.

No sooner had he gone, than Don Enrique leant over the low counter, and opening the drawer, seized the dish of broken meats and turned it into his handkerchief, bread and all, and dropping a dollar into the dish, he replaced it in the drawer, led forth his horse, mounted, and digging his spurs to the flukes, started off at a rapid run. Before he got out of sight, he heard the enraged

Spaniard yelling after him, but the cries grew fainter and fainter till they vanished.

After riding for an hour, he halted, and hastily ate, to him, this delicious meal, riding on as soon as the last piece of bread was swallowed.

After riding some hours, he came across a little farmer's *estancia*, covering about twelve acres of ground, in which grew Indian corn and a patch of vegetables, revelling in wild luxuriance. The planter and his horse were both famished, for the animal neighed when he saw the maloja *in posse* growing by the yams and sweet potatoes. Riding up to the house, a framework of sticks covered with palm leaf, Don Enrique called out "Hola !"

"Who is it ?" cried a voice, and a swarthy Spaniard, followed by a comely mulatta girl and several half-breed children, came to the door.

"Can I have some maloja for my horse, *caballero ?*"

"But yes, señor ; and do you want coffee ?"

"A thousand thanks, yes," said he, alighting and entering the house, the Spaniard taking the horse off to provide him with a feed of green corn-tops. Whilst he was thus engaged, Don Enrique talked to the good-looking mulatta, and patted the naked children on the head.

When the Spaniard returned, the wife produced a large gourd of beans and meat, and placed it in the centre of the table, but neither plate nor knife nor fork was there.

"Do you desire?" said the Spaniard, pointing to the food.

"Many thanks, yes."

"It is at your disposal."

And the family gathered round, dipping their hands into the dish, throwing the morsels into their mouths, and letting the beans run in as they passed a handful from the wrist to the finger-tips. The hungry planter took great handfuls, and followed their example as well as he could ; but his clumsiness caused much merriment to the children, for as many beans fell to the floor as went into his mouth.

When the common stew was finished, coffee was put on the table and served in gourds, the mulatta, dressed in a frock with a handkerchief about her neck, talking volubly about the next lottery as she sipped the beverage. She had bought part of a ticket, and believing seven was a lucky number, had bought part of ticket Number 777.

The horse chumped the maloja outside, and the naked children ran in and out, picking up the beans that had dropped to the floor and eating them.

When the planter had finished his coffee, and received directions for his road back to the estate, he offered to pay for his entertainment.

"No, señor," said the Spaniard. "Amongst gentlemen ? No, señor."

" Well, well, the children, then," said the planter, scattering a handful of reals fuerte amongst the naked brats who played about him.

That afternoon he arrived on the estate, but his revolver was never found. He had lost it whilst jumping some of the streams in the savannah.

CHAPTER IV

DYSENTERY

THE following day Caoba was ordered to ride hard to the little doctor, for Don Enrique had been taken ill early in the morning with fever, griping pains, and diarrhœa. The whole household was upset, and the administrator went about looking very grave, for the little doctor told the señora, when he arrived, that her husband was suffering from a severe attack of dysentery.

For a week the great planter lay in torments of pain, which the ever-watchful doctor tried to combat by administering huge doses of ipecacuanha. At the end of the tenth day Dr. Rios pronounced his patient out of danger, and at the end of a month Don Enrique went forth a haggard, shrunken man, from whose dirty-coloured skin his eyes shone unnaturally bright.

"You had better go north," advised the doctor.

"Ah, man, I cannot do that; grinding begins soon."

"Life is more important," said the doctor.

"Ah, well, next year," replied Don Enrique, dismissing the subject.

All through the grinding season the dysenteric symptoms kept coming and going, so that directly the last hogshead was carted, Don Enrique and his family went to the alum springs of Virginia to recruit his health.

CHAPTER V

CHOLERA MORBUS

WHILST drinking the astringent waters of the springs and gaining strength, Don Enrique received the following letter from the administrator :—

"INGEÑIO LA ESPERANZA, *Aug. 25th.*

"MY DEAR DON ENRIQUE,—I am afraid we must strengthen our hearts and put our faith in the Lord, for we are inflicted with that fearful plague, the cholera.

"Poor Dr. Rios took it on the Sant Anna, where they have already lost thirty hands, and rode over here, immediately going to bed in my spare room, where he died *three hours* after his arrival. I had him buried at once, and everything burnt, even the bed, thinking God, in His mercy, might spare us; but three days after Juan Laluz took ill, and died with terrible cramps in fourteen hours. I cannot tell you the terrible trouble I have been through, and regret to have to report that already eighteen hands have died—the best men being Nicolas, Fernando Ganga, Antonio, José Carabali,

Joaquin; and the best women, Henobeba, Juana, Maria Carabali, Florencia, and Salomé Criolla.

"No doctor has yet taken poor Rios' place, so that I am doing my best with opium and homeopathic remedies, but no medicine seems of use. I have had all the pigs killed, and all the styes removed, having recompensed the owners. I did this because as yet no Chinaman has taken the disease, and I thought the pigs being so close to the negro quarters might have something to do with it.

"The people are scared, and I should like to move them to some other place, even if they encamp in the woods, for I fear, if this goes on, we shall lose every hand. The people already dead represent a loss of 18,000 dollars, and they are still dying.

"Let me know at once what to do about moving the people, and whether you would like medical aid obtained from the city, which, as you know, would be very costly.

" I trust your own health has improved, and that your good lady is well, as well as the children.

" May the Lord, in His merciful kindness, look down upon us.

"Yours obediently,

"N. MARTIN."

Don Enrique sat for some minutes as one dazed, then, as he re-read the letter, he muttered,

"The canting old hypocrite! I see his girl, Rosa, is not dead yet." Then ringing the bell, he asked when the next steamer left Baltimore for Havana.

"Next Thursday, sir," said the waiter on his return.

And on the following Thursday the planter and his family were aboard the *Evening Star*, bound for Havana.

CHAPTER VI

THE MASTER'S EYE

Don Enrique left his family by the sea at the Boca, having advised the administrator that he would arrive on a particular night.

It was dark when the train rolled up to the little station of Santiago, where the administrator and six stalwart negroes, amongst whom was Caoba, were awaiting him.

When he alighted, the six negroes knelt on the platform, begging for a blessing.

"God keep you," said Don Enrique.

Then shaking hands with the administrator, whose single eye glittered beneath his panama, he asked eagerly, "How goes it?"

"A little better, but still bad. It has broken out in the Chinese quarters. That beast La Hu stole some carrion from a dead cow; he was seen to wash it in the river by Caoba, and ate it. You know how fond the Chinese and some of the negroes are of carrion."

"I know—the beasts!"

"Well, La Hu was the first Chinaman to take the disease and die."

"Come, come to horse. It must be a bad type. A healthy Chinaman got in with us at Havana, and he was carried out dead before we reached the end of the journey. A few cases broke out on the steamer *Nuevo Almandarez*, from Havana to La Boca, and the Spaniards sat up all night drinking rum—to frighten it off, as they said."

Don Enrique and the administrator mounted, and, calling the dogs, started for the estate, leaving the negroes to follow with the baggage waggon.

The roads were bad and the night dark, so that they did not speak much till they passed through the works of the neighbouring estate, *La Marguerita*, when the big dogs began to bark loudly, and some negroes, with torches, ran forth to see who the strangers were.

Passing the works, they forded the river, their horses sinking to the girths in the muddy shores, and it was nearly midnight when they arrived at the administrator's house, where, after a light supper, they retired to rest.

CHAPTER VII

DISMANTLED

THE next day Don Enrique made a minute survey of the negro and Chinese quarters, the result of which was that everything in the *Casa Grande* was hastily packed and warehoused in the deserted boiling-house. The administrator had to give up his house and go into rooms where the white employés lived, and Don Enrique took up his residence at the administrator's house with a diminished staff of servants. The stables of the big house were emptied, and the pigs, chickens, and sheep kept to be killed and served out as rations. In fact, the *Casa Grande* was dismantled.

" Here are thirty thousand dollars to make up," said Don Enrique, " and as many more to replace the old hands ; it must be done."

Amongst the small posse of servants retained were Caoba and Maria, his wife, the majority of the others being sent to join the field-hands or distributed where required. By this arrangement the dreadful gap made by the deaths was partially filled up, much to the disgust of the servants who had lived at the *Casa Grande*, for field-work was a different matter, but they soon fell into it. The *Casa Grande* itself was turned into an hospital, every suspicious case being at once carried thither in a cart, the invalids being distributed about the house in cots, under the charge of some old negresses. River water was prohibited for washing or drinking under penalty of severe flogging, and the people were compelled to draw water from one of the wells in a cane-field at some distance—being the chief well that supplied the engine with water in the grinding season—round which the horses tramped day and night, pumping water to the works.

These energetic measures, together with prompt treatment, and the broths and meat from the chickens and sheep brought from the *Casa Grande*, soon stamped out the disease, and before grinding began there was no longer any choleraic symptoms on the estate; but the plague had carried off forty-three negroes of different ages and sexes, and eight Chinamen, representing altogether a loss of some sixty thousand dollars.

Nevertheless, the energetic Don Enrique closed his lips and determined to make up for it. A fresh gang of twenty Chinese were engaged on the spot, each man receiving four hundred dollars, Don Enrique agreeing to pay him four dollars a month, and clothe and board him for eight years, when he was free to go where he liked.

The day before grinding began, the señora and the children arrived at the estate and took up their abode in the administrator's house amongst the orange trees by the river.

CHAPTER VIII

FRIENDS

PEDRO, who was now a tall boy, enjoyed the life in the little house on the *batey* more than he had at the *Casa Grande*, for there was more excitement. Every morning his horse stood saddled at the door, and he went for a ride with his father in the dripping dewy grass, where the delicious morning glories filled the air with scent, and the trailing thumburgias brightened the greenery with yellow dots. In the evening, too, they rode, accompanied by the señora, to the fields where the hands were cane-cutting, to the *corrals*, or to the more distant woods. During the day, the boy was out of doors, either gathering oranges and limes, which he stored in a palm-leaf hut he had built himself by the river, or gathering the eggs of the muscovy ducks that built on rocky boulders in the river, and roasting them in wood ashes in his hut, he and Caoba eating them, for Caoba, whenever he could get away from the house, came down to the boy's hut and told him strange stories of runaways that lived in the cave in the hill. Caoba used to take the boy, too, to the

negroes' allotments by the river, and show him
the humming-birds hanging, as if on wires, before
the sweet honey-trumpets of the plantain trees,
at which they would suddenly dart, rising per-
pendicularly, then darting down and skimming
away some fifty yards to the greenery.   On moonlight nights, too, Caoba would take him to watch
the turtles laying their eggs by the river, whence
they dug some and carried them back to the little
palm-leaf hut to cook.   Some days young Pedro
would spend entirely in his hut, cooking his own
chicken which he caught by running down, together with some plantains or sweet potatoes,
which he roasted in wood ashes.   In the heat of
the day he spent a great deal of time bathing in
the pools that reflected the rustling palms or
waving canes.   Furnished with a crossbow made
by the carpenter, he would sally forth and attempt
to shoot the snipe, or shags, or *jutias*, or galli-
nules that frequented the river, but he never got
much sport unless Don Pablo, the major-domo,
took his gun along.

In the afternoons he would often go with his
lasso to the *corral* and catch the younger cattle,
helping the bad-tempered Tomas and the pleasant
Ignatio.

Or else he would spend his days in the corn-
house, watching the yellow maize being ground,
or looking for rats or snakes, or else working in

the carpenter's shop, or lying hidden in the chasm below the saw-mill, smoking cigarettes, which the messenger, Ignatio, smuggled from the village.

Pedro was everywhere, and a general favourite with all, the girl gang smiling upon him when he met them filing past, like living bronzes, to their work, or surprised them bathing in the pools, near which the mice built their nests.

But Pedro loved most of all to be alone by the river, finding lizards' eggs, catching crayfish, or killing the ugly-looking water-snakes, or crushing the snakes' eggs, or swimming by the water-lilies, or setting traps for the meadow-larks and wild pigeons, or nesting amongst the trees, getting the nests of the Baltimore oriole from the palms.

In this contemplative life the lad drank in a love of nature and beauty which was indelibly fixed in his nature, and still further refined by the sculpturesque figures of the negresses, and the father, noticing his dreamy and contemplative manner, used to mutter—

"The boy is a dreamer; he'll never be a Stephenson,[1] which I should like him to be."

[1] The engineer.

CHAPTER IX

RUIN

TOWARDS the end of the grinding season, Don Pablo and Pedro took a walk up to the *Casa Grande*, which had been shut up for some time after it had ceased to be a hospital. What a change was there in so short a time! The grounds were overgrown with rank weeds, and the snakes and wasps literally overran the place. The day was hot, so Pedro climbed a leaning cocoa-nut tree, and pulling forth a little dirk, sliced off the green top of a cocoa-nut and drank the sweet cool water, scraping out the thin white lining of the fibrous green shell. When they got up to the house, they found the left portion of the piazza had fallen in at the spot where the fire had been. Snakes thrust their heads from holes in the stones, lizards ran all over the piazza, and the sandy covered tunnel under one of the doors showed that the red ants were already at work undermining the cedar rafters. On opening the door, the great room rang emptily, and the walls were rudely white-washed after the disinfecting. Walking through into the back garden, a tangled mass of weed, flowers, and fruit struggling for mastery met the gaze. Weeds choked the paths, creepers covered the iron bars of the windows, and nearly hid the old white cotton tree. Dead banana trees lay on the ground, and the peelings of the purple heads of the living bananas, together with the sweet, honey-laden, trumpet-like flowers. The corner where the fowls and meat used to be buried to make them tender was now rank with a crop of cañasanta. The gay, blue, papilionaceous *clitoria* held its own, and one side of the house was a blaze of azure blossoms.

Walking through the empty kitchens, the cold ashes still lay on the stonework cooking-range, and on the floor lay a pile of sugar-cane peelings and chewed bagasse.

"A runaway negro has been here : this is his work. Let us look in the tanks," suggested the major-domo.

Having drawn his dagger, the brave little Spaniard, followed by the boy, descended into the first cellar-like tank that opened into four others, the light from the trap-door above them, whence water was drawn, dimly showing their way. The room - like cisterns, now empty, sounded hollow and ghostly as they walked through them, but never a runaway was there. On their return to the garden, Don Pablo looked at the tempting manzana bananas, and again drawing his knife he cut down one of the trees, and choosing some of the finest fruit, they went up to the top of the watch-tower to eat it and view the scene.

There it lay in all its former beauty, the golden green cane-fields, the shining roofs and gleaming white walls of the neighbouring estates, the dark greenery of the primeval forest, from which the rounded outline of the mountain rose, the scene of Lorenzo's death, and now the home of run-away negroes.

As the landscape palpitated and glittered under the pure azure, Don Pablo said, casting his eye round on the fair scene, studded with the lonely royal palms, "Ay, ay! if the cholera had not come; if the cholera had not come!"—then pausing, he turned to the boy and said, "The old times will never come back, my boy," and the major-domo shrugged his shoulders; then, pointing to some birds, he said, "See them? Guinea-fowls flighting, the sun is getting low, and the birds are going down to the water; we must go. But what a pity this fine place should come to this."

"Oh, some day it will be done up, and we shall go back there and live," said Pedro.

"We shall see," retorted Don Pablo, with deliberation.

Leaving the old house reluctantly, they walked down to the estate, and the night was upon them when they arrived.

"Come and drink a panella and water, eh, Pedro?" said the kind-hearted little major-domo.

When they arrived at his rooms, they found the administrator, the Canary Islander, and the master-mason playing cards, and awaiting Don Pablo. The Spaniards greeted the planter's son effusively, but the one-eyed administrator asked him in a bantering tone whether he had been nesting at the old house.

"No, we have been hunting runaway negroes in dark tanks. I wonder if you would do as much?" retorted the boy.

"Is it true?" asked the carpenter of Don Pablo, for the *gaucho* was an arrant coward himself.

"It is true," said Don Pablo haughtily; "he is like his father."

"Is he?" sneered the one-eyed Yorkshireman. "I'll give him a dollar to buy *confite* with if he dare walk up to the gates of the house now in the dark and pick a cocoa-nut."

"You'll go, won't you?" asked Don Pablo.

"Of course I'll go; it's absurd; there's nothing in it," said the blue-eyed lad, taking up his little Panama hat and starting off.

The walk was nothing, and the boy gathered

the cocoa-nut and returned, walking leisurely across the *batey*, when a man burst with yells from the bagasse-house.

"All right, Don Pablo; I've got my knife," said young Pedro cheerily, recognising the major-domo.

"Ay, good; if *he* were as brave," said Don Pablo, coming up.

"Who? Don Martin?"

"Nothing, nothing," said Don Pablo quickly, and they returned together to the room, the boy placing the cocoa-nut triumphantly on the table.

"Ah," sneered the administrator, "Don Pablo went with you."

"No, sir," said Don Pablo hotly; "I tried to frighten the lad, but he is like his father, like Caoba; the *Esperanza* breeds *men*."

"Yes," said the administrator, with a simpering sneer.

"Come, the dollar, Mr. Martin," demanded the boy.

"No; there's half-a-dollar, that's enough for you to spend on sweets."

"Cheat!" cried the boy hotly, throwing the coin on the table—"you are no gentleman;" and taking up his hat he left the room in a temper, followed by the sympathetic glances of the two Spaniards, who are always admirers of pluck.

For a few moments the four men in the room

looked uncomfortable, and not a word was spoken, when Don Pablo impulsively ran after the boy and gave him a dollar from his own pocket, and said in a strange voice—

"Ah, child, may the one-eyed coward never cheat you of more than *one* dollar!"

CHAPTER X

THE grinding season was over, and propitious weather had favoured Don Enrique. A good crop and good prices had been realised, so that the usual dinner to the white employés, though it was held in the little dining-room of the administrator's house, looking out on to the orange grove, was more sumptuous than usual ; as was the negroes' dance, for, though many of them had lost mothers and sisters, fathers, brothers, or children, they heeded not, for many of them, when in Africa, would willingly have sold their children to neighbouring tribes, notwithstanding the sentimentalist who imagines the African has the same family affections as the civilised white man.

It was not long after the end of the grinding season, before the one-eyed administrator showed another side to his character. Don Enrique had been laid up with bilious fever, due to exposure to the sun, and one evening Pedro went with the administrator for a ride. They chose the road leading through some low black lands to the maize-fields. When they reached the patch, enclosed by a ring fence and a gate, to keep the stray cattle out, the administrator, who was ahead, said—

"What's that, Pedro, in the corn ?"

"What ?" asked the boy, reining up his horse, and leaning over his high-pommelled Spanish saddle, he peered into the corn patch.

"Why, that dark thing in the corn."

"A ceiba stump," answered Pedro promptly ; "I see it."

"No; I saw it move. Jump down and see."

The boy kicked his stirrups free and jumped from his horse. Opening the gate and walking towards the patch, he hitched his bridle over a stump, then walking into the maize, he made straight for the stump, as he thought, for the light was none too clear in the crop. Suddenly, as he approached, a huge negro jumped up and made a slash at the boy with his machete. Pedro, nimble as a cat, dodged the blow, and ran back to his horse—the negro breaking away into the heart of the maize.

"That's a nice job to send me on !" said Pedro, turning hotly to the administrator.

"You said it was a stump," sneered the man.

"Yes ; but you didn't say it was an armed runaway negro. Why didn't you get down yourself and look ? You're a coward !"

"Come, come, Pedro ; I thought it was an

animal of some sort. Ride to the estate and call the majoral and two or three of the people."

"Not I ; go yourself."

"I shall tell your father if you don't go."

"Tell him, and I shall tell him what a coward you are. I know he doesn't think much of you anyway. I have watched him."

"If you use such language to me, go home."

"No, I shan't. I will never obey a coward !" hissed the boy, and digging spurs into his horse, he rode off towards the river—a favourite place of his. Going down to the muddy shore of a large basin in the river-bed, he waded in with his horse, and was soon swimming across it, leaning well over his horse's neck.

The boy's temper burned within him so hotly that he must needs put the river between him and his enemy—a man he had never liked, but whom he had loathed ever after the incident of the cocoa-nut.

Riding along the opposite bank of the river, he watched the administrator returning at a quick canter in the setting sun. He kept pace with him, and they entered the *batey* from opposite sides about the same time. Pedro was just fording the river, when suddenly a magnificent cream-coloured stallion that had broken loose from the stables came galloping and neighing towards his mare. She stopped in the water and began to neigh too. Whilst the boy was deciding what to do, Caoba came running from the house, shouting—

" Dismount, child, dismount, and wade into the deep water and swim away, as the stallion will kill you !"

Pedro slid from the mare into the ford, and wading into the deep water, struck out, and began to swim across the big pool, scrambling out on the masonry in the centre that covered the feed-pipe of the boiler of the saw-mill. Standing up, he turned towards the ford, where a fierce struggle was going on. The stallion, with tail erect and pricked ears, was biting and kicking the mare, who was returning the compliment, the two animals neighing and splashing the water around them, like fighting sea-horses. While the horses were thus engaged, Caoba and the groom ran down with lassoes, each one trying to get a good cast when the animals were separate. At last Caoba made a good throw, and caught the stallion by the neck and one leg. He was a fierce beast ; so whilst the grooms held the lasso firmly, Caoba approached with a halter, with which he managed to bridle the animal, after which he was led back to the stable. . . .

" You would have been killed, elder child, had you not got off. He would have kicked or bitten you to death ; the animal is very vicious," said Caoba the next day, as they smoked cigarettes in Pedro's palm-leaf hut by the river.

" Why didn't the administrator gallop up and tell me what to do ? " asked the lad. " He was not far off."

" Why, elder child, because he is a coward."

" How do you know that, Caoba ? "

" My child, I know many things, but a slave must not speak."

" I hate him ! " said the boy.

" He is no man. Don Enrique will find him out some day," replied Caoba.

CHAPTER XI

IN THE TORRENT

WHEN Don Enrique recovered from his attack, he was an altered man. The recent worries and the disease had told upon him. He had grown quite thin, and his face was full of marks and dusky in colour.

Notwithstanding this, he did not deem it necessary to go north, because of the great losses from the cholera. Naturally a stern man, but also genial, the tropical disease which affected his liver made him irritable, and Pedro used to come in for some scoldings—for swimming the horses through the water, for crossing by the deepest and muddiest fords he could find. But this did not check the youth's rides. He would be about in all but the hottest part of the day, even after the rains, which had already begun.

But the boy's nerve was shaken a little in the height of the rains.

The river at this season was a roaring torrent, and although the boy was accustomed to bathe in a little backwater at this time of year, he never realised that the river itself was dangerous, but it was chiefly avoided by him on account of the quantity of mud brought down. Indeed the floods did not seem remarkable, unless the huge swing-gate below the ford, that kept the cattle from breaking through in the summer-time, was carried to an angle with its uprights of 45 degrees—then the river appeared to be in serious flood.

One day he went down with Caoba to bathe, when the torrent in the river did not look so great as usual.

"I should like a swim in it, eh, Caoba?" said the boy.

"No, no, elder child, you could do nothing in there."

"Oh yes; I'll swim down to the swing-gate; it's only about three hundred yards."

"No, no; you'll get bruised on the rocks or tree stumps."

"Bah!" said the boy, throwing off his shoes and hat and jacket.

"No, no, elder child, you must not go," said Caoba, catching hold of him.

"Caoba! let me go," said the boy hotly.

Caoba dropped him, and he jumped into the water, as it went roaring past.

"*Ay, Dios mio!* he'll be drowned," cried Caoba, jumping in after him.

The pair were swept over the rocks into the big pool that fed the saw-mill, when Caoba began shouting—

"Catch hold of a bush! catch hold of a bush!"

The boy was carried like a cork, sometimes head up, sometimes under water, across the big pool, over the ford where the water was now rushing three feet deep, on across another pool towards the swinging-gates.

"Catch the gate! catch the gate!" roared Caoba, as he was himself being carried across the ford.

On went the child towards the gate, when luckily a circling eddy took him in towards one of the great posts from which the water-gate hung, and he floated up to it, scrambling up the bank, and sat down very pale and silent.

Caoba, by a few powerful strokes, had reached a palm-tree stem growing in the bed of the river, where he rested ere he struck out for the shore, which was a few yards from him. The faithful negro came up to Pedro and said, reprovingly—

"Ah, that was a chase; but you might have got your head broken by the rocks, or by the water-gate, if you had been carried under it."

"*Caramba!* I never knew water had such power," said the boy.

"Yes, much power, like a machine," said Caoba, picking the *nino* up, and carrying him to the house for a change of clothes.

CHAPTER XII

JARS

DURING one of the fine hot days that occur at intervals in the wet season, the administrator's horse broke loose and galloped off to the *camino real*.

When the administrator heard of it, he sent Piehob, the only Chinaman then on the estate, to look after it.

Piehob went off on another horse about ten in the morning, and returned about three, wet with perspiration, and leading the lost animal.

"It is good," said the administrator, handing him a dime.

The Chinaman thanked him, and went off to his quarters, and drank quarts of water in his over-heated condition, dying in less than an hour afterwards.

When Don Enrique heard of the matter, he was wroth, and sending for the administrator, he asked—

"Who authorised you to send people after your stray horses, Mr. Martin?"

"I thought there was no harm in it," answered the man.

"No *harm* to send a freshly-imported Chinaman on such a wild-goose chase in the heat of
the day? I hear he found your horse, and you
generously gave him a dime for his trouble.
You have caused the poor fellow to lose his
life, and you have lost me four hundred dollars.
Take care, Mr. Martin.

"By-the-by," said Don Enrique, whose blue
eyes now flashed fiercely, "my boy has told me
of one or two things I do not like. Tell me, did
you promise him a dollar if he went in the dark
and gathered a cocoa-nut from the house? and
did you tell him to dismount and go into the
maize to see what you evidently suspected was
a runaway negro?"

"No, I only promised the dollar in fun, and
sent him into the maize because I thought a goat
had got loose there, or something of the sort."

"Bah, excuses ; I hate them worse than crimes,"
said Don Enrique, turning on his heel and leaving
the discomfited administrator to chew the cud of
shame.

CHAPTER XIII

MANUMISSION

ONE morning towards the end of the wet season Juana, a good-looking negress and a clever cook, came to Don Enrique and said—

"Don Enrique, I want to buy the freedom of my child just born."

"Yes, Juana ; his name is Alofio, I think. Have you the twenty-five dollars ?"

"Oh yes, señor, and I want to buy my own freedom."

"Hola, and where has the good-looking Juana been getting money ?"

"Ah, señor, by pigs, tobacco, honey, and doing sewing for the station-master's people."

Don Enrique smiled, and said—

"Well, Juana, I'll send for the syndico, who will get your papers made out. Do you know what you'll have to pay ?"

"Yes, señor ; Don Pablo told me I was bought for four hundred and fifty dollars. He says I shall have to pay that and another hundred dollars, because I have been taught a trade, and twenty-five for the child."

"A mulatto, eh ?" asked the planter ; "I have not seen it yet. Well, Juana, that's what you'll have to pay, and though you are worth double the money to me, the law states that you can buy yourself off for the price I originally gave for you, with another hundred dollars added, as Don Pablo says, because you have been taught a trade. It's a poor bargain, eh—for me ?"

"Yes, señor, but I shall be well off."

"Come, come, who is the father—who is finding the money ?"

"Gomez, my master."

"Oh, that old *picaro*. Well, may you be happy with him ; but, mind, you cannot leave the estate until the money is all paid. Is he going to pay down, or in instalments ?"

"He says he will pay in a year, my master."

"Good. I'll send for the syndico to see to the matter ; and now you can go back to your work."

"Thank you, my master."

"But, Juana, don't tell the other people. You see, Gomez might not pay in the year. Such things have been, child, and it would look foolish if you were not to go at the end of the year, eh ?"

"Yes, I should look a *bobo* then. I will keep it a secret. A blessing, my master !"

CHAPTER XIV

THE RUNAWAY

A FEW days after this scene, José, the carpenter's foreman, was found to be missing. He had not answered to the roll-call.

Pedro, who had been taking lessons in the shop with him, said that he was cheerful enough the night before, and no reason could be assigned for his flight.

Don Enrique rode over the estate towards Gomez's land, the administrator going in the other direction towards the woods, but neither of them succeeded in finding a trace of him, so they decided to track him by the bloodhounds the following morning.

Soon after daybreak next morning, Ramon and Caoba, with their machetes and the hounds, followed Don Enrique and the administrator on the horses to the carpenter's shop, where the hounds were given a " snuff " of some of José's old clothes. The animals began to bay, and started off on a trail, going down to the ford, where they stopped and bayed. They were led through the water, and on reaching the opposite shore cast about for the scent, which they soon found, and struck off towards the woods, where the horsemen had to dismount on account of the thick growth of creepers.

The hounds went snuffing and baying, when suddenly they stopped, and began scenting this way and that, then starting off to the left, they broke into a run, outstripping the negroes. Presently they could be heard in the forest baying loudly.

"They have treed him," said Don Enrique.

"Yes, treed."

Ramon and Caoba had meanwhile come up with the runaway, seated in an ironwood tree.

"Aha! twenty-five," said Caoba, looking up to him, "why did you run away?"

"Is the master coming?" asked the runaway in an anxious voice.

"Yes; he is close on us."

At that moment Don Enrique and the administrator broke through the bush and looked up at the tree, round which the hounds were still baying, saliva still streaming from their jaws.

"Secure the dogs, Ramon," said Don Enrique. Then looking up to the runaway, he added, "*Sinverguenza*, throw down your machete, and come after it."

The negro obeyed the order and descended, dropping on his knees, and crying—

"Pardon, my master."

" Secure him, Caoba."

Whilst Caoba was binding him with a light line, Don Enrique asked—

" Why did you run away ? "

" Oh, my master, Don Basilio, the carpenter, is so hard."

" *Que sinverguenza*, we'll leave it till by-and-by."

Don Enrique and the administrator returned to their horses, and the party marched slowly back to the estate, where José was taken to the stocks and shut up in a dark room with bread and water.

José was a native African, and dreaded this punishment much more than a whipping ; for to be left alone in the dark had to his disordered imagination great terrors ; and for this reason Don Enrique made much more use of the stocks than of the whip, as being more effectual and more humane; but running away, being a serious offence, was invariably punished with both.

The next morning the runaway was led up to the majoral's room, Don Enrique sitting at the head of the table, with the administrator and the majoral on either hand.

" Now tell us why you ran away ? " said Don Enrique severely.

" Ah ! pardon, my master.   Don Basilio asked me to saw wood all day."

The carpenter, who had been sent for, came in just in time to hear the accusation, and he retorted, " *Sinverguenza,*" as he took his seat.

"Is that all you have to say?" asked Don Enrique.

The planter looked at the negro, and said—

"José, you have always been treated well. You have been given extra time; you have been permitted to do private work in the carpenter's shop; and yet you run away, and give as your excuse that you were told to saw wood all day. You must have all the stripes the law allows, namely, twenty-five, and you must for three months wear the *grillos.*" [1]

The negro answered never a word, but darted a look of hatred at the carpenter.

That evening he received his punishment, and the *grillos* were publicly welded to his legs by the blacksmith.

[1] The *grillos* consisted of a couple of iron rings, joined by uprights, and acted as a hobble, so that the wearer could not run, and at the same time it was a badge of disgrace; but it caused no pain, and the wearer could walk quite well, for he always padded them.

CHAPTER XV

A few days before the grinding season began again, a dark-eyed, savage-looking Creole pedlar arrived on the estate on the negroes' holiday—a man not hitherto known in those parts.

The man brought his wares on a led horse, in panniers—cheap jewellery, coloured handkerchiefs, crockery, sweets, cigars, cigarettes, looking-glasses, knives, beads.

Young Pedro often went to the pedlar's to buy sweets and cigarettes, or boxes of guava jelly, and was always accustomed to be treated with great respect; but the boy soon saw by the cold looks of this man that he was unfriendly. He noticed, too, that the man had been talking eagerly to some of the principal negroes, and that they moved off uneasily on his appearance in the circle. However, he bought what he wanted, and went off; but late in the afternoon he was sent by his mother to buy some boxes of big beads for his little sister; and coming suddenly into the group from behind, he saw the pedlar handing to several of the negroes little paper flags with the single star.

"Oh, how pretty!" said the boy. "I'll have one of those."

"No! no! elder child; they are all sold!" said the pedlar, quickly secreting the rest. "Yes; all sold to the gentleman on the next estate for a children's party."

"Oh, then, I shall get one."

"Yes, yes," said the man.

Pedro bought the beads, and asked for the *contra*.

"*Tenga!*" said the Spaniard, handing him a lead pencil, and muttering something quickly to the bystanders; but the boy could not catch the words, though he spoke Spanish fluently.

That evening he told his father the story of the flags, and Don Enrique pricked up his ears.

"Flags with a lone star, eh? Are you sure, my son?"

"Yes; he had a handful of them."

"Ah!" said the planter to himself, and looked very grave.

CHAPTER XVI

SMUGGLED

THE grinding season had begun well, but dark care seemed destined to dog the energetic landlords of that miserable island.

Don Enrique was sitting in the piazza one evening, when Captain Baro and some of his men rode up.

After salutations had passed, Captain Baro dismounted, and giving his horse to an orderly, he entered the piazza and sat down by Don Enrique, looking very serious.

"Well, captain, what can I do for you?" asked Don Enrique.

"Señor, I must confess I am on an errand I do not like. From information received, I understand you have two barrels of gunpowder on your estate, illicitly landed from an American vessel."

"Why, certainly, captain."

"But you have no permit to keep powder, Don Enrique."

"True, but they have only just come up from Maravilla. I ordered them from America."

"Ah, from America?" said the captain, in a peculiar tone of voice.

"Yes, captain, there is nothing to conceal; they are for blasting rocks for my light railway."

"Ah, yes," said the captain, his eyes lighting up with new intelligence.

"That's so. The line is begun, and I can show you nearly a mile of permanent way."

"Well, Don Enrique, that is good, and I am glad to hear it. It gives me much joy to find you do not conceal the matter. The Government is suspicious of all foreigners, and especially of Americans, since the Lopez expedition. Filibusters are an ever-present object of dread, and since it has become known to the Government— through your consul, perhaps—that you were invited, when in the States, to have an interview with the President, you have been looked upon as a political suspect. I tell you this as a friend, and it must go no further. And I tell you also that some recent attempts have been made to land arms on the coast, and you are known to have powder. You will pardon me, but I must search the estate, and if I find no arms beyond those I know you have for your private use—and I am sure I shall not—and no more powder than you say—two kegs—the matter, which might have been very grave indeed, can possibly be set right, with a little——" and the captain

rubbed his thumb and index - finger together,
signifying money. "But, my friend, be careful
what you do in future ; you foreigners are not
loved here."

"Thank you, captain ; and kindly begin your
search at once, sparing not even our private
apartments."

Captain Baro told off a posse of men, and a
busy pretence was made to search the estate ;
and after a good dinner, he rode off contented
with a bag of ounces, for Captain Baro was a
shrewd man, and knew well Don Enrique was
no political intriguer, although the planter was
suspected in higher quarters—as, indeed, were
all foreigners. But the matter did not end there,
for after the captain had made his reports, Don
Enrique had to attend the nearest court, and
was sentenced to pay a heavy fine for smuggling
powder.

CHAPTER XVII

DURING that season Don Enrique had another attack of dysentery that threatened his life. But the new doctor—a clever Cuban, who had studied in Paris—pulled him through.

"But you must go north before the rains set in, or you'll die," said Dr. Ramon decisively.

.   .   .   .   .   .

When the grinding was over, the family packed, and the last day before starting north had come. That day Pedro spent with Caoba in his palm-leaf hut by the river.

"Well, so the elder child is going to the north, eh ?"

"Yes, Caoba."

"Where all negroes are now free, my little master."

"Yes, Caoba, and often starving."

Caoba smiled his good-natured smile.

"Ah, the elder child should stay here. He is growing to be a young man, and there are nice girls here. Salomé is pretty, and Virginia, the mulatta, loves the elder child. Ah, the *nino grande* would like to live here presently."

"What do you mean, Caoba ? I like it now."

"Oh, nothing, elder child. Wouldn't the little master like to fight ?"

"Fight who, Caoba ?"

"War, my little master."

"What for, Caoba ?"

"Oh, anything—the *Esperanza*, for example."

"Yes, if people came to take it."

"If Gomez came, elder child ?"

"Yes, if Gomez came, and Caoba would fight with us."

"*Quien sabe ?*" said the negro.

"Come, come, Caoba ; what's the matter with you ?"

"Oh, nothing, elder child, but tell the señora not to come back for many years."

"Oh, nonsense, Caoba."

"There it is ; I am done," said the negro ; "but the elder child will bring me back a revolver when he comes ?"

"Yes, Caoba, if my father will let you have it."

The great, handsome, intelligent negro laughed loudly with his deep voice.

That night Pedro could not sleep. A cockroach had got between two gourds, and kept ticking and scratching all night.

The next morning the party left in the travelling waggon, and arrived late at the station. The stationmaster and his wife stood on the platform.

"Quick! quick! the train is going," said the little official, who seemed to have suddenly lost all his usual politeness.

"Yes, the foreigner has delayed the train," said his thin-faced, half-caste wife.

"Go to the devil," said Don Enrique; "*sinverguenza.*"

"Ah, yes, it's very fine to talk big when one has estates," sneered the little woman; "but they will be divided one day, and my husband and I shall have our share of the *Esperanza.*"

Don Enrique stood and looked at the couple, amazed, and muttering—

"*Bobos,*" he got into the train, and said to the English engineer, who was walking up the platform, "How insolent these trashy whites are getting. What is the meaning of it?"

"That's so," said an engineer from a neighbouring estate, who was also going north. "The lower classes and the negroes themselves have suddenly become insolent. I think mischief is brewing—a general rising or something."

"Oh, nonsense," said Don Enrique; "what can brew?"

"A civil war," said the engineer, "or something of that sort."

"I think not," said Don Enrique, though in his own mind he had great misgivings.

"Well, I am not so sure," persisted the engineer. "I heard a good deal from a friend of mine who is on an estate near Havana, and incriminating letters have been found, showing that a plot of some sort is intended ; and in order to get the negroes to join, it was stated that they would have their freedom, that the land would be equally divided, that all foreign men and Spaniards were to be killed, and, if you please, the negroes were promised all the white women in the island."

"Ah, that sounds more like a negro rising, but they can never do that in Cuba. On the other hand, the Cubans would have risen long ago, if they had had any go, for I do not believe any colonials would stand the extortionate taxation without representation that these islanders do. Why, a Cuban has no civil rights, and lives always under martial law—even in times of peace."

"Well, old Spain will have to pay for it all one day," said the engineer, "and the clanking of the train drove the conversationists into silence.

CHAPTER XVIII

THE PLANTER'S DEATH

ABOUT three months afterwards the American Consul was sitting in his office, when a letter was handed to him from Alum Springs, Virginia. Breaking the seal, he read—

"ALUM SPRINGS, VIRGINIA, U.S.A., 1867.

"MY DEAR SIR,—We are requested by our client to inform you of the sad death of Don Enrique, proprietor of the *La Esperanza* sugar estate, on Wednesday last.

"It seems Don Enrique was suffering from internal ulceration, brought on by dysentery contracted in Cuba, and that unfortunately it resulted in perforation and death.

"His widow is so prostrated at this sudden death that she has requested us to communicate with you, and to advise you that you have been appointed sole executor by the will.

"Being assured that you will do the best for our client's interests, and those of your late friend.

"Believe me to be yours obediently,

"A. DUPONT."

PART III

WAR—BLOODY WAR

CHAPTER I

In the following October the señora and the children arrived at the Boca and took up their quarters at the little Spanish hotel, for there was much business to be done. The estate had been valued and offered for sale at 450,000 dollars, as the law demanded, and was bought in by the widow, who, after securing the children's portions by mortgages, was allowed 14,400 dollars a year for their education, the profits going to her, and the estates going to her when the mortgages were paid off, when the children came of age at twenty-five.

After these deeds were executed, the family was about to move on to the estate, when the news first appeared in the newspapers of the outbreak of the Cuban rebellion, and of a war tax of 25 per cent. to meet it. Most planters thought that every possible tax had been devised for robbing them, but this additional burden brought the taxation to over 50 per cent., so that ruin stared the landlords and their vast numbers of dependents in the face.

The news of the rebellion only incited the señora the more to go up to the estate, for now that she was in charge, her energy and business capacity showed itself.

But the American Consul protested.

"No, no," he said, "you must not go up to that lonely estate. The rebellion has broken out in the district. Indeed the volunteers— mostly our shopkeepers and the lower classes— are assembling. Spanish vessels are constantly arriving with fresh recruits, most of them destined to leave their bones here; and nearly all the Spanish navy, such as it is, has formed a ring round the island to keep out the American fili- busters. Things could not look worse."

And, indeed, such was the case. The Cuban revolutionists were massing in the country dis- tricts, whilst the volunteers were rudely fortify- ing the towns. Indeed skirmishes had already taken place between the Spaniards and the Cuban patriots, as the insurgents called them- selves, and savage acts of guerilla warfare had already been enacted. One estate had been burnt, and some murders had been committed with all the bloodthirsty brutality and unforgiv- ing revenge of the lineal descendants of Alva and Philip II.

The señora took the Consul's advice, and re- mained for a few weeks at the Boca, but was restless all the time, and finally insisted on going to the estate towards the beginning of December.

Grinding was in full swing when they alighted at the little house in the orange grove on the *batey*, taking their meal that evening in the little dining-room that looked into the orange trees. And a sad meal it was, for the señora's mind reverted to the last time she had eaten in that room, with her husband sitting proudly at the head of the table—a strong man to battle for his interests in a lawless country, whereas now all the cares and anxieties of this large estate, nearly seven square miles in extent, fell upon her shoulders, and she felt that she alone was there to shield her children, and protect her property in dangerous times, such as had never existed in her husband's life. But nevertheless she determined to face it.

CHAPTER II

SCHEMING VILLAINS

THE week before her arrival, Don Natan, the one-eyed administrator, might have been seen riding over to Gomez's *estançia*, a clearing in the woods.

When he arrived, the half-wild dogs flew out and barked at him savagely, but old Gomez came forth and welcomed him with profuse gesticulations : rascals always have a bond of sympathy.

In the cabin were his two sons, born in Spain, and his concubine, Juana, bought from the estate, with their mulatto child.

After dismounting, and hitching his horse to a bench outside the hut, the administrator entered, and was given a cow-hide chair, the family greeting him with profuse welcomes, and treating him with great civility.

"Will you take coffee, *caballero?*" asked old Gomez.

"No, thank you," said the administrator coldly, with his icy reserve.

"So the señora is coming next week?" began Gomez.

"Yes, and for that reason I wish to talk to you concerning the matter we discussed last week when you dined with me."

"It will delight me much, gentleman," said the old man, lighting a *vaquero* cigar. "Shall we go without?"

"As you like, Don Gomez."

Gomez made a sign to his sons, and led the way to an ample tree-trunk, lying some two hundred yards from the house, where the two worthies seated themselves.

Gomez opened the talk, and said—

"Well, Don Natan, is it agreed?"

"For five thousand dollars gold—yes."

"You must take less," said old Gomez.

"Not a peseta," said the one-eyed man. "Here have I to persuade the señora to buy fifty-three *caballerias* of uncleared land to-day with this rebellion before us, and to give 26,500 dollars for it, when, under the circumstances, its market value would not be more than ten thousand dollars. Besides, I shall have to use my arguments with the señora against that dog of a Consul, who is sure to persuade her not to buy."

"Ah, señor wants too much for his kindness."

"I must have the sum named, neither more nor less, and, moreover, you must be content to take less than you ask."

"*Valga, me Dios*, the señor wants five thousand dollars, and grudges me my price for myself."

"Yes, Don Gomez, and I won't act unless you do as I say."

"Why is the señor so particular ?"

"For the reason I told you. That American Consul was a great friend of Don Enrique, and if I should succeed in persuading the señora to buy, he will point out to her the price is absurd in these times, or he may grow suspicious, and the whole thing fall through."

"But he, too, takes money, eh ?" leered the Spaniard.

"No, the dog is an honest man."

"Is it true ?" asked the Spaniard, with an air of surprise.

"That's so."

"Well, then, what will you persuade the señora to give ?"

"Twenty-six thousand, five hundred dollars— neither more nor less. But *I* want five thousand dollars gold if you get it."

"I must sell, I must sell ; I want to get home to Spain, whined the Spaniard. This rebellion is going to be bad, bad. All the negroes will rise and kill the whites. My sons, too, wish to go home."

"And Juana and the child ?" asked the administrator.

"Will be left at the Boca—free."

"Well, Don Juaquin, that settles it. If I sell your land for 26,500 dollars, you give me five thousand dollars the day you are paid."

"It is a bargain," said the *montero*, taking him by the hand and shaking it, and the one-eyed administrator mounted his horse, and returned to the estate, where he ordered a negro twenty-five lashes for stealing maize from the corn-house.

CHAPTER III

LOS INSURRECTOS

A FEW days after her arrival the señora began to superintend the unpacking, Maria, Caoba's wife, being her chief maid. All morning they had worked in feminine fashion, arranging the muslin dresses and fine linens in the cedar presses. The still, hot afternoon was broken only by the songs of the negro children feeding the cane-stairs, the stamps and puffs of the engines, and the cries of the carters to their cattle, when suddenly the dogs arose and flew out, barking violently, towards the negro quarters.

Pedro, who was without, ran into the house, crying, " The insurgents ! the insurgents !"

" *Ay, Dios mio!*" said the señora, for reports of their brutal murders and outrages had become commoner every day. Then turning hurriedly to Maria, she said, "Tell Caoba to bar the doors."

But before Caoba could be found, the troop of insurgents, some thirty in number, ambled up to the house, all the horses with cropped tails, which was one of their badges, for it was the custom at that time for every one to wear their horses' tails long, dandies having them gaily plaited and dressed. A swarthy Cuban, in Panama hat, and armed with a machete, rode ahead, bearing the Cuban flag—the flag with a lone star—the rebel flag.

The commander, seeing the señora sitting in the window, took off his hat with a sweep, the little troop, dressed in the usual countryman's costume, drawing up with affected military order.

Pedro was in the verandah, looking on at this strangely-mixed group of Cubans, negroes, and mulattos, strangely armed—some with old fowling-pieces, some with old-fashioned carbines, and some with horse pistols, all "requisitioned," as they euphuistically called stealing.

So ignorant of firearms were many of these men that they did not know how to hold their antiquated weapons, one man, with much pomp and circumstance, holding his carbine the wrong way up; but they did know how to use the dirks and machetes that every man carried in addition.

The captain of the troop, with much officiousness, put a guard round the house, some of them, it was afterwards proved, being notorious criminals, giving orders that no one should enter the dwelling or molest any one, under penalty of death. Then going up to the verandah, he patted Pedro on the head, and said, "You will soon join us, eh, my little gentleman?"

"*Quien sabe?*" said the boy coldly.

Walking to the grated window, this guerilla begged the señora's pardon for disturbing her, and explained that he had received orders from headquarters to search the estate for arms.

As he was talking, the new engineer, a jovial, light-haired Englishman, ran across from the works, and tried to force his way between the guards into the verandah.

"Halt!" cried the commander severely.

"Go to hell, you marauding traitors, frightening a lady like this," cried the engineer in English.

The commander only smiled superciliously, for he could not understand a word of the speech.

"*Sinverguenza,*" then shrieked the engineer, in very English-sounding Spanish.

"Take care, the balls fly quickly," said the Cuban severely.

"What does he say, Pedro?" asked the engineer.

But the señora translated the speech, and begged the engineer to withdraw, as she was sure there was no danger, whereas, if he were to enrage them, they might proceed to extremities.

The chivalrous little engineer, seeing the sense

of what she said, withdrew, shaking his fist at the Cuban, who only laughed at his gesticulations.

The captain then proceeded to search all but the señora's private apartments, and found three old carbines that Don Enrique had kept in the old days of the bandits. Those the man "requisitioned" for the Cuban patriots, giving the señora some worthless paper money, hurriedly printed in some little town with ordinary letterpress type.

The rebels then went over to the quarters of the white employés to search, and the engineer again appeared in the verandah, asking the señora if she had been frightened.

"No, no, not at all; but I was fascinated. Did you see the face of that young negro who rode the bay, he whose eyes always looked over your head, never at you? Maria says he is from the Santa Anna, and has murdered four people already. Caoba knows him, and told her."

"The blackguard," said the engineer; "but we are in for bad times, and this is no place for you, madame. You should get back to the Boca, for Pedro here will be joining the rebels."

Pedro laughed, and said—

"Not much; they are only toy soldiers. We could drill better than that at the school I was at in Virginia."

Yet to conquer these amateur soldiers, Spain

sent to the island of Cuba, between 1868 and
1876, 150,000 trained soldiers, of which army but
a few hundreds ever returned home—not enough,
it was said in the Cortes at Madrid, to form a
single regiment ; and besides the loss in men,
the value of the property ruined was incalculable,
and it cost the Spanish treasury millions to subdue
that rebellion.

After searching the white men's quarters, the
rebels pranced off in the evening light, whilst
Caoba stood in the verandah, shading his eyes
from the evening sun, and watching them intently, wrapt in thought.

"*Que, que*, Caoba ; do you wish to join the
insurgents ?" laughed the señora.

"Ah, no, señora," said the negro, laughing ;
"but war is a fine thing."

That night the señora packed all her jewellery
into a tin case, and her husband's revolvers she
packed in another tin case ; and when she had
finished, she sent for Caoba.

"Caoba," said she, "Don Enrique, when he
was alive, said you were the most honest, the most
faithful, and the bravest slave on the *Esperanza*,
and when he was dying, 'You can always trust
Caoba.'"

"Ah, my master, my master," said Caoba, with
broken voice ; "he was a brave man, and I loved
him like a father."

This unexpected display of feeling moved the señora, and she said, in a gentle voice—

"Caoba, I am going to trust you to bury these revolvers in the cane-field across the river, and to hide these jewels in the roof. You can get through the trap-door in the *sala*. Will you do it ?"

"Señora, for your sake, for little Pedro's sake, as well as for the sake of my dead master, no one shall ever know from me where they are hidden."

"Thank you, Caoba ; take them, and may God protect us."

And the faithful negro took the boxes and hid them, as he had been commanded.

ANARCHY spread through the island. Manuel de Cespedos, the leader of the rebellion, and the first to raise the standard of revolt on his own estate, the Demajagua, in the October of that year, supported by only fifty men, must have been overjoyed by the quick spread of the rebellion.

Nevertheless, the rebellion was sporadic, and carried on by guerilla warfare, though report said that 12,000 men had already joined the Lone Star, but some desperate fights, in which no quarter was shown on either side, had taken place between Santiago and Cuifuegos—fights often disgraced by horrible mutilations of the dead, and brutal atrocities.

The troops were not long in following the rebels to the estate, for in less than a week after that first party of mongrel patriots had "requisitioned" the old rifles, a battalion of 500 Spanish regulars, dressed in blue dungaru, trimmed with red cuffs, with black caps and rifles, marched upon the estate and encamped upon the *batey*, the officers billeting themselves on the señora, with many polite apologies. Nevertheless, these 500 troops had to be fed at the expense of the estate, and the cattlemen were busy killing beasts for their consumption. In a few days the scouts belonging to the troops said that a large party of insurgents were encamped in the *La Esperanza* woods near Maravilla. On the other hand, the rebels knew well that the Spaniards were on the estate—for the poor whites and runaway negroes kept them well informed concerning every movement of the Spanish troops, who were mostly young recruits, unaccustomed either to the climate or this guerilla warfare.

On the seventh day of their stay on the estate, the Spanish scouts brought in a young Cuban innkeeper and a negro boy as prisoners.

The officers, who had just breakfasted with the señora and the children, were informed that a spy had been captured, and, after much gesticulation and talk, the bugle sounded, and the troops were drawn up in a hollow square, the officers sitting at a table, which had been provided, in the middle. A court-martial was about to be held. The negro lad, aged nine, was called as witness, and swore that Don Fernando, the innkeeper and his master, had been receiving visits from the rebels, and supplying them with food.

The young Cuban looked on at the proceedings sullenly, but the Spaniards' black eyes flashed, and there was much talking between the puffs of their cigars.

When the Cuban was asked to speak in his defence, he merely shrugged his shoulders.

After a hurried consultation with his brother officers, the chairman of the court-martial turned to the wretched prisoner, and said—

"You have been found guilty of acting as spy for the insurgents.   You will be shot at two o'clock."

"Cowards!" hissed the Cuban, but his further remarks were lost, for a guard had quickly been told off, who took him to the stocks.

At two o'clock the estate bell was rung, and the negroes and Chinese were formed into three sides of a square, opposite to the Spanish troops, who stood in the same formation.   At a signal from the commanding officer, the prisoner was brought from the stocks, followed by two negroes bearing a coffin.   The *cortège* stopped opposite the corn-house, and the rough coffin was placed on the ground, the pinioned prisoner standing by its side.   All the while employés of the estate had gathered round, and stood by the officers, looking very grave, and talking in low voices, but a bugle which was sounded caused all the negroes and Chinamen to turn their eyes towards the doomed prisoner.   When the last notes of the bugle had died away, the commanding officer, in a loud voice, said—

"This Cuban, Don Fernando Ochoa, has been found guilty of aiding the insurgents, on which account he is condemned to die. Thus will be treated all enemies of Spain."

Then giving a few hurried orders, a sergeant marched out twelve men, and took up a position some fifty yards before the prisoner.

"Bandage his eyes," ordered the officer.

"No need for that; I can face cowards and tyrants," retorted the Cuban.

Nevertheless, his eyes were bandaged, and he was forced on to his knees, with his *back* to the firing party—an indignity reserved for traitors.

"Ready, present, fire," commanded the officer, and twelve rifles went off simultaneously, the prisoner falling on to his face, shouting—

"Long live Cuba! down with the tyrants!" but the spurts of blood from his mouth soon choked him, his body twitched, and he was dead.

Two negroes standing by hurried the hot, still palpitating body into the rough coffin, and started off towards the Campo Santo.

"Dismiss," said the officer, and the tragedy was complete.

The administrator went pale to his room, whilst the little engineer stood swearing loudly, and calling the Spaniards cowards.

"Take care, Don Juan; the Spanish bullets fly quickly," said Caoba.

CHAPTER V

THAT same night, Louisa, the magnificent negress in charge of the feeding-stair gang of children, sought the señora in her bedroom, and said—

" Señora, my mistress, there is bad news, bad news. After the shooting to-day, Sabicu, Juan de Dios, Tomas, Pablo, and Ramon, and ten of the girls, have run away to join the rebels. They have gone to the woods by Maravilla. But worse times are coming. My mistress had better go to the Boca."

" No, no, Louisa ; my place is here with my people. Why should I fly ? "

" Ah ! my mistress, I cannot tell. Bad times are coming, and I have a letter for the señora."

" From whom, Louisa ? "

Louisa's eyes sparkled, and she replied, " I do not know, my mistress."

The señora took the letter with trembling fingers, and read, in feminine writing and illiterate Spanish, the following message :—

" DEAR SEÑORA,—Pardon a poor girl's letter, but out of love for the dead master, I warn you

that the insurgents are going to burn *La Esperanza* on Tuesday night next.—LOLA."

"Who is Lola, Louisa?" asked ;the señora,
turning from the letter."

"A girl at Maravilla—the innkeeper's daughter."

"So she loved the master, eh, Louisa?"

"Ah, my mistress, what do I, a poor negress,
know? Perhaps he gave her presents when he
went down to the Almaçen."

The widow bit her lip, and replied—

"It is well—go!"

"Good night, my mistress," said Louisa, as she
left the room.

The señora redressed, and going to the saloon,
sent for Captain Diego, who was playing cards
with his brother-officers in the little dining-
room that looked on to the orange grove,
whence sweet scents were wafted through the
jalousies.

The captain left the table, and, going to the
saloon, greeted the señora with all the courtesy
of his race, asking her of what service he could
be—as he took his seat.

"Captain Diego, I have had a private letter
warning me that the estate is to be fired on
Tuesday night by a party of rebels coming
from Maravilla way."

"*Caramba!* is it true ?   *Sinverguenzas!*   The señora may rest assured it shall not occur."

.   .   .   .   .   .

On the following Sunday the soldiers started off towards Maravilla, following the highway, as the tracker suggested, for they were entirely in the hands of native scouts, who were often none too loyal.

CHAPTER VI

LAND-HUNGER

ON this same Sunday the American Consul arrived on the estate for a short visit; and after dinner, the administrator, who had been invited, began cautiously to open the subject of the purchase of Gomez's land. Said he—

" It's by far the richest land about here. It is covered by rare and choice woods, and Gomez, who, by-the-bye, I hear, has been taken prisoner with his two sons, by the rebels, is only too anxious to sell, and is frightened to death, and offers it at a very cheap price. The land lies close to the estate, and will save much carting, which in these unsettled times is most desirable. The rebellion, I feel sure, will soon blow over."

" What is Gomez's price ? " interrupted the Consul.

" Twenty-six thousand, five hundred dollars."

" Positively the lowest ? " persisted the Consul.

"Yes," said the one-eyed man, shifting in his chair.

" My husband once did make a bid for the land. What did he offer ? " asked the señora.

Q

"Some four thousand dollars more than Gomez asks now," replied the administrator.

"Considering the times, it seems a very high price now," said the Consul; "but I know Don Enrique always wanted the land, and were there no rebellion I should urge its purchase."

"To my mind, the purchase is now more urgent than ever," retorted the administrator. "If the rebellion continues, it will be unsafe to grow cane at a distance; and if the troops and rebels continue their raids upon us, there will be neither horses nor cattle left to draw cane, and it will all have to be carried by the people. The rebels reached the Santa Anna last night, and carried off all the provisions in the Almaçen, threatening to shoot the administrator and major-domo because they opposed them; and to add insult to injury, they paid for it with their worthless paper money, demanding a receipt from the major-domo."

"The outlook is certainly serious—very serious," said the Consul; "if horses and cattle grow scarcer, the work of the estates must stop."

"That is so," acquiesced the administrator; "but by buying this land near at hand we are laying up treasure in heaven."

"Well, I'll consider it," said the Consul.

"I shall be ruled entirely by you," finished the señora. "I know my husband wanted the land."

CHAPTER VII

THAT same night the big bell of the *Santa Marguerita* rang out in alarm, and a bright and ruddy light flared up under the violet sky. Fast and furiously rang the great bell, calling urgently for aid, for the cane-fields were afire—the work of the rebels.

All the white men of *La Esperanza* arose, and, dressing hastily, met in the *batey*, all gazing towards the ruddy glare that filled the northern sky towards the woods.

"It's a big fire," said the majoral. "Well, Don Natan, what are you going to do? They want help."

"Yes, there is no time to lose," said the Consul.

"I don't know," said the administrator, in a shifty manner. "We have been warned that they intend to burn us, and it would never do to leave the señora unprotected; and if we take negroes, they will probably run away and join the insurgents."

"Can't you trust any of them?" asked the engineer.

"Yes, some dozen or so."

"Then I'll go for one," volunteered the engineer.

"I am in authority here," said the Consul, "and we must help those poor people. Let the administrator and engineer take twelve of the trustiest negroes, with machetes, and go and help; the majoral and I will keep watch here."

"As you will," said the administrator coldly; and turning to Don Leonaldo, he said, "Call out the trustiest twelve, and arm them with long machetes."

Still the alarm-bell rang on, and the roar of the fire could be heard like a gale in the distance.

The help party started, Caoba showing the way to *La Marguerita*. As they neared the ill-fated estate, walking under the bright stars in the cool night, the peals of the bell grew louder and louder, mingled with the roar and crackling of the fire and the shouts of the people.

As they came upon the scene of the conflagration, they became aware that never a hand was raised to stop it. There was no gang cutting a long lane through the cane to prevent the fire spreading; there was no counter-lane being burnt—nothing but the bright, dancing flames flickering against the forest, and the choking smoke, that blew in their direction.

Not knowing what to do, the administrator ordered the party to halt; but Caoba and the engineer got separated from them in the smoke, and made for the point whence voices came.

When the administrator saw that they had gone, he ordered the other negroes to remain where they were, and calling the Canary Island carpenter, he pretended to go and look for the two strayed men.

The negro party waited as ordered for some half-hour, when the administrator and carpenter came crashing back through a young cane-field on the left, crying, "Fly, fly; the insurgents have got charge of the place; the buildings are all on fire, and they are shooting and murdering people." And mounting his horse, he dug his spurs in, and galloped back to the estate, followed by the panting carpenter, who ran all the way.

The American Consul was sitting in the piazza, waiting anxiously for their return; and when the administrator drew up, soon followed by the fleet negroes, whom the majoral took off to their quarters and locked in, the admininistrator began in a hurried voice to tell how the estate was entirely in the hands of the insurgents, that all the buildings were on fire, and that the rebels were shooting and murdering people as fast as they could.

"God help us all," murmured the Consul. "Is it so? But where are the engineer and Caoba?"

"We lost them—got separated in the smoke. They'll soon be back," said the trembling Canary Islander.

CHAPTER VIII

TWO STORIES

THE anxiety on the *Esperanza* was terrible all that night, and it was only laid with the daylight; but even then no people were sent to the fields to work, in case of an emergency.

About nine o'clock, a small party of horsemen rode on to the estate from the highway. The lookouts stationed on the roof of the boiling-house reporting them to be Spanish soldiers, about twelve men with an officer.

As they neared the *batey*, the white employés could recognise the engineer and Caoba riding with them, Caoba mounted on a sorry insurgent's steed with cropped tail.

The body of men drew up before the admini-strator's door; the officer, a young lieutenant, in charge of the party, handing Don Natan a letter.

The administrator read the letter, and said—

"Good! I am glad, lieutenant, to have a posse of your men stationed here. Don Pablo there will give you and your company rations, and find you quarters."

The engineer, who had dismounted, then came up, and said, "Nathan Martin, you are a coward."

"Take care, sir," retorted the one-eyed man.

"No, I won't; you are no man;" and turning on his heel, he went to his rooms.

The little major-domo found it necessary to move the Chinese to the *Casa Grande*, and after cleaning out and white-washing their quarters, the lieutenant's troop were billeted there, where they were kept and fed at the expense of the estate.

The Consul, who had witnessed the scene between the engineer and the administrator, went over to the engineer's quarters, and asked for an explanation.

The engineer lit a cigar, and told his story as follows :—

"When we got to the *Santa Marguerita*, and saw the rebs in possession, that one-eyed York-shireman turned tail with that old woman of a carpenter—they had left the niggers in the bush, you know. I whispered to the lad Caoba, who is a brave boy, to follow me. We ducked and ran along a ditch by the edge of a burning cane-field, until we got clear of the smoke, and soon found our way to the *batey*, where there were a lot of rebs and niggers riding and running about in the firelight. All the buildings were on fire, and the roof of the administrator's house had fallen in. There were fights all over the place with machetes and knives. Some of the faithful niggers were fighting the rebs ; some of the rebs were fighting each other. They had broken into the still, you see, before it was set afire. A lot of the niggers were half-drunk, and those that weren't fighting were chasing and ravishing the negresses — some of the women seeming to like it, too. You never saw such a sight—it was hell let loose ; but some of the white rebs kept sober, and sat quietly on their bob-tailed nags, watching that no one should put out the fires. They took no notice of the fighting or raping, but if any drunken chap came near them they cut him down or shot him. Some of them had Remingtons, I saw. The boy Caoba looked on with greedy eyes. I thought by his face he was mad to go and join in the sport ; but I knew it was certain death to go in there, so we lay low in the ditch.

" Suddenly, in the middle of these orgies, came a volley from the bush on the opposite side of the *batey*, some of the bullets whizzing over us. Then we saw the troops advance at the double with fixed bayonets—we could see it all as clear as daylight by the fire. The rebs began to shout, and shoot, and form up ; but it was soon over.

The regulars broke them, and they turned and made for the bush, the soldiers going like mad for any one who came in their way, bayoneting them, nigger women and all.   You never saw such a scene: the cries were terrible.   Caoba kept shouting 'Cowards! cowards!'   That lad's already a rebel at heart.

"Presently the bugle sounded, and the soldiers formed up, and found twenty-three of their men were missing, some being killed and some wounded.   When they had formed up, I told Caoba to follow me, and we walked up to the captain; but I could not speak much of the lingo, so Caoba told them how we had started to help, and how the administrator had run away with the people.

"'English coward,' hissed the officer.   Then he asked Caoba a lot about the fire, whether it would catch the woods.   Caoba said the river would stop it.   Then the officer said there was nothing to do, and he wrote that letter and sent us on with the troops, himself going on to Santiago with the wounded and captured horses."

"By Jove, it looks bad," said the Consul, as the narrator finished.

"Yes, and the captain told us we should have been burnt, only Lola, a Maravilla girl, told them three hundred soldiers had just come on to the place."

"Aha, it is the same who warned us about Tuesday," said the Consul.

.   .   .   .

The lieutenant in charge of the company, with much stroking of black moustaches, told the Consul his story as follows :—

"We made our way to the woods where the Insurrectos were encamped, and three of us were sent forward to scout. We crawled through the chapparal with a black tracker, and watched them all dancing with negresses and drinking. There was a Cuban flag sticking out of a tree stump, and a lot of young Cubans dancing round it and shouting. It was a regular *mascara.* We saw some prisoners tied to a tree too ; then we went back and reported."

"And you attacked them ?" asked the Consul eagerly.

"No, no ; the captain thought——"

"What, not attack them—why not ?" interrupted the Consul.

"Well, well, señor, money—money goes a long way, even in war."

"Is that so ?" said the Consul, with astonishment.

"Yes, but few words are best just now," replied the lieutenant.

"Just so, just so."

"Yes, for a gentleman this is no war. That butchering on the *Santa Marguerita* was horrible. Hist—it was purely accident that we came across them there. The captain thought they were safe in the woods, half drunk. By-the-bye, that lad Caoba told me that some of the negroes and negresses from the estate were there—at the burning of *La Marguerita*, and that two were killed by the troops, a mulatto Tomas, and Juan de Dios."

"Yes, they'll all go if this keeps on," said the Consul.

"Yes, señor, ruin stares the country in the face, and this is dirty work for an officer and a gentleman, and it will never end till Cuba is free," finished the young lieutenant.

CHAPTER IX

BUTTERFLIES AND BULLETS

THE American Consul stayed on for a week, for it had been decided that the señora and children should at once go to the Boca, for outrages and murders were growing commoner every day.

One day, about the middle of the week, a horde of some fifty rebels rode on to the estate, and drawing up before the major-domo's quarters, demanded rice, maize, and *tasajo*.

The major-domo, thinking the guard were in their quarters, refused.

"Take care, the balls fly quickly; get the stores at once," said a great negro from the Santa Anna.

"*Sinverguenza*, not for you; go back to your work."

"Ah, you wish to die then," said the negro, drawing his machete.

But no troops came; it seemed they had ridden off towards Gomez's woods.

The shrewd Don Pablo saw he was in a corner, so he at once went to the Almaçen and provided the stores.

"We'll remember you, accursed Spaniard," cried the tall negro, as they rode off the estate with the stolen goods.

When the rebels had left, the administrator went off to look for the guard, and the old negress cook, in their quarters, said that they had ridden off some time after the engineer and Pedro had gone off towards Gomez's woods to catch butterflies, for Pedro was an ardent collector.

.   .   .   .

After the entomologists with their pocket-boxes and green gauze nets had ridden some half-mile through the yellow cane-fields, with their tossing tassels and sentinel palms, they arrived at the edge of the forest, and were busy slashing right and left with their nets, when suddenly they were startled by the "crack, crack," of a couple of rifles, almost immediately followed by five more shots. The naturalists were startled, but as they could not see whence the shots came, and all became silent again, they concluded the guard was target practising, so they resumed their butterfly catching.

In a few minutes, however, they were interrupted by the young lieutenant and his posse dashing up to them, the lieutenant shouting excitedly—

"At last we have got you, Don Juan. So, señor, you are the person who makes signals to the insurgents, and who shows them our troops, to be fired upon from ambush. Traitor! I arrest you." Then turning to Pedro, the lieutenant ordered him to ride home.

Much surprised, and somewhat fearful of the result, the engineer indignantly denied the charge. However, he had to follow them as their prisoner, and he was escorted back to the estate, being allowed, after entreaty, to eat his breakfast—under guard.

Whilst thus occupied, an orderly galloped over to the captain of the *partido;* and amidst great excitement amongst the employés, Captain Baro arrived towards noon with the orderly.

Captain Baro was a shrewd man, and in cases of life and death a just man, and suspecting some error of judgment on the part of the lieutenant, he informed the engineer that he would be treated fairly, and he forthwith proceeded to take the depositions.

The two soldiers who had fired the first shots gave evidence to the effect that they had been told off to watch the engineer; that they followed him, and presently saw him signalling to the enemy, when one of them had fired a couple of shots to show their presence, whereat some ambushed rebels to whom he was signalling had in return fired five shots, luckily missing them.

The prisoner then gave his story, which was simply to the effect that Pedro had asked him to go butterflying, and being a collector himself, they had gone to the woods and begun capturing the insects ; and in proof he showed his pocket-box, with some gorgeous butterflies pinned to the cork, and his green gauze net.

Captain Baro and the lieutenant examined these articles carefully, and the lieutenant said, with a sneer—

"A pretty story. What does a *man* want with butterflies ?"

But Captain Baro held his peace, and after some moments of thought, the men were ordered to produce their rifles.

Whilst they were getting them, the lieutenant explained that he had inspected the rifles that morning, and they were all clean. Captain Baro went round and inspected the rifles himself, and when he came to those belonging to the two men who had given evidence, he found them *both* very dirty.

The captain then ordered the lieutenant to remain and guard the prisoner, and the troop to procure machetes, after which they mounted their horses, and the captain directed the troopers to take them to the spot whence the soldier had fired the two shots as he had sworn.

On arriving at the spot, the captain said, in a light manner—

"Now just explain how you stood, and where the rebels were."

The trooper replied—

"I stood here, and my comrade there. I fired my two shots from here, where I am standing, and the enemy fired upon us from those trees about a quarter of a mile off."

The captain then ordered the two men to stand aside, and the rest of the troop were told to chop the grass closely and shake out each handful.

The men began the work, and presently two cartridges fell from a handful ; then another soldier found another, and so on, until all seven empty cartridge-cases lay before the two crest-fallen soldiers, who changed colour and trembled visibly.

" *Esta bueno !* Arrest those two men, and take away their arms," ordered the captain, pointing to the culprits.

Returning to headquarters, the captain said—

" Don Juan, you are free. These two soldiers under arrest fired all the seven shots themselves. That there was an enemy in ambush is entirely disproved by the fact. They are liars. But it is rather strange that a man should catch butterflies. You had better be careful, Don Juan, for these are rough times."

The two perjured soldiers received short terms of imprisonment, and the engineer, much to his surprise, a few days afterwards, received an order from the alcalde of the district, commanding him to appear before the courts with his butterfly-boxes and nets, and the case was again formally tried, and he again formally acquitted.

Indeed, had there by chance been rebels in ambush who had fired upon the guard, no doubt the engineer would have been shot upon the spot as a spy.

CHAPTER X

SELF-MURDER

At the end of the week the señora and family went with the Consul to the Boca, where they took up quarters in the old - fashioned hotel, leading a dull life in the little provincial town by day, or listening at night to the tramp of the volunteers, or the musical cries of the night watchman, who, with halbert and lantern, went the rounds every half-hour, crying—

"Sereno de noche, los dos y medio, esta lloviendo !" or some such cry.

.   .   .   .

The American Consul had well considered the proposal to buy the land, and after weighing the pros and cons, had, with considerable misgivings, given his sanction for the purchase of the fifty-three *caballerias*. 'Tis true, Gomez had come down another thousand dollars, for he dreaded the rebels worse than ever since his capture, for they had threatened to shoot him, with his two sons, the morning after the capture, as Spaniards ; but one of the sons had managed to cut his ropes with a knife, which he had secreted about his person, and waiting till the guard was asleep with fatigue or drink, he unbound his father and brother, and they managed to crawl away unseen, returning to their hut, where they lived in constant dread of their enemies. Their joy, then, when they received the news of the purchase, was extreme. They cleared up all their live-stock, and sold them at once at any price, and came down to the town, bringing Juana and the half-caste with them.

The deed of sale was duly drawn up, signed, and the money paid, the old man, intoxicated with joy, going round the *posadas*, bragging of his acuteness, and the part that the one-eyed administrator had played in the sale, for he grudged paying his bribe, which, however, he had already been compelled to do by the sharp Yorkshireman.

The Consul got wind of the story, and going to Messrs. Maton, commission merchants, he asked them, as the privilege of an old friend, whether Don Martin had lodged any money lately to be transmitted to England or America.

" Yes ; in confidence," said the merchant, " he has just placed five thousand dollars gold to his credit, to be sent to Philadelphia and invested in railways, and I cannot conceive where he got it."

"Is it possible !" said the Consul; but keeping his counsel, he left the merchant and sought out Gomez, whom he found with his sons already aboard the steamer for Havana, *en route* for Spain.

After making the Consul swear he would not cause his detention in any way if he told him, old Gomez made a clean breast of the matter, adding contemptuously—

"The man is a dog, and a cowardly one as well!"

"Great God ! what have I done ! Allowed the widow and children to be robbed!" reiterated the Consul to himself as he returned to his home.

.   .   .   .

The next morning the American Consul was found dead in his bath. He had opened a vein and bled to death. But none knew the reason of his suicide at the time—that transpired afterwards.

CHAPTER XI

KIDNAPPED

THE señora was much upset on receiving the sad news, as indeed was the whole of the town, for the American Consul was a man of honour, just and kind.

After his funeral she was compelled to give her power of attorney to the administrator, who pretended to be much shocked and grieved at the Consul's death, but who was secretly delighted (for the greatest enemy an honourable gentleman has is a dishonest cad, even if their interests do not clash; but if they do, as they did in this case, the hatred of the rogue passeth the understanding of an honest man).

Altogether, the administrator was joyful at the turn circumstances had taken ; nor went he now in such bodily fear, since the guard had come to live on the estate, but his days of peaceful-mindedness were short-lived.

One night he was awakened by shots being fired round the guard's quarter, followed by cries and the clash of steel. He lay in a tremble, gripping his revolver. At length, when the noise had subsided, he dressed leisurely, and ran out in apparent haste, to find the little guard all gesticulating and swearing excitedly.

"What is it ?   What is it ?" he asked.

" The *Insurrectos !*   They have carried off Don Pablo, the major-domo, and killed two of our men with machete cuts, and the negro, Caoba, was with them."

"Yes, señor," said the lieutenant.   "Caoba : he it was who cut this poor trooper down."

"I thought he'd go," said the administrator. "They have been calling him *caballero*, and begging him to join for some time past, and——"

"Well, sir, what ?" asked the hasty lieutenant.

"Well, he was spoiled by Don Enrique. . . . And you hit none of them ?"

"Not one.   But surely you heard the shots ?"

"No ; I am a good sleeper.   The carpenter called me."

"It seems you both slept remarkably well," said the lieutenant coldly.

"Yes ; we work hard," retorted the administrator.

At daybreak the lieutenant ordered out the guard, and they scoured the country to find traces of the rebels, but never a trail could they hit upon ; so they returned, discomfited, to the estate, to learn that, besides Caoba, some thirteen more of the *Esperanza* people had gone to join the rebels.

A few days after this night attack, much to the surprise of everybody, Don Pablo walked into the *batey* at mid-day, dressed in a pair of trousers, his feet naked and bleeding, and never a shirt on him.

His brother employés crowded round him, but the poor major-domo was so faint that he could scarce utter a word; nor did he give his report to the lieutenant until he had eaten and slept nearly twenty-four hours, after which he gave the following account of his adventure :—

" I went to bed as usual, and awoke suddenly, to find Caoba bending over me with a long machete in one hand and a lantern in the other, by the light of which I could see there was fresh blood on the machete.

" ' Get up ; you have got to go with us,' he said.

" ' Go where ? ' I asked, ' and with whom ? '

" ' The Insurrectos.'

" ' What, you an Insurrecto, Caoba ? ' I said. ' *Sinverguenza.*'

" ' Come, no words,' he said, ' or I'll cut your throat. Get up. You have insulted a Cuban patriot.'

" ' What, that long negro from the Santa Anna,' I said.

"'That gentleman,' he said; 'and you've got to pay for it.'

"I saw it was useless to resist, so I got out of bed and put on my trousers, and no sooner had I got them on than several men rushed in, bandaged my eyes, lifted me off my legs, carried me out, and placed me across a horse. I could hear some of them fighting with the soldiers, but I was told to hold on tight to the saddle, and we started off at a gallop, some one leading my horse. When we had gone some distance, Caoba came up and pulled off the bandage roughly, and then I beheld him riding a magnificent white charger, and armed with a Remington. He looked handsome, I can tell you.

"'Don't attempt to fly, or I'll kill you,' he said, with a laugh, as he threw me the reins, and I knew he meant it.

"I heard one or two shots behind us, and the rest of the band came riding up at a gallop, and then we all started as hard as we could go for the forest, after reaching which we slowed down, and went single file through a narrow road that seemed to have been recently cut. Presently we reached the rebel camp, where everybody seemed asleep, for I saw no sentry of any kind. They tied me to a tree, and, after eating some cold pork and plantains, they, too, lay down to sleep.

"When the day broke, some of the negresses

made fires, and roasted plantains and broiled *tasajo*. Then they kept waking and getting up, and some of the negroes from *La Esperanza* came up and began to jeer at me, saying they were the masters now, and they were going to cut up all the Spaniards, and ravish all the white women. Then they began to joke among themselves as to how many lashes they should give me—twenty-five or forty; but Caoba came and cleared them off, and told them they were cowards to jeer at a tied-up man. I counted out thirty *Esperanza* negroes there.

"After breakfast the white men and some of the negroes, amongst whom was Caoba, held a council before my tree. Some of them were for shooting me for insulting a Cuban patriot, whilst others were for flogging me and letting me go. A few said I had done nothing, and should be let go free. Well, they couldn't agree, so they gave me some plantains and a little water, but they never loosened my ropes.

"I had to stand there all day, dozing off at times; and at night the negroes began to drink *aguadiente*, and I thought my time would soon come then; but they seemed too much taken up with the negresses, dancing and carrying on in the most libidinous manner. There was no shame in that camp; indeed, they seemed to forget me altogether until next morning, when they held another council before me, when Caoba, who has somehow become a great man amongst them, took my part. He said that, although I was a Spaniard, I had always been fair, and had never treated anybody cruelly, which was unusual for a Spaniard. His speech got me off, for they talked together for a bit in a low voice; and then a man they called 'the General,' a Cuban, said 'that since the gentleman, Caoba, had given me such a good character, although I was a Spaniard, they would let me go free, on condition that I would at once leave the *Esperanza* and return to Spain, but that if I was caught after a week, I would be killed at once.'"

The little lieutenant took down every word and sent it off to headquarters, whilst Don Pablo packed all his things, and going to the administrator, briefly told him his story, saying that he must go at once; but he added, "I shall not go back to Spain. I shall go to Havana, and get a clerkship, and join the volunteers. I should like to have *my* turn at these people."

And so ended the faithful little Spaniard's career on the estate. It seemed as if the fates were removing all the honest men from *La Esperanza*, and leaving it to the mercy of cowardly rogues.

CHAPTER XII

SENTENCED TO DEATH

AFTER much vexation and anxiety, that grinding season, in which the rebellion opened, passed, and the estate escaped being fired, though pieces of phosphorus embedded in balls of lard were sometimes found in cane-fields, left in hopes that the sun would ignite them; but fortune favoured the *Esperanza,* and beyond being robbed alternately by the troops and the rebels, and the loss of several people who had joined the insurgents, serious as these matters were, that most dreaded enemy, fire, had hitherto kept away.

But a few weeks after the end of the grinding season the *Esperanza's* turn came, and early one morning clouds of smoke were seen belching from the still, where there was a considerable quantity of rum stored; and immediately the great alarm-bell began to ring, and presently a large posse of people from the Santa Anna came, armed with machetes, and headed by the majoral. Luckily there was close by the still a cachassa ditch, now filled by the early rains, and a hose was fitted to the pump of the saw-mill, and this supply, aided by hundreds of buckets, extinguished the fire before reaching the purging-house, where there was still a valuable lot of sugar stored; and Don Enrique's foresight was now evident, for the very thick walls that he had built round the still showed up in the gutted ruin, and doubtless had saved the rest of the buildings.

It transpired after the fire that a party, headed by Caoba, who was now called captain, had broken into the still that morning and stolen several demijohns of rum; and it was agreed that the fire was the result of their carelessness in moving about with lighted candles rather than intended arson, but nevertheless the damage done was considerable.

The lieutenant reported that the outrage was due to Caoba and his band, and at headquarters Caoba was now looked upon as a most dangerous rebel, for reports kept following each other that Caoba, on his white charger, with his Remington, was the leader in many thefts or "requisitions," arsons, and, worst of all, cold-blooded murders; and the report got around from the rebels that he was the coolest, the bravest, and the most bloody of all the guerilla patriots. Never was there a skirmish with the troops either but this bold, good-looking negro was in the thick of it, using his Remington and machete with deadly effect, often laughing as he cut down a foe, taking it all as a great joke.

Two or three other *Esperanza* negroes had already also made their names, the fame of the two big Ashantis, Sabicu and Ramon, being nearly as great as that of Caoba; but they were one day surrounded, with some thirty other rebels, by the troops in ambush, and captured, Caoba being away at the time with another party.

This capture took place a few days after the burning of the still, and immediately it was reported to Captain Baro; he sent word to *La Esperanza*, informing the administrator that Sabicu and Ramon would be executed on the estate before the rest of the people, to act as a deterrent, and with them some of the Cubans, whilst the other negroes would be taken to their respective estates and treated in the same manner. But when the party of prisoners arrived, no Cubans were to be seen amongst them, the officer in command having given them *quatro tiros* on the roads to save trouble.

When Captain Baro arrived, the people were drawn up in a hollow square, and two shells that had been hastily constructed were placed against the stone wall surrounding the *batey*. The bugle sounded, and Captain Baro, in a loud voice, said—

"People of *La Esperanza*, your old fellow-slaves, Sabicu and Ramon, have been captured, after committing many atrocious and cowardly crimes, for which they are to be shot in your presence to-day.

"The negroes of this estate seem to have a remarkably fierce and desperate character, but that will not save you, for every one who joins the insurgents is sure to be taken and shot, unless they are killed by the rebels themselves, as two of the people of this estate have been killed, for insubordination. But the biggest villain is still at large, Caoba. The Government have given me orders to pay the sum of one hundred ounces to any person—white man, or slave, or Chinaman—who brings this man, dead or alive, to any of the authorities. Printed proclamations to that effect will be posted all over the country.

"I warn you all not to be lured away to your destruction by those who have already joined the rebels, for you will all be surely taken and shot, but I advise you to go on quietly with your work."

Then turning to the sergeant and men drawn up ready, the captain said—

"March the prisoners to the coffins."

All eyes were turned upon the powerful Ashantis as they walked, surrounded by the guard, to their death.

When they reached the stone wall, Captain Baro cried, in a loud voice—

"Halt. You, Sabicu and Ramon, kneel and turn with your backs to the soldiers, for so we shoot cowards and traitors."

The great negroes obeyed sullenly, and the twelve men, already formed in line some paces in their rear, were given the order to present; and as Captain Baro's sword flashed, a volley rang out, echoing back from the house on the hill, the prisoners falling forward, pierced by the bullets.

"So perish all traitors. Long live Spain and the *siempre fiel Isla de Cuba*," shouted Captain Baro, his last words being lost in the cheers of the soldiers.

The two dead rebels were thrown into the shells, and borne off by some of the negroes to the little graveyard by the river, and so perished Caoba's rivals.

As night was drawing on, the remaining prisoners were secured, under a strong guard, in the stocks, after the people had been dismissed, and rations given out by the major-domo for the troops; whilst Captain Baro sat down to dinner with the administrator in the dining-room overlooking the orange-grove; for, since the señora and family had gone to the Boca, the administrator had resumed his residence at his former house.

"A stern but useful lesson, Don Natan," said Captain Baro.

"Yes, but a great loss, captain. Those negroes were worth 1500 dollars apiece. This rebellion is ruining the estate."

"Ay, and the island too," said Captain Baro. I rode past *La Marguerita* the other day. Only the great rollers of the mill were left —an ugly ruin, upon which sat a turkey-buzzard, like a pelican in the wilderness—an emblem of desolation."

"Yes, may God protect us from these cowardly cut-throats of insurgents!"

"Yes ; and, by-the-bye, take care of that English engineer of yours. He was nearly shot the other night at Santiago."

"How so, captain ?"

"He was riding past the fort, and was hailed by the sentry, when he muttered something in English, and rode on. The sentry cried, ' Halt, or I fire.' He seemed to understand that and stopped, or he would undoubtedly have been shot."

"Yes, it is no use my saying anything to him ; he is rashness itself, and—between ourselves—is, I believe, in league with the rebels."

"How ? What is that you say ? I never could understand a man running after butter-flies. What does a man want with butterflies ?" said the captain doubtfully.

Don Natan shrugged his shoulders.

"Well, we must keep a close watch upon him. Traitors are easily disposed of nowadays. *Quatro tiros*, and nobody asks any questions," said the captain.

"Well, well, he is my countryman, so I won't say much," said the one-eyed man, with affected generosity.

"Oh, that's very good of you," said Captain Baro, with a sneer; "but have you seen that villain Caoba lately?"

"Yes, captain—last Tuesday. I was returning from inspecting the new land bought from Gomez —"

The captain's eyes twinkled.

"When the fellow suddenly came upon me from the cane, mounted upon his white horse, with his Remington, as usual. He looked grand —a real guerilla chief, with a broad, good-humoured smile on his regular black face. I was on foot, having left my horse tethered to the fence."

"'Hola, *caballero*,' said he, in his deep voice, keeping me covered with his Remington, although it lay across the pommel of his saddle.

"'Hola, Capitan Caoba,' I replied."

"You called him Capitan?" sneered Baro; "why didn't you draw and shoot the villain dead, and take the blood-money—I know you like money?"

The administrator did not notice the sneer, but went on.

"Had I moved my hand towards my revolver, he would have shot me dead first."

"I see," said the captain coldly ; "continue."

"'I want a couple of ounces, *caballero*,' he said.

"I felt in my pockets and gave him all I had— one ounce, a medio onza, and a doblon."

"What did he say to that ?"

"He then asked me how the señora and little Pedro were, and if his wife Maria, who is a servant here, was well. I told him yes.

"'That is good,' he said ; 'so long as the *Esperanza* belongs to any of my old master's family, it is well.'"

"He loved his master, then ?" said the captain.

"Certainly. The señora told me that she actually gave him her jewels and a box of revolvers to hide, and he never told a soul, and the box of revolvers is in the cane-field now. I looked myself only last week."

"And the jewellery ?" asked the captain, with a malicious twinkle.

"Has gone to the Boca. I took it myself last week, and the rascal knew it, for he told me as much, and said that I passed within twenty-five yards of him on the way to the station ; but he would not touch them, because they belonged to the wife of his old master, and so they were safe."

"A strange character. It seems unbelievable of the bloodiest cut-throat that ever joined a set of butchering guerillas."

"Ay, 'tis strange, but true. The man evidently loved Don Enrique, and that is why we have not been burnt and murdered, for he is often about here. He was on the estate only last night, and nearly shot our friend the engineer on the *batey*, for the guard were all occupied in gambling."

" Hola, how was that ? " asked the captain.

"He demanded money, and that hot-headed fool of an engineer refused, and told him to go to the devil, to which Caoba replied—

"'Take care, the balls fly quickly; but as you are brave, I forgive you this time.'"

"That does not look as though the man were in league with the rebels," said Captain Baro coldly, looking the one-eyed man in the face.

The administrator shrugged his shoulders, and suggested a walk round to see that everything was right for the night.

CHAPTER XIII

BUTCHERY

THE chief merchant at the Boca, a canting Scotsman, who had lived some years in the little town, farming a poor little sugar estate on the outskirts, and holding slaves, though a sanctimonious Presbyterian, made it his business to get to know the affairs of *La Esperanza;* buying some of its sugars as commission merchant, to effect his ends, for *La Esperanza* was actually making money, notwithstanding the heavy drain on its resources; and no sooner did this Scotsman and the one-eyed administrator meet, than the natural sympathy between rogues drew them together.

And there were no people more interested at the beginning of the grinding season of 1871, when the cane looked most favourable, than these two worthies, and they both wished the señora and her family well away.

The señora was just in the mood, too, to go, for the very dull life, with all the conventionalities that hedged in a woman in that country, grew unbearable; and the children's education was being neglected, for there was none to teach but a broken-down American gentleman, who acted as clerk in one of the offices, teaching Pedro the rudiments of mathematics and Latin in his spare time, so that the boy had too much time on his hands, and soon began to get interested in the gallos, but perhaps more so in Juanita, the pretty daughter of the shopkeeper Nargas, who supplied the estate with clothes, the father giving him presents, and encouraging him to visit the house, the wily Spanish tradesman thinking he might inveigle the boy into marriage later on with his pretty little daughter, so the old shopkeeper kept him supplied with cigarettes. But the señora got to hear of this through the canting Scotsman, who talked largely of the bad moral effect cigarette smoking would have on the boy, interlarding his barbarous English with Scriptural quotations. Indeed, he tried one of these lectures on Pedro himself, but the boy told him to mind his own business, and from that day they were sworn enemies.

But, nevertheless, the señora, from a sense of duty, still lived on in the miserable little town, and Pedro found a new amusement in riding the circus ponies which often came to visit the town.

The señora received favourable letters from the administrator ; the grinding was progressing favourably, and the visits from the rebels had not been so frequent. Indeed, the whole of that rebellion consisted of spasmodic spouts of volcanic activity, followed by long spells of desultory reprisals—bribery and the rains compelling such jerky procedure.

The *Diario de Marina* reported all fights, murders, burnings of estates, raids; but unfortunately, owing to the censorship of the press, they were nothing but one-sided accounts, calculated to tickle the Spaniard or mislead the reader. But one thing even the *Diario de Marina* had to allow, and that was the daring and blood-thirstiness of Caoba. He was already an historical character well known throughout the island, and his reputation had even travelled to the United States, every one knowing that a price was upon his head.

But the spell of comparative inactivity, in which the grinding season began, was soon ended; and the world was horrified by the barbarous murders of the Cuban students, one of the deepest blotches on the Spanish escutcheon, which was already besprinkled with the blood of disgraceful deeds from the dawn of history.

An American merchant from the Boca, who had been to Havana on business, saw the whole tragedy, and when he returned to the Boca, he was besieged on all hands for his version of the affair, for the newspapers had the usual garbled accounts. And the merchant told his story as follows :—

"I went up to Havana, as you know, on Monday the 20th, to transact business with Messrs. Zaldo & Co., to sell them some sugar, and I heard nothing of the affair till Saturday evening, when I heard at the Telegrafo Hotel that forty-one students had been imprisoned for desecrating Castañon's grave.

"I went out and found the city in an uproar, the streets full of volunteers, drinking, and shouting, 'Long live Spain ! down with the traitors !'

"From what I could gather, it seems that on Wednesday last, a class of the University of San Dionisio were waiting for their professor close to the cemetery. The professor was late, so some of the students strolled into the grave-yard, and began to read the names on the long courts, where the niches are let into the walls for burying people in quicklime."

"After they had wandered about for a bit, the boys—for the oldest was but seventeen—began frolicing, one boy plucking a flower, two others playing with a cart.

"The caretaker saw them and rebuked them, and the youngsters stopped at once, the boy who had picked the flower dropping it, and they all slunk away to their college.

"They heard nothing more of the affair, and

thought nothing more of it, and were sitting quietly at class on Saturday, when, who should walk into the room but the Political Governor of Havana, Don Lopez Roberts, followed by two officers and a body of *guarda civiles*, a company of volunteers keeping guard at the gate.

"The professor arose in surprise, and the governor, with a brief apology, took his chair, and addressed the class in a solemn voice, saying—

"'Gentlemen, it has been reported to me that on Wednesday last, between two and three o'clock, some of you were playing in the cemetery, and that you desecrated the tomb of Genzalo Castañon, a loyal Spaniard. I have been myself, and examined the glass over the tomb, and I find scratches upon the glass. You all know what occurred : which of you is the criminal ?'

"A dead silence fell on the room, and the boys looked at each other in amazement and dismay.

"An American boy stood up and said—

"'Señor, what you describe never happened, and no one desecrated anybody's tomb.'

"A Spanish boy then got up, and also denied the accusation.

"'Enough !' said Lopez roughly ; 'the culprit is amongst you ; tell me his name.'

"Several of the youths replied it was impossible to give the name of the culprit, for none of them had done such a deed.

"'Give it yourself, since you are so sure,' called the American boy boldly from his seat.

"The Governor's temper rose, and he said harshly—

"'Unless you confess his name, every one of you goes to gaol.'

"None protested, save the American, who persisted that no such thing had taken place.

"'Take him off to gaol, *sinverguenza*,' said the Governor, pointing to the American boy.

"After the American had been removed, the Governor interrogated each lad separately, in this way eliciting the names of all who had played in the cemetery, and of the boy who picked the flower ; but each one denied having scratched the glass covering over Castañon's tomb.

"'Then march them off to prison,' said Lopez Roberts, the Governor. 'The inspector of the *guarda civiles* shall make them speak.'

"Two or three of the boys protested they were at home on the Wednesday.

"'It does not matter: you all go to prison until I know the name of the criminal,' said the pompous Spaniard.

"And the boys were formed in two files, and marched between the volunteers to the civil prison.

"As they were leaving the room, Triay, one of

Roberts' company, called out with a sneer to Alonzo Alvarez de la Campa, the lad who had picked the flower—

"' Neither your father's money nor your father's influence shall save you from merited punishment.'

"It was eight o'clock when they entered the prison; and after being enrolled in the prison register, they were led to a private chamber before an inspector of police, who began to interrogate them. Alvarez de la Campa and another, a boy of seventeen, confessed to playing in the court, whereupon they were immediately sent to the convict cells; the remainder, maintaining their innocence, were finally sent to the Jaula, where they were provided with bread and sardines.

"All Sunday they were left in the Jaula without chairs or food, nor were their friends permitted to communicate with them.

"Well, the desecration of the tomb was all the talk on the Sunday—at the Union Club, in the hotels, in the cafés. Some said that the glass over the tomb had only been broken; others maintained that remains had been dragged out of the columbarian—and all this over a man who was shot in a duel at Key West. So I thought I would go myself and see, and I found Castañon's tomb untouched, save for a few scratches on the glass made by a diamond, and they were old, as any one could see.

" But the volunteers—chiefly tradesmen and the low classes—got it into their heads that the tomb had been desecrated, and they went mad with rage ; and, as everybody knows, the 10,000 volunteers in Havana have ruled the city ever since they got Dulce sent home to Spain. There they were, galloping about and marching round, singing and drinking ; and when they came to parade before General Crespo in the evening, many of them shouted, ' Death to the traitors !' Crespo didn't like the look of things, so he hurried off to the palace after the review ; but deputations from the different corps followed him, and complained bitterly that twenty-four hours had passed since the traitors had been arrested, and no steps had been taken to try them. Further, they complained that the authorities intended to wink at the outrages, and demanded that the prisoners should be shot as traitors at once ; the main body of the volunteers having in the meantime collected in the Plaza de Armas, where they were all shrieking ' Death to the traitors !' their cries being carried to the prisoners, who were horrified at their situation.

" I went to the Plaza, and never saw such a fearful sight as to see these low-born people yelling for the blood of the poor Cuban boys—

boys amongst the flower of Cuban youth—the sons of refined, rich, influential, and well-born fathers.

"However, nothing happened for some time, and the volunteers got mad, and the buglers began to sound their Moorish calls all over the square, some of the drunken ones rushing off to try and break into the prison, whilst the others met and sent another deputation to the palace, and said they would burn it down if the traitors were not brought out and shot. The Plaza was a scene indeed. All the cafés were full of volunteers, smoking, and shrieking for the blood of Alvarez de la Campa.

"Then a message came that Crespo had agreed to begin the trial that night, and that he had selected a tribunal composed of captains of the army, with a colonel for chairman.

"Directly this report went round, the shrieks of 'Death to the traitors!' were simply deafening, and the crowd, with a roar and a rush, amid the shrieking of the bugles, forced its way to the Prado, where the prison is situated, and where Crespo had told the deputation the trial would take place.

"The report of the serious turn that affairs had taken spread like wildfire over Havana, and many of the horrified relatives hastened to the prison to try and beg or buy off the prisoners. Whilst this was going on, some of the chief officers tried

to pacify the crowd, but they were promptly seized
by the volunteers, and locked up in a room ; and
the guardian of Castañon's children—who, to his
credit, loudly proclaimed the innocence of the
prisoners—was hooted, and had to disappear ;
whilst one of the governor's horses was bayo-
neted as he drove to the prison, and his hat knocked
down over his face, his guards probably saving his
life, for they hid him when they got him into the
prison.　Crespo, be it said to his disgrace, kept
away from the scene altogether, hugging himself
at home.

"It was a little after midnight when the report
circulated that the court had opened, and it soon
got about that no accusers had appeared, the cus-
todian's declaration alone being read.　Captain
Frederico Rey y Capdevilla, a Spanish gentleman
and officer, was chosen to defend the boys, and he
did his duty like a man ; and if wretched Spain had
many Capdevillas, she would again be amongst
the first nations of the world.　He spoke loudly
and clearly on behalf of the boys.　I have his
speech in my pocket, and I will read it to you.
By Jove, he was a man.

"'My obligation as a Spaniard, my sacred
duty as a defender, my honour as a gentleman and a soldier, compel me to protect and
shield the innocent — and there are forty - five
to be defended—to defend these children, who

have hardly emerged from boyhood — have just entered upon that youth in which there is yet no hate, no vengeance, no passion. What are you going to expect from children—for you cannot call them men? You cannot judge them as men, these striplings of fourteen, sixteen, eighteen, more or less. But even if you judge them as men, where is the accusation? where is the proof of the crime? Gentlemen, from the opening of the session I have been present; I have heard the reading of the report, the declarations, the verbal charges; and either I am utterly incompetent and ignorant, or there is nothing, absolutely nothing, of culpability. Before entering this hall, I heard rumours without number that the students had committed sacrilege and desecration in the cemetery; but in the name of truth, be it said, nothing of this has appeared in the proceedings.

"'Gentlemen, before all things we are honourable soldiers; we are gentlemen. Honour is our motto, our pride, our device, and, like Spain, always honour, always nobleness, always gentility, never passion, baseness, or fear. The punctilious soldier will die at his post. Well, then, let them assassinate us; but the lovers of order, of society, the nations of the earth, will dedicate to us an immortal memory.'

"But in response to this noble and brave speech,

the volunteers, who had crowded into court, only yelled, 'Death to the traitors!' and one excited fellow struck at the speaker ; but Capdevilla gave the fellow a smart rap with the back of his sword, when they all began to yell for *his* head, and so serious was their attitude that his friends dragged him from the court and hid him away in the prison, much against his will.

"Then, amid ceaseless uproar, the court found the prisoners guilty of profanation, and sentenced them to be fined and imprisoned.

"The volunteers, on hearing this, and being thus balked of their prey, grew madder than ever, and sent off a deputation to Crespo, demanding the death of the traitors or a new Council.

"The cowardly Crespo, ignoring all law and justice, appointed a new court under a colonel, made up of six regular officers and some volunteers.

"The volunteers crowded the hall, and their eager faces showed that they now felt sure of their victims.

"The lads were given a list of persons from whom they might choose defenders, which they did ; but most of their defenders were unknown to the boys, who were now drawn up in file in the council hall, surrounded by their relatives, the volunteers glaring at them, hissing curses in their faces, and showing them the bullets with which they would be shot. The defenders turned cowards, and said there was no defence ; and for a long hour these tender sons of gentlemen, with their lives in their hands, had to put up with the brutal insults of the bestial populace, and yet no proof during all that time was brought against them. After this, they were marched off again to prison, when I hurried off to the Telegrafo and got breakfast, when we heard that they had discharged the American boy and another, who was a Spaniard by birth and also a volunteer. When I returned to the Prado, people said that the court had decided to execute eight of the students.

"I asked a quiet-looking volunteer standing near me if the sacrilege had been proved.

"'Proved ? No ; we want them to die—that's enough,' he said.

"'The tomb is untouched,' I ventured to say ; 'I saw it myself yesterday.'

"'Who knows ?' he said, shrugging his shoulders, and walking off.

"Presently the Council came out on to the verandah, and the bugler blew a long blast. There was a dead silence, broken by occasional cries of 'Death to the Council !'

"The bugler blew a second blast, and the crowd began to yell, 'Death to the Council !' The bugler kept on blowing blasts between cries of 'Death to the Council!' until they numbered eight, when the wretched and fickle mob cried, 'Viva el Consejo!'

"It was then passed about that the lad who plucked the flower, and that the four who had played in the court, had been sentenced to death; and lots had been drawn for the remaining three to complete the eight, as represented by the bugle blasts—one of the three doomed lads, drawn by lots, not having been at the University on the Wednesday afternoon.

"It was past mid-day before the death sentence was signed and carried to Crespo for confirmation, and the coward signed it at once. Then some official brought it to the balcony and read it.

"I never saw people so mad with fierce joy. They nodded their heads joyfully at each other, patted each other affectionately, slapped their thighs, yelled "Viva Crespo," "Viva el Capitan-General," throwing rolling Spanish oaths at the heads of the Cuban boys, who were led to the cells of the condemned criminals.

"There the band struck up wild Moorish music, and the cafés were filled with laughing, half-mad volunteers.

"I went down by the prison after getting a meal at the San Carlos, and got into the square just as the eight boys were marched out to their deaths ; the young De la Campa, who had plucked the flower, walking at the head. They were brave youths, those Cuban aristocrats, for they smiled as they walked to their doom before their brutal enemies, who were now formed up in battalions.

"The firing-party was already drawn up, and you might have heard a pin drop as the manacled prisoners were marched before them and told to kneel with their backs to the firing-party, an indignity reserved for traitors, and the last in-dignity to which they could be put. I looked at the faces of the volunteers, and could see nothing but hate gleam from their black bright eyes. Suddenly a drum beat, and all eyes were turned towards the poor victims. A dead silence fell on the crowd, and an order was given in Spanish, and three volleys rang out, the mangled children falling with cries on to their faces, the blood spurting over them."

"By God, the whole world ought to avenge this butchery," interrupted an excited bagman.

"Immediately the bands all struck up their wild music, and the mutilated corpses were roughly huddled into shells ; and these tradesmen soldiers filed past the corpses with bands playing, many of the brutes hurling curses at the mangled remains. After this shameful proceeding, the corpses were carried off to the cemetery, the friends not being allowed to see them again.

"It was a sight I shall not forget to my dying day.

"Then the rest of the prisoners were brought forth, manacled two by two, and marched through the streets to the quarries, where these delicate boys were sentenced to labour with convicts, in constant companionship with the foulest criminals, and under the cruel goadings of taskmasters especially appointed by the volunteers to look after them, and to make their lives a misery; and in addition all their property was confiscated, which I am told is illegal."

"By God, it is enough to make every man, woman, and child in the island rise and cut every Spaniard's throat," said the new American Consul, who had heard the recital of the tragedy.

"This will strengthen the rebels," added another.

"Yes, yes, but few words are best in this island just now," said the narrator. "Let us go and have some *panales:* I am hot."

CHAPTER XIV

PILLAGED

THIS terrible butchery relit the smouldering embers of the Revolution, and from all parts of the island came reports of reprisals, of rapes and mutilations, of burnt estates, of wholesale murders.

Don Natan, the administrator, went about in fear and trembling, and in his reserved way was plotting to place his worthless skin under protection, and to fill his dirty pockets. For long he had been brooding over a scheme to these ends, when an incident befel which at once decided him to try his plans.

One day a party of insurrectors came on to the estate, and riding straight to the *Casa Grande*, robbed the Chinese, who now lived there, of all their valuables and money, afterwards departing by the road that led to Maravilla, no doubt to one of the permanent encampments in the high woods round about that seaport.

When the Chinese went home to dinner and found what had happened, they were mad with rage, and seizing their machetes, with Tangu at their head, they ran down to the *batey* and demanded to see the administrator, who was taking his siesta in a rocking-chair.

When he heard the hubbub and angry voices without, he walked pale and trembling into the piazza, being dismayed when he saw the crowd of yellow faces contorted with anger, their eyes flashing, and all of them gesticulating and talking wildly.

On the appearance of Don Natan, Tangu raised his stick as a signal for silence, and addressed the administrator thus in Spanish :—

"Don Martin, we have been robbed of everything by the insurrectors. The soldiers kept on the estate are cowards and worth nothing. We demand to be led against the rebels, who have gone to their camp in the woods near Maravilla ; we intend to kill them and get back our property."

"Come, come," said the administrator ; "who is to lead you against the rebels?—and in any case you would only embroil the estate, and we should be burnt out."

"We don't care, señor ; we are determined on revenge."

"But it is impossible ; I sympathise with you, and cannot make out where the guard was when the insurgents came."

"Why, with the negresses in the cane, of course, as they always are," said Tangu bitterly.

"Well, well, Tangu, I will do all I can for you, but you must give up this idea of revenge. If you will be honest, and get a list of the property stolen from each man, I will send it on to the señora, and ask her to make good your losses."

Tangu told the Chinamen in their own tongue the administrator's proposal, and immediately their countenances changed. Their machetes dropped to their sides, their eager fierceness disappeared, and they began to talk together in low voices.

"Well, Tangu, what do they say?" asked Don Martin, after an interval.

"They say the administrator is very good, and they will do as he desires."

"Good, let them go back to their quarters," said the one-eyed man, much relieved. . . .

The generous señora ordered everything to be made good to the Chinese, including the money of which they said they had been robbed; and from the modesty of their claims, it was thought for once the heathen Chinee was honest.

CHAPTER XV

THE end of the grinding season of '72 had come, and Nargas, the Boca storekeeper, came to the estate with his handsome daughter, to bring the usual clothes for the people, and to have his accounts settled, as was customary ; but on this occasion he was received as a guest by the administrator, though hitherto he had only been considered worthy of the major-domo's society. That evening the Spanish storekeeper, a little, dark, weasel-eyed man, with a Jewish nose, led his daughter, a handsome, cream-coloured Cuban, dressed in white muslin, with a spray of orange flower nestling on her magnificent bosom, into the little dining-room that overlooked the orange grove.

Laura had a sensuous form ; large, black eyes, that flirted with every one ; ripe, full lips, and an exquisitely-modelled neck and bosom.

The administrator took the head of the table, placing Laura on his left, facing the open windows, through which the purling of the little falls in the river could be heard, mingled with the voices of the cicadas, and through which the delicate perfume of orange blossom stole with the night air. She could see, too, a patch of the violet sky, star-besprinkled.

"How beautiful is the night!" she murmured, looking archly at the administrator, as her father took his seat opposite her.

"Yes, señorita, but not so beautiful as its *vis-à-vis*," said the one-eyed man, with a mischievous twinkle.

"Hola, Laura," said the father jocosely.

"And how is the señora, Don Nargas ?" asked the administrator, helping the fideo soup.

The little Spaniard shrugged his shoulders, and looking furtively at the administrator, answered : "I never see the señora now. She is too proud even to enter my shop. She goes to Hildago's store."

"How is that ?"

"Well, well, señor, we are men. Young Pedro, who is a brave lad" (the administrator made a move that did not escape the weasel eyes of the storekeeper), "and I were good friends. He has an eye for the points of a gallo, the boy, and beat all the boys on the little horses when the circus came to the Boca. They had a race got up by the circus man, Pedro gaining a case of scent. Well, the señora did not like his coming to my house, for Pedro, *carajo!* is a little man, and can smoke his cigarette with the best; began to make love to Juanita, my youngest—but only as children, you know, Don Natan."

"Yes, as children, Don Nargas," sneered the administrator. "But Pedro is a dare-devil—he is like his father—cares for nothing, but has been spoilt. He was insolent to me : used to ride my horses through the rivers and mud, and make them in a fearful mess."

"Yes; ah, he should have had the rod," acquiesced the sycophant.

"He did when his father was alive ; but go on."

"Well, one day he came with a long face, and said that his mother had forbidden him to come near my house again, and she left off dealing with me."

"Yes," said Laura, ogling the administrator ; "if we had been gentry it might have been different, but you see we are only shopkeepers."

"Ah, Laura, never mind; you may be a señora yet — you, with your good looks," said Don Martin jollily.

"Ah, get along, Don Natan," said the girl, giving him a most bewitching glance, and letting her magnificent bosom rise and fall with a sigh.

"I have often thought I should like to be a *hacendado*," said the tradesman ; "but we must be so rich. Ah, if I could but buy an estate and get made a marquis ! My brother, General Nargas, bought his commission ; and if I had an estate, 25,000 dollars would buy me the title."

"Well, Don Nargas, stranger things have happened. Estates go cheaply nowadays ; and what a contessa Laura here would make ! There is no girl that goes to the Captain-General's balls who is so *linda* as this señorita."

Laura bowed, and began to use her fan vigorously.

The administrator then turned the conversation to the rebellion and the execution of the students, and the time passed so quickly that the table was soon cleared, and the coffee and fire brought, when Laura, pleading fatigue, retired to her room.

"A grand girl, your daughter, Don Juan," said the administrator.

"Ah, *si*, señor ; she would make a fine lady."

"Hermosa," said the one-eyed man, smacking his lips. Then turning to Don Juan, he added, "So you would like to buy an estate, eh ?"

"I should," said the Spaniard decisively.

"And you would not mind living in an out-of-the-way place like this, for instance ?"

"Not I. I am no coward," said the Spaniard, putting his hand on his heart.

"Then why don't you buy *La Esperanza ?*"

"Buy *La Esperanza ?* Whew !" gasped the little storekeeper.

"Yes, it might be arranged," said Don Martin, looking at the ceiling.

"Come, man, what are you driving at?" asked the Spaniard.

"Well," said the administrator, turning towards him, "in private, the señora is tired of living in that hole of a town, and wants to go to the States to educate her children. She is tired, too, of the worry and anxiety."

"Ha!" said the Spaniard, "do Morez and Agurio know this? I know they have always had longing eyes on the *Esperanza*, and they are very rich."

"No, nobody except Don Juan, my friend, knows it."

Don Juan bounded to his feet and shook the administrator by the hand, then relighting his cigar, which he had allowed to go out, he sat down and fixed the administrator with his weazel eyes, and asked bluntly and boldly—

"What are Don Natan's terms? I see the clever señor has been thinking it over."

"Yes, señor, I too am tired of the life, and if it were made worth my while, I'd——"

"I understand," said the tradesman, sitting back in his chair and puffing hard at his cigar; "come, let us talk like men—what are the terms?"

"Well, Don Juan, as man to man, listen. The children's money is tied up in mortgages payable when they come of age. They are now thirteen and eight. That will give you twelve years and seventeen years before they are twenty-five, and many things might happen before that."

"I understand."

"But, of course, those mortgages will have to stand. Then you will have to give the señora something down, and you can promise to pay the interest on the mortgages till the children come of age. Do you see? Say you offer the señora 50,000 dollars down, which you can easily borrow on another mortgage."

"Ah, Don Natan is very clever; and what little present does he want for his kindness?"

"Fifteen thousand dollars down the day the deed is signed—no more, no less—and——"

"What, señor?—speak," said the Spaniard excitedly. "Laura?"

An expression of chagrin passed over the Spaniard's face, but quickly recovering his composure, he said grandiloquently—

"Come, come, señor; a father cannot dispose of·his daughter's heart."

"Nor can an administrator dispose of his master's property," said the man coldly.

"Well, well, Don Martin, let me think over it to-night—it has all been so sudden. To-morrow we shall see."

"As you will," said the administrator.

Then these two worthies parted for the night, the little storekeeper pleading fatigue, and going to his bedroom, whilst the administrator, who was heated with wine and excitement, went out under the stars for a turn, and as he passed the kitchen, he saw a deserted swing, that Pedro had put up, was moving, some one having evidently just risen from it, and then he saw a woman's figure run into the house. Recognising Maria as she stepped into the lights of the dining-room, he walked quickly to the steps, and called her to him, saying severely—

"Caoba has been here to visit you to-night; you know it is forbidden."

"I must see my husband," said Maria saucily.

"Well, go in, and do not let it occur again, or I shall send you to the Boca to wait on the señora."

Maria laughed, and went and lay down on the mat before Laura's door; and the administrator, calling a servant to lock the house up, retired to rest.

CHAPTER XVI

THE COMPACT

NEXT morning the administrator and Don Juan were closeted for hours in the major-domo's office, ostensibly settling the storekeeper's accounts — in reality overhauling the estate books.

"You see it pays well even now, and in a year or so, when the rebellion is over, things will be at the old pitch," said Don Natan persuasively.

The Spaniard thought for a long time, and then he said decisively. "I'll do it on one condition—that I pay the sum down to the señora at the *expiration* of the first year. This is May—say I take possession on July 1st, for my head-man will buy my shop from me—he has money. I will pay the señora her sum down on July 1st, one year hence, together with the interest on the mortgages."

"And my 15,000 dollars gold, the day the papers are signed, and Laura?"

The Spaniard made a grimace, and said—

"As to the money, good. As to Laura, señor, if I give her to you, you will marry her — according to the Catholic Church, of course."

" Marry her, señor ? Come, Don Juan is no fool. I don't wish to marry her at all."

The tradesman got up in a furious temper, and said pompously—

"Señor, do you think a Spanish gentleman can sell his daughter ? "

"Yes," said Don Natan coolly ; "they have often done it—and real gentlemen, too."

"What would her mother say ?" pleaded the Spaniard.

"*Carajo !* I am not dealing with women, but with a man. Without Laura I do not move," finished the administrator curtly.

"Ah, señor is too clever for a mere shopkeeper," said the Spaniard, with a grimace.

"Well, is it a bargain ?"

"Yes," said the Spaniard, with some reluctance, extending his hand, which the one-eyed man gripped.

.   .   .   .

Early the next morning, the administrator started for the Boca to visit the señora and propose the sale ; and the little Spaniard spent the day walking and talking with his handsome daughter, who, in reply to his devilish schemes, said—

"Ah, if it had been Don Enrique, he was a man, but this one-eyed beast! . . . Well, we must play with him." And so the compact between father and daughter was made.

CHAPTER XVII

LAURA

LATE that night the administrator returned from his journey in high spirits, and informed Don Juan, who had sat up for him, that the señora was in a mind to sell.

"In truth, señor, it is as good as done," said he, thumping his fist with glee on the table.

"Ah, Don Natan is very clever, very clever," said the Spaniard, rubbing his hands ; " but he is tired, and if the *caballero* will permit me, I will go to bed."

·   ·   ·   ·   ·   ·   ·

A few days afterwards a letter came from the señora, expressing her decision to sell, and saying that she was tired of life in the little town, and considered it her duty to take the children north to educate them.

The two rogues were delighted beyond their wildest hopes, and that night they drank much wine and many liqueurs at dinner, the administrator leering at Laura until she went to her bedroom, that opened from the dining-room.

After she opened the tall cedar door, she turned and stood framed in the doorway, and looking archly at the administrator, said—

"Good night, *caballeros.*"

The administrator, inflamed with wine, kept his single eye glued upon the cedar door after her disappearance, answering Don Juan's questions absently, for all his thoughts were fixed upon Laura, who was then taking off her red morocco boots and spotted muslin dress, exposing her lovely figure to the moonlight that streamed through the open windows. As she undressed and got within the mosquito-nets, the love-lorn administrator arose and bade his guest good night—Don Juan taking the hint, and retiring to his room, heavy with unaccustomed wine.

After the father had disappeared, the administrator returned from a stroll in the orange grove, and reseated himself at the table, drinking more maraschino, and looking intently at the cedar door that separated him from his love.

"By God, I'll try it," he muttered to himself, and forthwith began to remove his shoes. When he had kicked them off, he walked stealthily towards the bedroom door; but as he went his heart failed him, and he turned out into the night, where he stood looking at the sleeping dogs; then, moving stealthily down the steps, he went all round the kitchen, and assuring himself there was no one present, he crept towards Laura's window, the jalousie shutters of which were ajar; and below he stood listening intently, and he could hear her regular breathing in the room. Gently pushing the shutters ajar, he climbed up on to the cedar ledge, the moonlight streaming over him and falling on to her mosquito-nets, through which he could discern her luxurious black hair; but his heart failed him still, and he was all of a tremble as he hesitated on the cedar window-sill.

"But," he said, "I must do it;" and giving a last look into the court where the dogs slept, he climbed gently over the cedar panelling, and stood in the room.

The girl was restless, and evidently heard the noise, or was awakened by the moonlight; but still she must have been drowsy, for the guilty wretch succeeded in reaching the mosquito-nets and pulling them gently apart, where he stood in a cold sweat, gazing intently upon the beautiful Cuban girl, whose magnificent form was outlined under the sheets.

"By God!" muttered the man, as a gust of passion swept through him.

The girl's eyes slowly opened, and she looked steadfastly at him for a few moments, when she broke the silence by a loud shriek.

"Ah, little Laura, do not cry out; it is I, your

affianced husband," said the man, broken with passion.

But the athletic girl sprang to her feet. She seized the mosquito-nets and drew them together, standing within her gauze cage a magnificent and irate Venus, hissing "Coward !"

"Come, come, Laura: your father must have told you all. I have done my part of the bargain," said this old Don Juan.

The girl realised the great stake for which she and her father were playing, and recovering her presence of mind, she said in an altered voice, "Ah yes, Don Natan ; but you make love in such a funny way," carrying it off with a laugh, as only a Spanish woman could.

"Ah, señorita, I am English, and do not understand the ways of Spain," pleaded the administrator.

"No, not at all," exclaimed a loud, exuberant voice from the window, and the speaker burst into a deep, guttural laugh.

The administrator turned, and in the bright moonlight recognised the laughing face of the terrible Caoba, and could only stammer in reply, " *Como*, Caoba !"

"Caoba ! murder !" shrieked the girl, hiding her face in her hands.

" *Caramba*, she looks lovely," said Caoba, who had vaulted lightly into the room. "Come, shall we share, Don Natan?" said he, with a leer at the administrator.

" *Vaya, hombre,* I'm going to marry her."

Caoba laughed ironically ; but suddenly stopping, he listened for a moment intently, then said in a loud voice, " *Caramba,* the soldiers ! Goodbye, señorita ; a *man* shall tame you one day ;" and with this farewell he dropped lightly from the window, and fled towards the river like a deer.

The administrator hastily drew the shutters of the room together, and disappeared by the door into the dining-room, where he drew his revolver and ran out behind the house, amid the barking of the dogs, and came upon the guard, the young lieutenant asking anxiously, on seeing him, "What is it ?—what is it ? We heard shrieks."

" That *sinverguenza,* Caoba. The señorita caught him climbing into her bedroom."

" *Ay, carai,* but he is a daring fellow. Which way did he go ?"

"Towards the river."

" But the dogs — they did not bark till we arrived."

" No, he knows them better than we do."

The soldiers then scattered towards the river, where they presently found fresh footprints in the soft mud of the banks ; but they did not follow, for they knew that long ere this the guerilla chief had mounted his white charger, and was galloping like the wind towards the high woods.

.	.	.	.	.	.	.

Next morning Laura gave her father a full account of Caoba's attempt to enter her room, and said that Don Natan had gallantly come to her rescue, for she knew that, sordid as her father was, had she told him the truth his passion would have got the mastery of him, and she never would become a señora, the daughter of a *hacendado*.

The wily Don Juan made this incident an excuse to take his daughter back to the town, whence he said he would not bring her until the deed of sale was signed.

CHAPTER XVIII

AT the end of May the administrator received the following letter from the señora, which made him anxious :—

> "HOTEL DE QUATRO NATIONES,
> "*May 13th*, 1872.

"DEAR SIR,—The news that I propose selling *La Esperanza* estate to Don Juan Nargas seems to have got about, for since your visit I have received two offers from Messrs. Hernandez & Olivier and from Don Pedro Gomez, both wealthy planters.

"The offers are not so good as Nargas's on the whole, but there is more ready money to be had from them.

"I hardly know what to do in the matter, as I would like to keep my promise to Nargas, though I detest him and his family personally ; but one must take into account my promise, and the fact that they have served the estate faithfully for some years. Will you come down and talk over the matter ?—Yours very truly,

"J. ENRIQUE."

The administrator read the letter carefully, and said to himself—

"By God, I wonder how it has got about. I wonder if Caoba heard our talk. He seemed more impudent than usual that night. However, I must go down and work upon her sentiments and upon her love of money, for all women are greedy in business."

The villain succeeded in his mission, and on June 22nd the document was signed selling *La Esperanza* estate to Don Juan Nargas, on the terms agreed upon between the two rogues, as given in a preceding chapter.

Don Juan paid the administrator the 15,000 dollars gold at once, and it was immediately forwarded by the administrator's merchant to England for investment.

It had been arranged that Don Juan should take possession on July 1st, and the one-eyed man made himself gay with a new eye, the better to woo Laura with when she came up with her father upon the 1st.

When the administrator returned to the estate, after witnessing the deed of sale and sending off his bribe, the English engineer waited upon him at his own house.

"Well, what can I do for you?" asked the administrator coldly.

"Take my notice to quit at once. Every one

knows that the family has been sold, and I refuse to work under an upstart Spanish tradesman who will never be able to pay any one."

"Well, if you wish it," said Don Natan.

"It is not a case of wishing it.   I am going, and you can draw me a *libranza* for my salary at once."

The administrator went to his writing-table and drew the cheque, taking the engineer's receipt in return.

"Now, before I go, I wish to tell you, as man to man, what I think of you.   You are a damned coward and a rogue, sir, and I am ashamed to think you are my countryman.   Living about the world has taught me one thing—there are brave men and gentlemen, and cowards and villains in every country, and you are an English coward, an English cad, and an English villain."

"Come, come, what's all this about?" said the man, turning pale.

"What's it all about, eh?   I know enough to send you to prison for the rest of your life in any damned country but this.   Who made the señora buy Gomez's land on the top of a rebellion?"

"Mind your own business, sir."

"Ah, yes.   Well, perhaps it is not my business after all, but I won't stand by and see the widow and orphans of a good and brave man robbed."

"Take care, sir ; you go far."

"Ah, cur, the mills of God grind slowly, but they grind very small. Mark my words—they are my last on this estate to you—you will all receive your punishments in this world as well as the next for robbing the widow and orphans." And the engineer turned on his heel and went to his quarters to pack his valise, leaving the estate on horseback at once.

By the same steamer that took the señora and her children to the north the engineer was a passenger, and on the journey he told her the whole truth, but, much to his chagrin, she would believe never a word of it, and replied coldly—

"Don Natan is a good Christian man. I have perfect faith in what he has done."

"May you never regret the day you gave him your power of attorney, madame!" said the engineer, turning away; and these two never spoke to each other again.

CHAPTER XIX

CAOBA'S COMMISSION

On the last day of June Don Juan, his wife, two daughters and two sons, now young men, arrived on the estate and took up their residence in the administrator's house, inaugurating their arrival by a merry dinner given in the dining-room overlooking the orange-grove.

Laura looked lovelier than ever in the soft candle-light, and the administrator tried to make himself more agreeable than hitherto. But Laura seemed to have changed, and she no longer flirted with him with her eyes, and seemed rather to avoid him.

After the women had retired, Don Juan signed to his two sons also to leave, and the two worthies were again left alone.

"Well, Don Natan, it is done; it was a brave move," said the little Spaniard.

"How done?" asked the administrator, aghast.

"Done! why, of course it is done, *caballero.*"

"But about Laura?" stammered the administrator.

"Aha!" laughed the little Spaniard, "she sleeps in that room. You are at liberty to go to her; but with Spanish women, señor, it is better to win their favours by courtship than by force, or else their love is as cold as a stone."

"Yes. Well, I'll try to win her, señor; she is a beauty."

"Yes, just like her mother in the old days," said the little Spaniard reflectively. . . . "Now to business. You have had most of my ready money, but I have plenty of stock to feed the people with, and my brother, General Nargas, will lend me enough at 12 per cent. to pay the white men's wages and the Chinese until crop time, and you say the prospects are good."

"Yes, excellent; and should we not be burnt out by the insurrectos, you will make a handsome profit."

"Aha, yes; the insurrectos, they fear us Spaniards," said the little tradesman, blowing himself out like the frog of old.

"*Quien sabe?*" replied the administrator, shrugging his shoulders.

After some further talk about estate matters, the two rogues went to bed, the wily Spaniard already scheming how to get rid of Laura's repulsive lover, now she was a grand lady and he had gained his object. He already felt himself an important man, too. He was now Don Juan,

the *hacendado*, one of the Cuban landed aris-
tocracy, and here was a one-eyed English ad-
venturer demanding *his* daughter as a plaything.
" He shall never have her, though," said the little
man to himself decidedly.

The next few days were spent by Don Juan in
riding about the estate and informing every little
Spanish *sitero* and *montero* that he was now the
proprietor of *La Esperanza*. Moreover, he had
all the people assembled on the estate, and the
vain little man made them a speech, in which he
promised them that they should *now* be treated
with kindness and justice, and have more food
and clothes than they had in the days of the
foreigner.

Nevertheless, more negroes than ever ran away
to join the insurgents, and the little tradesman
was beside himself with rage, and thought of
every possible scheme by which he could stay
the secession of the people—for the little man
had one only virtue, and that was courage. He
rode about the estate armed with revolvers; nor
did he quail when one day, in a lonely cane-field,
Caoba broke from the tall crop, and reining up
his white charger, said—

" Good morning, gentleman."

" Good morning, gentleman. Whom have I
the honour of addressing ? " asked the Spaniard
coolly.

" *El capitan*, Don Caoba," replied the guerilla chief.

"Ah, señor," he replied, "what can I do for you ?"

" Four pounds of *tasajo*, twelve pocket-hand-kerchiefs," jeered the jocose negro.

" *Que hombre !* I'm proprietor of this estate now," said the little fellow, with pride.

" A *caballero ?* " sneered Caoba.

" Yes, at your service, señor," replied the Spaniard, who began to dislike the dark mouth of the Remington with which Caoba kept him covered.

" Can you fight ? " asked Caoba, with a guttural laugh.

" No, no, señor ; I am a man of peace.

" Yes, a cowardly shopkeeper," said the negro, laughing. " My master was a *caballero* and a brave man. I often think of him. He was not afraid of a dozen *bandoleros*. I try to be like him. Ah, poor master ! And the señora, and Pedro ? Where are they ? "

" Gone to the North."

" Ay, I know. When will they be paid ? Poor family," said the negro solemnly.

Don Juan winced, but regaining his composure, said—

" See here, capitan ; you are a brave man. Every one has heard of you, even in the United States."

Caoba laughed, and asked—

"What good will that do me?"

"Well, I like a brave man," said the store-keeper. "I will give you fifty ounces if you do me a favour."

"Is it to murder?" sneered the negro.

"Perhaps."

"Who is it, then?"

"Don Martin."

"Hola!" said Caoba, with a laugh. "He is a coward; he isn't worth the trouble. Besides, he never did me harm. Why does Don Juan want him killed?"

"See here, Don Caoba. He loves my daughter" (Caoba smiled). "She does not love him. I wish to be rid of him."

"It is good; I understand. Make it fifty ounces, and I will rid you of him—twenty now, and thirty after he disappears."

The Spaniard drew a bag from his pocket, and counted out twenty ounces, and gave them to the negro, saying—

"*Ya esta!* We shall always be friends, eh?"

"But Don Juan is a Spaniard," said Caoba coldly.

"No, no! Here, I am an insurrecto. My children are Cubans."

Caoba laughed his good-natured, exuberant laugh, and replied—

"*Veremos! Adios, caballero;*" and digging his spurs into his white charger, he disappeared towards the woods.

Three days afterwards, some cattle got into the cane, and the administrator rode out to drive them forth, taking the dogs with him.

He reached the edge of the wood whence they came, when suddenly Caoba appeared on his white charger from amongst the trees, exclaiming—

"Good morning, Don Martin."

"Good morning, Don Caoba," returned the administrator, turning white.

"Ah, I have a little account to settle with Don Martin," said Caoba, drawing up close, and keeping the administrator covered with his rifle, as it lay carelessly across the pommel of his saddle.

"And what is that, *caballero?*" asked Don Martin.

"But how is Laura?" asked the negro, changing the conversation, with a laugh.

"Very well, she is a grand woman, is not she?"

"Yes, a *man* shall tame her one day," said the guerilla chief, with a far-off look.

"*Como?*"

"*Veremos!*" replied the negro. "But to the account. I have been paid to kill you."

"To kill me, Caoba ? What for and by whom ?" said the man, turning to a cold sweat.

"It does not matter. I get fifty ounces to kill you. Give me fifty ounces more, and I will let you escape the knife." (The cowardly administrator shuddered). "But you must go straight off to England. You are English, eh ?"

"Don't make a joke, Caoba."

"Joke, eh ?" said the negro, drawing his horse up still closer. "As God is my witness, I will cut your throat where you sit, if you don't pay me fifty ounces."

The man shook like a leaf, and instead of drawing his revolver and shooting Caoba dead, and taking the price of his head, he merely muttered—

"Well, you must have it, of course, but I have only half an ounce with me."

"It is good. Give Maria the fifty ounces to-night. I will take the half-ounce you have for the *contra*. To-morrow morning, start for England, and never let me see your face again. You do not please me ; you are a coward," finished the negro, and held out his hand for the half-ounce, which the trembling administrator gave to him ; after which he said—

"Good day, Caoba," and with hanging head turned his horse towards the estate.

"See you," yelled Caoba, "you sold the family

of Don Enrique. I will avenge my old master. You are too much of a cur to kill. Go back to your own country, and eat out your heart until the great Spirit eats you up, and wait and read of Caoba's revenge on the *Esperanza.*"

The shameful man rode with hanging head to the estate, and alighting at his old house, went in and asked for Don Juan.

"With the major-domo," said Maria curtly.

The administrator walked across to the Spaniards, and entering the room, said with dreadful seriousness—

"Don Juan, I must leave you. I met that villain Caoba to-day, and he tried to assassinate me, but I saved my life with my revolver ; but he escaped, and has sworn to kill me before the week is out. I don't mind the man alone —an Englishman is good enough for three of such, but he will probably bring a large party, and fire the estate, and kill us all."

Don Juan smiled, and said coldly—

"Don Martin, it gives me great pain that you must leave us ; your salary shall be paid to date. Don José here will write you out a cheque for 2040 dollars — your year's salary. With such threats, the bravest cannot be expected to stay. Laura will be grieved, too, to hear of your departure," finished the weasel-eyed man.

"Who knows ?" sighed the broken admini-

strator. Taking his cheque, he went to his rooms
and packed ; and then going across to Maria,
he handed her the fifty ounces for Caoba in
a bag, and mounting the horse awaiting him,
he said—

"Good-bye, Don Juan. Where is Laura ?
I should like to say good-bye to her."

"Laura has a headache, but sends her best
wishes and good-bye to you, Don Martin. May
God take care of you."

"Give her my horse, Don Juan," said the man,
"and may God bless her."

They then shook hands, and Don Martin
rode off, followed by a negro boy on a horse,
who carried his valises in a *seron*. The little
Spaniard gazed after him, and muttered to himself—

"'Twere better had he been given the knife :
dead men tell no tales."

The wretched man looked furtively from right
to left as he rode through the lone cane-fields
to the station, where he arrived mad with fear ;
nor was his mind relieved until he had reached
Havana, and shipped aboard a tramp that
carried him to Liverpool, whence he made his
way to his native village, where he took up his
residence with his sister, and lived for many
years, eating out his heart in misery, but always
attending divine service at the village church

on Sundays, where he was loudest in his responses, so that he passed in that rustic little society as a God-fearing and religious man, and died and was buried in all the odour of sanctity—but, as the engineer said, perhaps the worst lies before him.

CHAPTER XX

BEFORE the new grinding season set in, Don Juan had arranged his estate according to his ideas. A Spaniard had been appointed administrator and engineer in one, thus saving 1500 dollars a year. A new majoral had taken Don Leonaldo's place, he having joined the rebellion from conviction. The sneaking carpenter, Don Basilio, had left and gone to Havana, in fear of his life, José, his negro assistant, taking his place. The people's rations had been cut down to half their quantity, for Don Juan said a handful of ground maize was enough for any nigger. Floggings became more frequent, for whenever the vanity of the little tradesman was hurt, he ordered twenty - five lashes and the grillos afterwards. He was determined, he said, to show that a Spaniard knew how to rule. Nevertheless the people were often insolent, as all dependents had become since the beginning of the rebellion.

Meanwhile the exacting temper of his wife and

her daughters alienated the sympathies of the negresses in the house, and the two sons, dapper, clerkly young men, who could neither ride nor throw the lasso, and, in short, knew nothing of country life, were looked upon with supreme contempt by the negro men and lads, who called them women; though, to be just, some of the young negresses liked them, for these youths spent much time in their company, and were pretty free with presents to their favourites.

Laura spent most of her time in flirting with the young lieutenant in charge of the guard. She was thoughtless and insolent to the servants, so that altogether the majority of the people soon grew discontented with the little tradesman's *régime*.

The country round the estate had become a little quieter, for the volcanic reprisals that followed the execution of the students now gave way to a more peaceful reaction. Indeed, the rebels so rarely showed themselves for a few months that Don Juan talked of applying to the Government to withdraw the guard, in order to save his purse. But he was anticipated by the captain of the *partido*, who, being short of troops, owing to numerous deaths during the wet season, commanded the guard to return to their quarters at Santiago, much to Laura's disgust; yet the lieutenant made some amends by riding over sometimes to dinner.

But notwithstanding the tradesman's niggard policy, an ill fate overtook the estate in the shape of a tornado; and on the 11th January of the following year, soon after the beginning of the grinding, the wind shifted to the east-north-east, and heavy rain began to fall, black clouds rolling up, charged with lightning, the vivid flashes and loud thunder terrifying the superstitious negroes. The sky was as black as night at ten o'clock in the morning, and the wind quickly increased to a gale, hurling down palm trees, and ripping the zinc from the roofs, scattering it over the *batey* like a pack of cards. All work was stopped, and the terrified negroes sought shelter in their low huts, crouching in the gloom, whilst the rain poured down in a deluge, the wind increasing to a hurricane, which came whirling across the estate, cutting a track through cane-fields and forests, killing many cattle in its path.

By noon the gale had spent itself, but the buildings were without roofs, the bagasse-house was blown down, and damage, finally estimated at 70,000 dollars, had been done in that short space of time.

Don Juan went wild with despair, wringing his hands, and saying that he was ruined; and indeed it was a serious matter, for if the crop was to be harvested, the necessary repairs had to be done at once, and the little man would have to borrow money from his brother, for none else would trust him.

The incompetent Spanish administrator and engineer began in a bungling way to repair the buildings when Don Juan's brother had advanced him some money; but this was not sufficient to pay the white carpenters, masons, and roof men that had to be employed, so that the proud little upstart was compelled to borrow money from some of the negroes, which he did by promising them outrageous rates of interest which he never meant to pay.

By such shifts the boiling and purging-houses were re-roofed, but the engines and feeding-stair were still roofless, the negro children having to work in the broiling sun.

The tradesman's brother, the General, could not be persuaded to lend another peseta, so the little man, in despair, invited the General and his wife, with their son and daughter, to come and visit him, hoping that the sight of the roofless buildings would have the desired effect; and it was his last chance, for his brother and family were going home to Spain immediately, the General having been invalided, and having, during his tenure of office, squeezed sufficient for them to retire upon from the ' *siempre fiel*' islanders.

They accepted the invitation, and the following Friday arrived on the estate, jocund and smiling, to pay their farewell visit to their planter brother, of whom they were now proud, though formerly they had given the tradesman the cold shoulder.

CHAPTER XXI

THE next evening at dusk, Maria closed the cedar shutters over the big grated windows in front of the house as usual; but she did not leave the postigos open, as was her custom, for the mosquitoes to go out, but shut them too.

Dinner was late that night, for Don Juan had been to the Boca to borrow money to pay some of the white workmen, for his brother proved to be inexorable.

The little tradesman was busy after his return paying them their wages, ere they rode to their homes to return on the Monday.

The four servants that Don Juan allowed himself for the house, for he had no idea of the style kept up on an estate, laid the dinner in the little *comedor* opening on to the orange grove, for eleven people—six of the family, four of his brother's family, and the Spanish administrator and engineer.

At half-past six the candles were lighted, and the dinner served, all the dishes being placed on the table at once, Spanish fashion.

The little tradesman took his seat next the door at the foot of the table, whilst his wife sat at the head, with the General at her left, and the administrator on her right. The General's wife was on Don Juan's left, and his nephew on his right, Laura and the others filling up the rest of the table.

The meal began, and the party was soon talking excitedly and gesticulating, after the manner of provincial Spaniards. The old General was relating some of his experiences of the Peninsular War to the black, hard-featured administrator, who kept looking at Victorine, the General's daughter, as fine a woman as Laura herself.

"So you have seen the great Caoba," said the General's wife to Don Juan.

"Oh yes, señora; I met him once in the lonely part of the estate. He seemed a jovial, good-natured young fellow; it is marvellous he is such a scoundrel."

"He has a bold, bad face," said Laura, flushing at the thought of the night when she saw him in the moonlight.

"But he is good-looking, eh, Laura?" asked Don Juan.

"*Vaya*, for a *negro* he is handsome;" and Maria, who was pouring out the wine, looked intently at the girl as she made the remark.

So the conversation ebbed and flowed until the coffee was brought in and the cigars lighted, Laura and Victorine each accepting cigarettes from the administrator.

"Will the señora want anything more?" asked Maria.

"No, negress," said the woman haughtily, "you can go."

"*Si*, señora," replied the servant calmly, disappearing into the kitchen, followed by the others.

The men having drunk well, smoked silently, whilst the cousins chatted and flirted together, the light from the candles streaming through the open windows on to the dark orange trees, lighting up here and there some of the white waxen flowers or golden fruit hanging under the violet, star-sown skies.

In the lulls of the conversation could be heard the cries of the night gang at the boiling-house, and the musical songs of the negro children as they piled the cane into the feeders, together with the short, regular puffs of the engine; whilst nearer at hand the purling river, with its monotonous voice, soothed the ear, or the sharp cry of water-fowl startled the night.

"How do you like the cigars?" asked the little tradesman of the administrator.

"Very good," said the man; then suddenly turning in his chair, he said, "What's that?"

Every voice was silent, and all sat listening with open mouths, for various movements could be heard in the adjoining rooms and round the house.

"*Ay, Dios mio!* what is this?" said Don Juan, rising and turning pale, for he saw several men gliding through the front door, and then he heard it shut and barred.

"*Los Insurrectos!*" yelled the administrator, drawing his revolver, as the face of a great negro appeared framed in one of the open windows.

In a moment several men with naked feet and drawn machetes ran up the steps from the back, or vaulted in through the open windows, fastening the doors and windows behind them.

The family had risen in consternation, paralysed with fear, so sudden was the attack. The General was the first to recover, and he began to shout— "Fly, fly! we shall all be murdered where we are." Then, turning to the administrator, he said, "Fire upon them!" but the man was dazed with fear, and the revolver fell from his nerveless hand; and, at the same moment, he received a stab in the back from a knife, and fell forward with a groan on to his chair.

The room was crowded with fierce negroes and villainous-looking whites, and beside every woman two of the *Insurrectos* had taken up position with knives in their hands, cautioning them to keep silent on penalty of death. At this juncture Don Juan's young daughter came running out of the bedroom, shrieking. A knife flashed in the candle-light, and the poor child fell to the ground, stabbed through the arm, the blood pouring over her night-dress.

" Mercy, mercy," moaned the poor mother.

" Coward," hissed the General, "to stab a child."

" *Carajo*," said Caoba, jumping towards him with his long machete, "take back your words."

" Never," said the brave old General.

"Then take that, Spaniard," roared Caoba, whose form seemed to expand as he cut down the old man with his machete, cleaving his skull like a cocoa-nut, and at the same time cutting the arm of the old man's wife, who had in vain tried to jump to her husband, for the villains held her firmly.

Don Juan's wife was moaning, leaning against the panelling, whilst two great negroes held Don Juan himself, his eyes starting from his head.

The two girls had covered their faces with their hands, and hid them on the table, having dropped into their seats, where they began praying amid these awful scenes.

The poor child whose arm had been stabbed began to shriek hysterically, when Caoba made a sign to a dark-faced, villainous-looking white man, who, drawing a dirk from his belt, approached the child, who began to struggle and shriek for mercy; but the murderer, seizing her by the chin and forcing her head back, cut her throat, her eyes opening widely and her lips working as she fell upon her side on the floor.

"Oh, *Madre de Dios*, kill me, kill me," shrieked the poor mother.

"No, kill no more women now," said Caoba sternly; "take the two old women to the *sala* and stuff something in their mouths, and if that doesn't stop them—well, then you can——" and he drew his hand across his throat.

Caoba's good-natured look had gone, and his features were sternly set like those of a statue. After the two women had been removed, he approached the little Spaniard, who shrank before his bloody machete and rigid features.

"Don Juan Nargas," he said, with his deep voice, "the Council has sentenced you to death. I am about to kill you."

"Mercy, mercy! you can have my estate—anything."

"*Your* estate?" sneered the negro; "no, señor. Money will never buy back the lives of the boys, slaughtered by you Spanish volunteers. You are a volunteer, and your brother was a Spanish officer. For that we have killed him, and for that we intend to kill you, and your sons, and his son. But I have kept you to kill myself, because you cheated the widow and orphans of my old master, Don Enrique—he was a man, and had he been here to-day, Caoba would never have left his side—and because you have treated the *Esperanza* people cruelly."

Then drawing his knife, the strong negro dashed his left hand over the little man's face, seizing it between his palm and fingers, and, with cold deliberation, drew his weapon across Don Juan's throat, hissing into his ear—

"Spanish coward and cheat! Your daughter is for me!"

The murdered man's eyes opened with a wild stare, and he fell forward on to the floor.

"Now finish off the rest," he said to his men, who promptly killed the young men in the same manner. Then pointing to the girls, he said—

"Rip off their clothes."

The poor girls said not a word, but kept praying as the wretches ripped through their dresses with their dirks and knives, which were dragged from them with many lewd jests, and they sat naked, cowering before their tormentors.

"Laura, look up," said Caoba sternly; "your lives shall be spared, but you, Laura, will be mine. I told you that night that you should be tamed by a man, and, *per Dios*, you shall."

Then going up to the girl, he seized her, and carried her in a fainting condition to the next room; his lieutenant, a villainous-looking mulatto, seizing Victorine in like manner, the rest of the band, with fiery eyes and low curses, crowding round the door.

.   .   .   .

When the negro cook came the next morning from the *bohea* to cook the breakfast, he was surprised to find the house silent, and no servants moving; so, going up the steps to the dining-room door, he pushed it open and looked in, staggering back with a cry; for dead bodies lay about the room, and two naked girls, with the eyes of mad women, sat like stone statues gazing at him, yet uttering never a word.

Running off to the major-domo, he gave the alarm, and soon the few white men on the estate crowded round the scene of the tragedy.

The major-domo sent for some old negresses, who hastily wrapped clothing round the girls and took them off to the majoral's rooms. They then found Don Juan's wife crouching, mad with terror, under one of the beds, and her, too, they sent with the girls; but the General's wife was dead, having bled to death.

The *boyero* was sent off to the captain of the *partido*, who arrived about mid-day with a large posse of soldiers, who immediately surrounded the house.

.   .   .   .

The day after, the General was buried, with military honours, in the little graveyard by the river, and the rest of the dead were laid also in graves beside him.

"And all they ever got of the *Esperanza* was six feet apiece of its soil," said Caoba bitterly, when the burials were reported to him.

The price set upon Caoba's head was immediately doubled.

A guardian was appointed for Don Juan's surviving wife and daughter, who took possession of the estate, now protected by a strong guard, and from that day the names of Caoba and *La Esperanza* became historical.

CHAPTER XXII

BLOOD-MONEY

FOR a year nothing of note happened beyond occasional murders, captures of prisoners by the troops, who met their death always by *quatro tiros*, a few skirmishes between the troops and rebels, and an occasional burning of an estate— but no great wholesale crime like the massacre of the students or of the Nargas startled the island.

Indeed, the rebellion seemed to be waning, and some of the guerilla bands broke up, the members obtaining free pardons for giving themselves up. Many of the negroes, too, left the insurgents, now that the law to abolish slavery had come into force. The rebellion was evidently dying, though it had cost enormous capital and life to the Spanish Government.

Amongst the clear-headed countrymen who saw that the game was nearly up was Joaquin Rodad, a criminal who had escaped from Spain and joined the insurgents, and who made it his boast that during the rebellion he had killed thirty-eight people with his own hands, to say nothing of negroes. Joaquin had been in Caoba's band for some ten months, and he knew that in any case, if caught, he was doomed to death, either for his crimes as an insurgent or his original crime in Spain, for which he would not get the free pardon if he gave himself up as an insurgent. So it occurred to this ingenious villain that if he could make terms with the captain of the *partido* to betray his chief, he might obtain a free pardon and some money to boot.

Disguising himself as a country peasant, he rode into the fort under the pretence of selling fruit and chickens, and sought an interview with the captain, representing himself as a messenger from Joaquin Rodad, and submitting Joaquin's scheme to the captain. The acute captain immediately acquiesced, and gave the messenger a written promise for Joaquin of a free pardon and the stipulated blood-money if he produced Caoba, dead or alive.

Joaquin sold his produce and returned to the rebel camp, when he began, with all the low cunning and treachery of the low-class Spaniard, to flatter Caoba. But Caoba knew his men, and would have none of them as intimate friends, keeping them all at arm's length.

But at times his usual high spirits and jovial bearing deserted him, and he grew morose, for he could see for himself that the days of the rebellion were numbered; and, apart from the chances of being taken and shot when the rebellion ended, he realised that he could never live at peace with his fellow-men after the wild life he had been leading; so at times he allowed some of his comrades to talk to him more intimately than he had hitherto done. These fits of humour did not escape the acute Joaquin, who was always near at hand to profit by them by giving consolation and advice to his chief on such occasions.

One night they were riding along the Maravilla road by moonlight, when Caoba, who was in one of these fits of spleen, unbosomed himself to Joaquin.

"You can always be a *bandolero*," suggested Radod.

"Yes, señor, but that is not war; 'tis good for cowards," retorted Caoba.

As they rode along the silent way, with the forest on one hand and the prickly-pear fences of *La Esperanza* on the other, Joaquin asked—

"Why are *bandoleros* cowards, capitan?" edging his horse at the same time a little closer to Caoba, ostensibly the better to converse together.

"Why? I saw Don Enrique once stand up to a dozen of them, and Lorenzo was their chief."

"Ah, so? Don Enrique must have been a brave man, *caramba!*"

"He was; God keep his spirit," said Caoba solemnly.

They rode on in silence for a short time, disturbing a *campanero*, who sounded his bell from the sleeping, moonlit forest.

Caoba was buried in thought, and gazing at the bright tropical moon that rode high in the skies.

"Que linda esta la luna," said the Spaniard, also looking up at the bright orb.

"*Si*," grunted Caoba, his bold face fixed upon it.

Suddenly a knife flashed in the moonlight, and with unerring precision pierced the big negro's chest.

"Ha, *cobardi!*" hissed Caoba, turning his bold, regular features upon the murderer, and attempting to draw his machete.

"Die, dog of a negro," returned the Spaniard, again stabbing him in the neck before he could draw.

"Coward! coward!" gurgled the dying negro, as he fell from his white charger to the highway.

The Spaniard caught the riderless horse's bridle, and having vaulted from his saddle, tethered the animals to a guava bush.

Then he approached Caoba, who was already dead, and drawing his machete, he knelt by the corpse and hacked off the guerilla's head; and having wrapped the ghastly trophy (which was the last face that many had looked upon on this earth) in a bandana handkerchief that he took from the crown of his hat, he returned to the horses, and mounting the white charger, leading his own horse, he started off at the *marzo* through the moonlit tropical night for the fort of Santiago, some two miles distant, to render unto the captain of the *partido* the head of the famous outlaw, and to receive, in return, a free pardon and the blood-money.

And at daybreak the next morning loathsome turkey-buzzards were tearing and gorging the flesh of Caobo the guerilla chief—*Sic transit gloria mundi.*

THE END

Printed by BALLANTYNE, HANSON & Co.
Edinburgh and London

Marsh Leaves

Royal 8vo. A magnificently printed volume, from the press of Messrs. T. & A. CONSTABLE. Illustrated with Sixteen Photo-Etchings from Plates taken by the Author.

Edition de Luxe, printed on the finest Dutch Hand-made Paper, with the Plates on Japanese. Bound in White Linen and Morocco. Only 100 copies printed. A few left, price £1, 5s. net.

Ordinary Edition, with the Plates on Dickison's Art Paper. Bound in Cloth. Only 200 copies printed. The few remaining copies, 12s. 6d. net. All Plates destroyed.

SOME PRESS NOTICES

"To those who have ever felt the melancholy compelling charm of the marshes this book will come with a peculiar attraction. It consists of a series of vignettes or essays, of varying length, each dealing with a separate aspect of earth or sky, of death or life, as known and loved in the green marshland. The weird pallor, the delicate, subtle colouring, the quiet sounds, the savour and the smell of it, are rendered with convincing faithfulness and true artistic instinct. It vibrates with the suggestiveness of a Millet or a Corot. . . . The glimpses of human and animal life are also strong, treated, as a rule, with both sympathy and humour, and betraying a close and loving observation of nature."—*Pall Mall Gazette*.

"Nothing in the latest of Dr. P. H. Emerson's always acceptable volumes is more delightful than its cunning discursiveness. . . . Open the book where you will, it is certain that you will find either an unconventional but delicious photographic suggestion, or else some quaint or humorous jotting, which is, to the full, redolent of the East Anglian Fens. Dr. Emerson has closely watched and incisively set down the habits and foibles of a strange medley—thus, cats and women, upstarts and decadents, snobs and braggarts, come in for some hard hits."—*St. James's Budget.*

"Mr. Emerson is thoroughly imbued with a sense of the beauty of Fenland scenery—a beauty denied by many, and appreciated as it deserves by very few. . . . Altogether the book, with its many charming photo-etchings by the author, will revive very pleasant memories in the minds of those who know the region of which he writes."—*Morning Post.*

"A collection of prose idyls and character sketches of the Fenlands and Fen-folk, by one who has wooed and won the beautiful but mysterious spirit of the marshes. . . . The illustrations are well in harmony with the spirit of the book, and altogether it is a welcome volume."—*Westminster Gazette.*

"For the photo-etchings from plates taken by the author which accompany the text we have nothing but praise. They seem almost to have in them the very atmosphere of the tranquil scenes they represent."—*Daily News.*

"But the letterpress is, after all, not the main attraction of the book. That is found in the illustrations, which are wonderful alike in subject, feeling, and in reproduction."—*Yorkshire Post.*

"In a beautifully bound and illustrated volume Mr. Emerson gives us a characteristic spread of fact and fancy, legend and lore, and nature studies and reflections. They are set among the Fens and Broads in the districts Mr. Emerson has made his own by right of discovery, and of fresh, forcible, and entirely original treatment."—*Literary World.*

"Written with a wonderful felicity in translating into words the dominant impression of this or that aspect of nature."—*Scotsman.*

"These photo-etchings are most of them so very beautiful that we have doubts concerning them. . . . Perhaps the best of all is that entitled the 'Waking River,' a still sunrise scene on a river reach in which the luminosity of the sun through the misty air is most wonderfully represented, and the feeling of the sleepy river bearing a motionless barge moored to the bank is very beautifully expressed. . . . The short chapters accompanying the drawings are quaint and original; the spirit of the English country, or rather of such part of it as is to be found on our flat Eastern coast, inspires the writer, who thoroughly understands peasant life and thought."—*Liverpool Daily Post.*

"Some passages in their poetic feeling remind one of Madame Michelet; others, in their minute observation, recall Tourgenieff. In 'Marsh Leaves' there is abundance of good writing, a thing often sadly to seek nowadays ; there is abundance, too, of material which constructive imagination might have wrought into a popular novel of the Fen country."—*Illustrated London News.*

"Mr. P. H. Emerson knows the Land of the Broads more intimately than any other writer with whose works we are acquainted, and he can write of it with such freshness, such elegance, and withal bright humour, as make a volume of his papers particularly welcome. 'Marsh Leaves' will recall to mind one of the most distinguished of all nature writers, Henry David Thoreau."—*Observer.*

"It is just in his ability to resist the temptation of carrying his pictures too far that Mr. Emerson teaches his fellow-photographers an invaluable lesson."—*British Journal of Photography.*

"Nothing presents such an antithesis to the senseless rush of present-day existence as the marsh life of which Mr. Emerson writes."—*Cardiff Western Mail.*

"A handsome volume with exquisitely-finished photo-etchings worthy of a place with *editions de luxe.* The descriptive text, containing many quaint incidents of marshland and moorland, cleverly evades the commonplace, and is inspired by sympathetic observations of Nature in men and animals. 'Town Mouse and Country Mouse,' 'The Horse-dealer's Death,' 'Country Cockneys,' 'Visions,' 'Fine Ladies,' and 'Voices of the Night,' are very choice specimens of the author's style, and exhibit great powers of attracting attention to minute phenomena in the world's life which the unobservant pass idly by."—*Broad Arrow.*

"It is very rarely that a book which is at once a joy to the artist and to the book-lover is published. But in 'Marsh Leaves' there lies great pleasure for both temperaments. Sixteen dainty photo-etchings of the Fen-lands illustrate some delightful descriptions of the Fen country and its dwellers. Both in his prose and in his etchings Mr. Emerson has caught the elusive charm of the far-stretching marshlands with their teeming life, their glorious effects of colour, and their tender melancholy. In summer, in autumn, in winter, and in spring, Mr. Emerson knows them well, and loves them, and in 'Marsh Leaves' he has built a veritable monument to their beauties and their fascination. This is a book to possess, for it holds the restful atmosphere of a district and a people of which we know too little."—*Gentlewoman.*

"Dr. P. H. Emerson is a prolific writer upon nature in general, and the Norfolk Broads in particular ; and this book, like the others, realises the flat outlines and grey tints of that land, and is salted with a certain humour. . . . The book in its binding and printing is one of those goodly specimens of the publisher's art that Mr. Nutt can give us. It is illustrated by sixteen interesting plates which our author-artist, in whom the impressionist and photographer are happily married, calls photo-etchings. . . . His books have their own public, who will appreciate the shrewd and kindly insight into the character of the somewhat bony type of humanity that appears to predominate among the race of Broadsmen, and who will imagine his landscapes with the proper co-efficient of association. There are, however, a number of the character-sketches which are touched with rough humour and yet with directness and grip at the distinctiveness of life in this amphibian environment."—*Newcastle Chronicle.*

"Mr. P. H. Emerson's 'Marsh Leaves' is another of this eminent photographer's delightful books dealing with the life and character of the inhabitants of the Broads and Fen-Country. The wordsketches are deftly and lightly filled in. . . . The sixteen photo-etchings from plates taken by the author are charming studies of landscapes. . . . It is a handsome book—the printing and binding being all that can be desired."—*Magazine of Art.*

"Mr. P. H. Emerson has done much in many previous volumes for the glorification of East Anglian landscape, of the Fens, and of the East Coast; and he has now added another very pleasant volume. . . . The plates are, in fact, little removed from photographs, but of their kind they are very good indeed; while Mr. Emerson's literature consists of a number of stories, some amusing and all fairly characteristic of life in the marsh lands of Eastern England."—*The Times.*

"I would recommend Mr. P. H. Emerson's 'Marsh Leaves,' clever sketches of peasant-life with sixteen photo-etchings of extreme delicacy by the author. Mr. Emerson's beautiful experiments with the camera are, of course, well known."—Mr. R. LE GALLIENNE in the *Idler.*

"Dr. Emerson has done more to make the placid beauties of East Anglia in general and the Norfolk Broads in particular known to the rank and file of his countrymen than any one else, and his latest book, 'Marsh Leaves,' betrays the same intimate knowledge of the district, and is not less artistic than any of his predecessors. Dr. Emerson's pen-and-ink sketches, slight though the majority of them are, are not lacking in a touch of rough humour, and are racy of the soil. He understands life on these English lagoons, and knows how to bring vividly on the printed page much that is characteristic and picturesque in local custom and the talk of the people. The charm of the book, however, consists largely in its illustrations. There are nearly a score of them, and they are all full-page photo-etchings from plates taken by the author in the course of his rambles. Dr. Emerson is skilled in the interpretation of nature, and he has the eye of a true artist for its passing glories. One of the most exquisite pictures in the book is 'A Winter's Sunrise,' though scarcely less beautiful are 'A Winter Pastoral,' 'A Wayside Inn,' and 'The Lonely Fisher.' Dr. Emerson's success

with the camera in these instances is nothing less than remarkable."
—*Leeds Mercury*.

"'Marsh Leaves,' as his book is called, contains much of Mr. Emerson's best work. The charm of the Marshland is one which few London folk have felt. The colour, dreaminess, mystery of the marshes are suggested by Emerson with exquisite fidelity."—*The Echo*.

"This elegantly-produced work, with its sixteen exquisite photo-etchings from plates taken by the author, is a series of short papers on various aspects of Fen life, all of them very readable, and many of them—such as 'A Moonlit Midnight,' 'A Study in Gold and Blue,' 'Blackthorn Winter'—couched in a diction which is simply poetic prose. The author has, indeed, in these pages portrayed the natural history of the Broads with a skilfulness and a lightness of touch which can only be the outcome of an intimate acquaintance with all phases of his subject, with the result that a delightful book is before his readers. His philosophy is at times, though, of the cynical order, and his chapter on 'Marsh Cats' will prove a shock to many of his lady readers. The contents of the book, however, are well diversified, and the natural history is accompanied by 'The Fenman's Clock,' 'Broadsmen's Frolics,' 'Polly's Valentine,' and other entertaining items. Of the beauty of the illustrations it is impossible to speak too highly, their clearness, yet delicacy of shading, being most artistic."—*Rural World*.

"'Marsh Leaves,' by P. H. Emerson, with sixteen photo-etchings from plates taken by the author, is a most beautiful book. Not only are some of the plates, such as 'A Winter Sunrise,' 'A Water-side Inn,' 'A Corner of the Farmyard,' and 'The Lone Lagoon' simply exquisite, the writing is so poetical, so full of sympathy and insight. Mr. Emerson lays his scenes in East Anglia, and he is satisfied with sketches rather than stories of East Anglian life. . . . The pictures are beautiful, and the writing is so charming that, though the book is 12s. 6d., it seems to me remarkably cheap."—*The Queen*.

"The distinguished writer of 'Naturalistic Photography' has long since been acclaimed by those cultured in pictorial art as one whose productions, albeit they come from a camera, are instinct with a larger proportion of graphic quality and suggestion than is usually associated with a photograph. The photo-etchings in 'Marsh Leaves' will go far to widen the existing gulf which yawns between the crowds who depict too much of everything with harrowing insistence, and the few, such as Dr. Emerson, who impose upon their records an impressive reticence."—*Studio*.

"A large, very well printed book, tastefully covered in blue canvas and adorned with photo-etchings from plates taken by the author, is Mr. P. H. Emerson's 'Marsh Leaves.' Book, we say, for it is a little difficult at first to define off-hand, except by negatives, what kind of a book Mr. Emerson's 'Marsh Leaves' is. It is not a story nor a series of stories, neither should we describe Mr. Emerson as an essayist. Each of the sixty-five chapters, which are of all lengths, bears the stamp of an impression received directly from nature, and set down in beautifully chosen and impressive language, quite undis-turbed by any hint of the inevitable artificiality of the story-teller's art. In his sense of the remorseless self-perpetuation of nature we are sometimes reminded by Mr. Emerson of 'La Faute de l'Abbé Mouret.' But in Zola's story there are figures and a background; in 'Marsh Leaves' no such distinction is defined—nature inanimate, animate, and human are completely harmonised. . . . The occasional sketches, that occur from time to time in the volume, of the East Anglian Marshmen are often touched with a humour that is very finely grim. The book will be very direct in its appeal to those who love artistic writing, and writing of a kind that has only become possible at this end of the nineteenth century. The photo-etchings are in every way satisfactory and fitly adorn a notable book."—*St. James's Gazette.*

"I have had within my vision for the last month or two a book evidently inspired by the broads, rivers, and marshes of East Anglia. Only during the past week have I had the opportunity to glance through its pages. It is entitled 'Marsh Leaves,' and is written by Mr. P. H. Emerson. It is published by David Nutt of the Strand, and is dedicated to Alfred Nutt, the author's friend and publisher. In printing, paper, and illustration it is a perfect *edition de luxe.* A more expressive title would I think have been 'Marsh Idyls.' Each of the idyls—and they are sixty-five in number—breathes the breath of the reeds and the meadow flowers, or is suggestive of wintry skies and lowering clouds, while the description of the human originals that people the lonelinesses, and the birds and the beasts that haunt the wilds are given with a free natural grace. Sixteen photo-etchings from plates taken by the author enrich the volume. Lovers of the fens and the marshes will find it a treasure."
—*Eastern Daily Press.*

"This very handsome volume is one which will win the hearts of all nature-lovers who delight in picturesque descriptions of scenery. Mr. Emerson has with previous volumes gained the good-will of many readers whose prized possessions include such diverse works on nature as those of Gilbert White, Thoreau, Richard Jefferies, and John Burroughs. Although we class him with these, Mr. Emerson is by no means their imitator, although his manner most nearly approximates to that of the 'Hermit of Walden.' 'Marsh Leaves' consists of a large number of pen-sketches of scenery, life, and character in East Anglia. The author has long since earned a name for himself as a keenly observant and sympathetic observer of nature and human nature as seen in the land of fens and Broads, and his new book will, no doubt, add to his reputation. On the whole, it is admirably written. The sixteen photo-etchings representing scenes in the marsh lands are among the most beautiful examples of book illustration which we have had the good fortune to come across. The work will win almost unqualified approval from all who know and love the peculiarly fascinating land of the Broads."—*Publisher's Circular.*

" All readers conversant with this writer's works will be delighted to learn that he has sent forth a fresh volume. The book, despite its name, is another collection of 'Broadland' idyls, but its range will be found wide enough for all readers. Of Mr. Emerson's sympathy with all the moods and tenses of Nature it is needless to speak, save to say that it is again exemplified with all the writer's grace and power in such chapters as 'Lilac and Green,' 'Cuckoo-time,' 'The Tide-pulse,' and 'A Study in Gold and Blue.' But human nature is not neglected, and the stories of 'The Ways of Woman,' 'Old Wrote,' 'Fine Ladies,' and 'A Country Child' display alike humour, keen observation, and appreciation of all sorts and conditions of life among the inhabitants of the marshes. The sixteen plates of the work are things of beauty in themselves, and they have the additional charm of embodying some of the rarest and most evanescent aspects of nature, the winter scenes especially having this quality. The whole volume, as a record of nature in her loveliness and solitude, is admirable."—*Manchester Courier.*

" These sixteen photo-etchings are all, or nearly all of them, views taken by the author at various times and seasons on the Norfolk Broads. They are all exquisite examples of the mystic, mysterious, misty charm, in representation of which Mr. Emerson is *facile princeps.* . . . The text of the beautiful book is expressed in sixty-five pen-pictures, many of them little prose poems, gems in their way. . . . 'Marsh Cats' is a fair example of his vigorous style and facility of expression. . . . One might truly say that this is a singularly pleasant book, and one that will be read with delight and satisfaction by all true lovers of nature."—*Fishing Gazette.*